Gwen

E. D. Lippert

Fulton Books, Inc.
Meadville, PA

Published by Fulton Books 2020

ISBN 978-1-64654-599-5 (paperback)
ISBN 978-1-64654-600-8 (digital)

Printed in the United States of America

Chapter 1

2015

You're Not Getting Anything

Gwen stopped breathing when the next customer walked into her bank.

"David." She sighed. Even though she immediately knew this wasn't her David, her heart was already pounding fast in her chest. The pain was nearly unbearable. She closed her eyes and took a deep breath.

"He's in New York, Gwen, living a happy life with his ugly wife and two fat sons. This isn't him." She desperately wanted it to be David, even if on seeing her here he turned and left. She felt that one sight of him might fill her empty heart. One sight of him might save her.

Gwen took another deep breath and opened her eyes.

"Are you okay?" Gwen's customer, an elderly lady simply trying to make a deposit, was looking at her with concern.

"Yes, I'm sorry, Mrs. Kelso. I just have a headache today." She smiled reassuringly at her customer but then turned her gaze back to the man still standing just inside the door. He looked unsure and nervous. Something was wrong, and her heartache turned to curiosity and maybe even compassion. Part of her wanted to help him, and part of her was just curious what this guy was up to.

Gwen shook her head and turned back to her customer. "I'm new here, Mrs. Kelso, and with my head pounding like this, I'm drawing a blank on how to process your deposit. Can you please go back to the line and let one of the other tellers help you?" This was only half a lie. Gwen was indeed new at the bank; she'd only been here for two weeks. But she knew exactly how to process this deposit. Mrs. Kelso nodded and obediently picked up her deposit slip and cash and walked away. Gwen felt only a twinge of guilt for having lied to the older lady, but then her attention was turned back to the man who looked so much like David. Something was off.

*****

Larry had stopped just inside the door to get his bearings and take a deep breath. He'd been through this in his mind a thousand times. This was going to be simple. He'd be out of here in five minutes, home within the hour, and relocated out of state within a few weeks. It was going to be okay. "Just clear your mind and focus, Larry. You got this." He straightened his back and surveyed the bank.

It was a relatively small branch with only three teller stations, all manned, plus a drive-through in the back. The front wall was all glass, looking out onto the parking lot. There was a ledge along the glass for customers to fill out their deposit slips and other forms. The manager's office was off to his right. The teller counter stretched across the back of the bank and was chest high, except for at each station where it dropped a foot or so. There was a walkway to the far right and a good eight feet between the teller counter and the back of the building.

In addition to the three tellers, there was a guard to Larry's right, a manager sitting at her desk and one customer, and an elderly lady at the teller station to the far right. He saw the teller look at him, say something to her customer, and then saw the customer walk off with a confused look. The customer then stood beside the "Wait here for next teller" sign.

That same teller then addressed him, "I can help you, sir."

Larry hesitated, considering one last time whether he should just turn around and leave. "I can help you," the teller said a little louder.

He took another deep breath and headed her way, taking a quick look at her nameplate—Gwen Marsh. Sizing up Ms. Marsh on his few steps to her station, he at first felt confident. She was just a short, plump, middle-aged woman. Easy prey.

Then he met her eyes, and the way she watched him made him wonder if this was such a good idea. His heart started pounding again, and he broke out in a sweat. He could hear the squeaky sound of his sneakers on the tile floor and could hear the brushing of his pants, one thigh against the other. And above it all, he could hear his heart beating, pulsating in his ears. Every fiber of his being warned him to turn and leave. He kept walking.

When he reached the teller, he put both tightly fisted hands on the counter but remained silent. He tried to control his breathing, reminding himself that as far as anyone here was concerned, he was just a middle-aged man here to make a deposit. There was still time to say, "I forgot my check," or "Sorry, I left my deposit in the car. Be right back," and then head out. But that would mean that once again he failed. Once again, he would feel like a loser. *I'm tired of losing*, he thought to himself.

He looked at the teller.

Gwen didn't smile a greeting but just raised her eyebrows as if to say, "Well?" Up close, he didn't look so much like David. They were built alike, but if she was honest, this guy was slightly more handsome. He had thick glasses like David, but more hair, and only two chins rather than three or four. Judging by the pictures she saw on Facebook, David's wife fed him well. What this new customer didn't have that David had was a charming smile that would melt her heart. Just as well, she took a deep breath to show her impatience.

He reached out his right hand to her, opening his fist to reveal a tightly folded note.

She took the note, knowing what it would say before she slowly lay it down on the counter, smoothed it out, and silently read, "This is a robbery. I have a gun. Put all the cash you have into an envelope and hand to me."

Gwen froze for a moment and reread the note. *There* is *a God*, she thought, then looked up with an almost pleased look on her face, met his eyes, and whispered, "Let me see the gun."

Larry pulled his coat back just enough for her to see the butt of the gun tucked in his waistband. Gwen, being a bit short, had to stand up on her toes to get a look.

"Is it real?" she asked in a lowered voice.

"Yes, it's real. Now get moving."

This is my chance. Put me out of my misery, dude, Gwen thought with relief. She leaned forward over the counter, getting right up in his face, "You're not getting anything. Shoot me."

Larry stared at her in disbelief.

"Shoot me, you worthless son of a bitch."

He finally blinked. "I'm not bluffing. If you don't start empty-ing that drawer, you're dead," he hissed.

Gwen pulled her head back, stood up straight, shrugged her shoulders, and said, "Go ahead. Do it."

Larry looked at her, puzzled. She seemed almost eager. "You're crazy."

"Yes," she said, nodding her head, "yes, I am. Now shoot me." "Please" was on the tip of her tongue, but that was said silently.

Larry put his hand on the butt of his gun but froze there. This was not how things were supposed to go. In the thousand times he'd gone through this in his mind, not once had he been challenged. The teller was supposed to just do as he asked. They were trained to not make trouble if they were robbed, to just do as asked, and to do what they could to stay safe and ensure the safety of everyone in the bank. This woman was not supposed to challenge him. He didn't know what to do, and worse, it was clear from the impatience he saw flash in her eyes that she knew that he didn't know what to do. *All the banks in this city, and I pick one with a lunatic teller*, he thought.

The bank manager, Karen, was in her office a few yards away. The front of her office was all glass and looked out into the lobby. She could watch her tellers and normally kept one eye on things so that if the tellers couldn't keep up with the traffic or seemed to be in trouble, she could come out to help. She noticed Gwen leaning over the counter toward the customer. Gwen had only been there two weeks, but there had already been complaints. In the words of one of her coworkers, Gwen was "less than pleasant" to work with. Based on what Karen was seeing here, Gwen was "less than pleasant" with customers as well. She made a mental note to have a conversation with her new teller later that day. For now, though, she would just keep an eye on things.

"Pull out your gun. Point it at me, right about here"—Gwen pointed at her chest and tried to keep her voice low so as not to attract attention—"and pull the trigger. Once I'm down, everyone else here will be scared enough to do whatever you want. And if you're quick enough, you might even get out of here before the cops arrive."

Larry started to back away. Gwen held up her hand. "Oh no, we're not done here. You don't get to leave now. You need to finish this," Gwen said, looking him right in the eye. "Shoot me." Though Gwen's heart was pounding and her hands shaking a bit, she was not afraid. The shaking was a result of her rising anger. This was taking too long. She hissed. "Shoot me, you son of a bitch."

Larry froze in place. "Look, lady, I didn't want anybody to get hurt. Just let me get out of here, okay?" As he said this, he noticed a look of disappointment on the teller's face, as though she were saddened by this turn of events. They held each other's gaze for a moment. Gwen sighed.

The other people in the bank were beginning to take notice that something was off at Gwen's station. Both Larry and Gwen knew that something had to happen soon. Gwen thought for a second and then, with her head, motioned Larry to come closer, which he did.

She leaned back over the counter, just slightly this time, and with a low voice said, "Listen, we both know you're not getting out of here without a police escort, but I can change that. I'll help you, but you have to do as I say. I can get you through this. You'll leave here with about twenty grand. I can make that happen." She knew she could do that too, but she had no intention of fulfilling the promise.

She had her own agenda here. Whatever compassion she felt towards this nervous man was overcome by her desire to just die.

Larry thought for a second. He partially believed her—she wasn't going to let him get out of here unless he did as she said. How the hell did this happen? He had the gun. He was supposed to be in charge of the situation, but here he stood, fully at the mercy of this woman.

So okay, what was the alternative? She could make a scene now, and he knew he wouldn't make it out of here. Unless he was willing to use his gun, the guard would stop and hold him until the cops came. Or he could see what this woman proposed and hope she would really help him. She was crazy though; should he trust a crazy person? The worst that could happen in that case was that he ended up in jail. The best was that he got what he came in here for and went home to his sons.

"How much do *you* want? One minute ago, you said I wasn't getting anything," he asked.

"I'll get what I want, and you'll still get probably twenty grand."

He looked doubtful, but really, he only needed about $5,000, so he didn't mind sharing if he got $20,000. He rubbed his hand over his face and gave a sigh of resignation. "Okay, what do you want me to do?"

Gwen leaned back over the counter. She wanted him to shoot her, but that obviously wasn't going to happen without a lot of manipulation. She was the queen of manipulation, but she needed time to think. She refused to let this opportunity pass. "I want you to take out that gun and point it at my head and then yell, 'This is a robbery. Everybody, put your hands up and move towards the wall.'" She nodded her head towards the wall on her left. "'If all hands don't go up, I shoot. If you don't start moving immediately, I shoot.' Keep your eyes on the guard and the manager. She has a button to notify the police. Make sure her hands go up. Guard is armed; do not give him a chance to pull his gun. They won't want you to shoot me; they'll do as you say. Let's get them the hell out of here. Once they're all against the wall, escort them into the back. There's a supply room. Put them in there. There's a lock, but it can be unlocked from inside, so you'll need to block the door. You can use the copy machine for that. Don't forget to take their phones first. And the guard's weapon. Got it?"

Gwen could feel the eyes of her manager on them. "It's now or never, shit for brains. Time is running out." She raised her eyebrows, "You don't have much choice, do you?" Gwen hadn't thought through what she was going to do once they had the others locked up. She would find a way to get him to shoot her; she just didn't know how yet. She briefly wondered if he had ever shot a gun before in his life. She knew she could take his gun, or the guard's gun, but wasn't sure she had it in her to shoot herself.

Larry didn't know if it was the fact that she called him "shit for brains," which really pissed him off, or the fact that he knew she was right—he didn't have a choice—but he pulled the gun, pointed it at her head, and shouted, "This is a robbery. Everybody put your hands up." He turned slightly, keeping the gun pointed at Gwen's head but facing out. He looked right at the manager to be sure her hands went up. He also kept an eye on the guard, making sure he didn't do anything stupid. What he couldn't know was that Karen had already pushed the panic button.

"Everyone over here!" he shouted, pointing to the wall on his right.

Larry watched as the terrified women moved quickly to the wall. One was already crying, and he felt pity for her. He wanted to drop the gun and tell them all that it was okay, that this was only a big mistake, but things had already gone too far. Squaring his shoulders, he hardened his resolve. This wasn't going as planned, but he was doing this for his boys. He would not fail. He had no choice.

He noticed the guard was slowly walking toward the others. "Hurry up, asshole," Larry growled at him. Larry was surprised at the tone of his own voice, at his fierceness. He turned to Gwen and motioned her to get moving too.

When everyone, including Gwen, was lined up, he motioned Gwen with the gun to come around the counter. He pulled a plastic bag from his coat pocket and instructed her to hold it open. "Okay, each one of you is going to put your cell phone in this bag. And don't try anything because I know that everybody has a cell phone. If you left it at your desk, get it."

Gwen shook her head in disgust. *Don't send them back to their desks, you moron*, she thought, but everyone pulled out their phones, and Gwen immediately knew that if Karen didn't use this as an excuse to go back to her desk, she had already pushed that button. That meant there wasn't much time.

With the gun pointed at her head, Gwen went down the line and held the bag for each person. She made her hands shake and tried to look terrified. The others didn't have to try; they *were* terrified. Gwen didn't feel bad for them. Their fear had no impact on her at all. She knew they would be okay. Today would give them a story they could tell for the rest of their lives.

"Get his gun," ordered Larry, nodding in the guard's direction. Gwen carefully removed the gun from the guard's holster. She briefly considered turning on Larry, aiming the gun at him and forcing him to shoot her, but she knew he wouldn't. And being a hero was not her endgame here.

Once the phones and the guard's weapon were collected, still holding the gun to Gwen's head and pushing her along in front of him, Larry moved the group to the back of the bank. "Into the closet."

Karen knew she had to stall for time; she was the only one there who knew that help was on the way. She turned to Larry and put her hands on her hips, hoping to exude some authority, "We can't all fit in there."

"Then squeeze in," Larry replied dismissively. "You stay here," he added, pointing to Gwen. He herded them all in, shut the door, and looked at Gwen. She silently pointed to the copier, and Larry, laying his gun on top of the machine, pushed the copier to block the storeroom door. He picked up his gun. "If I hear this door move, I kill her and then come and kill all of you!" he yelled.

Turning to Gwen, gun down at his side, he started, "Do you…" Gwen quickly held her finger up to her lips, admonishing him to be quiet. She nodded to the front of the bank, and they walked that way.

Once out of earshot of the storeroom, Gwen whispered, "You need to be more careful. They can't hear you speaking to me unless you're shouting orders, okay?"

"Got it, sorry." Any sense of power Larry felt when holding the gun on everyone was gone.

She dropped the bag on the counter. "What's your name anyway?"

"Larry."

"Lesson one in bank robbery." Gwen sighed. "Don't ever tell anyone your name. You're robbing a bank, for God's sake." She was trying to piss him off, but instead of looking angry, he just looked ashamed.

"Okay, shit for brains, listen to me." Bingo! *That* pissed him off.

"Hey, I don't need your insults, you little smart-mouthed bi—" And that was when they heard the sirens. He grabbed Gwen by the shirt. "What did you do?"

"Nothing! Karen must have hit the panic button." Larry looked blankly at her. "The manager," Gwen said, again rolling her eyes and shaking her head.

"How?"

"She's stupid, but she's not a complete idiot." Gwen pushed him off her. "You took too damned long. Anyone paying attention would have known. She must have been paying attention."

Larry was nearly frozen in panic. This wasn't exactly going the way Gwen had hoped either. She briefly considered pulling the guard's gun out of the bag, shooting this moron, and then shooting herself. But when she looked at the total despair on this guy's face, she saw David again. So instead, she ran to Karen's office, grabbed the keys, and hurried to the doors to lock them. She needed time to think. She realized she couldn't kill Larry, and now she wasn't sure she could allow him to face the consequences of killing her, not when he still reminded her of her David. She needed a plan. *Why does he have to look like David?* she thought.

"Get behind the counter and down on the floor. We need to be out of sight," she ordered.

Once they were both safely out of view from the front window, Larry turned on her. "I should have just shot you, you crazy bitch!"

"You should have, and you still can. But you're not going to, so just shut up and let me think."

Chapter 2

Let Me Enjoy These Last Few Quiet Moments

Two years earlier…

Gwen leaned over the coffin and gazed at her daughter. Leah had always been beautiful, but lying here, with her face completely relaxed, no tension, no anger, and no wild-eyed look, she was radiant. Gwen gently traced her daughter's cheeks. "My beautiful girl, my sweet beautiful girl."

Leah's long strawberry-blond hair fell over her shoulders, the color accentuated by the dark blue of her dress. Gwen knew how important it would be for Leah to look beautiful and had spared nothing in getting the perfect dress. Even the shoes were top-notch, though no one would see them. Gwen reached in and touched a strand of her daughter's hair. She twirled the silky strand around her fingers as she thought back over the years, to Leah's first haircut, a sampling of which Gwen still had in a small envelope she kept in her dresser; to brushing Leah's hair before her first day of kindergarten; to taking Leah to a beauty salon to have her hair done for her first high school dance; to attending Leah's graduation from beauty school; and finally to telling the funeral director just how to style

Leah's hair for today. She pulled the strand of hair to her lips, kissed it, and then carefully put it back in place.

Gwen moved her hand away from her daughter's hair, remembering how angry Leah got the last time she had dared to touch her hair. Leah had come out of her room ready to head out to catch the school bus to middle school. Gwen was always taken aback when she looked at her daughter. She was so beautiful. When she kissed her girl goodbye that morning, she had reached up with both hands and gently rearranged Leah's hair so it was behind her ears.

"Mom! I just got my hair the way I wanted it, and you messed it up!"

Gwen was shocked by Leah's anger and look of pure hatred and took a step back. She had done this a million times before. "I'm sorry, sweetie."

"Don't ever touch my hair again, okay?" Leah stared at her mother with disgust. Gwen didn't answer, not sure how to respond. After a few seconds, Leah said, "Now I have to fix it again. Thanks, Mom. If you want to fix somebody's hair, worry about that rat's nest on *your* head!" She then stormed back to her room, fixed her hair, came out, and left the house without saying another word.

Gwen remembered feeling upset that entire day. She remembered fixing Leah's favorite meal that evening for dinner. She remembered realizing for the first time that day that she was a bit afraid of her daughter—not physically but emotionally. And she remembered that when Leah returned home that evening, they both acted as though nothing had happened.

Gwen never touched her daughter's hair again, until today.

"Excuse me, Mrs. Marsh." Gwen looked up to see the serious, dour mug of the funeral director.

"It's miss." She wanted to add *again* as this was probably the fifth time she had corrected him, but she bit her tongue.

"Sorry, Miss Marsh. Is there anything we can get for you? Guests should be arriving shortly to pay their respects."

Gwen wanted to scream, "Yeah, you can give me my daughter back! What could you possibly do for me?" Instead, looking back down at Leah's face, she quietly replied, "No, just let me enjoy these last few quiet moments with my daughter, please." Leah was always embarrassed when her mother was rude, which was often. Gwen was determined not to be rude today. "I won't embarrass you today, I promise," she whispered to her daughter as she leaned over and kissed Leah on the forehead.

Gwen grasped the side of the coffin to maintain her balance; she rested her head on her hand and sobbed silently. Her entire life was lying in this coffin and tomorrow would be buried beneath the earth. For twenty-two years, she lived for her daughter. She wondered how she would get through these next few hours, the burial tomorrow, and the rest of her life. How could she possibly be expected to do that? She desperately wanted to crawl in and lie next to her daughter, to just lie there and die. She should have brought a knife or a razor so she could slit her wrists. She could picture the shock on the funeral director's face when he came back in to find her there. She imagined the looks on the faces of Leah's friends when they saw both Leah and her mother lying there.

"Just let me die, Lord Jesus, please. Just let me die. Now." But she didn't die. She kept breathing. Waves of pain kept sweeping over her. Tears kept flowing.

Gwen stood up straight and forced herself back to reality and thoughts on how to get through this. There would be no family today as they didn't have any family to speak of. Gwen was an only child, and her parents passed when Leah was young. Leah's father had been a one-night stand. Gwen had only one friend in this world, and she hadn't yet told her about Leah's death. She didn't know who to expect really. She had only met a few of Leah's friends the last few years. She wasn't sure if Leah didn't bring them around because she was ashamed of her mother or because she was ashamed of her friends.

Probably the former. People were always surprised when they realized that Gwen was Leah's mother. They usually assumed that Leah had been adopted.

She remembered a time when Leah was still young and had invited a friend over to play. When the girls had gone back into Leah's room, Gwen heard the friend say, "Is that really your mother? You don't look like her! She's—"

"I know," she heard her daughter reply but walked quickly away, not wanting to hear the rest. She couldn't bear to hear her daughter call her ugly.

Gwen, however, understood the little girl's confusion. She herself was amazed that a short, fat, ugly woman like herself did indeed give birth to the tall, slim, drop-dead gorgeous goddess that was her daughter. Go figure. Genetics were amazing. Somewhere in Gwen's lineage, there must have been a good-looking person. Leah's father for sure was handsome. When Gwen thought of him, she referred to him as T&H—tall and handsome. Gwen met him at a bar one night when she was in her early twenties. She wasn't sure at first why this guy had come over to talk to her. Men *never* approached her. Never. Not since her David anyway. She guessed he was probably just horny and figured she was an easy target. In a way, she was right, though the reality had been even more painful.

Chapter 3

1993

Well, That Was a Disappointment

Gwen was about twenty-two. Two days after receiving her college degree, she had moved out of her parent's house in Towson and into an apartment in Baltimore. She doubted her parents missed her. They were busy with their own lives, both science professors at Dulaney University. Both had wanted Gwen to continue in school and get her PhD, but she was done. She wanted to be out on her own. She wanted a change. She had picked her major, accounting, with that very plan in mind. CPAs made good money, and she could graduate in four years. She was good at math and was a quick learner, so the courses were easy for her. She had no desire to follow her parents into teaching. Standing in front of a group of people every single day was not for her, and besides that, she knew that *not* continuing her education and not following in her parents' footsteps would let them know that she was an adult now, able to make her own decisions. Their time of making decisions for her was over. She wanted control over her own life.

Gwen's parents, Dr. and Dr. Marsh, had been good to Gwen from a financial standpoint. She never wanted for anything, but otherwise, she felt they had failed her. Gwen's early childhood was a stream of day-care workers, most of whom she could not remember. And from the age of eleven on, she was a typical "latchkey" kid.

She could only remember a few times that she truly felt her parents understood her, only a few times that she could remember coming first in her parents' thought process. When thinking of her parents, though, her focus always turned to the times they failed her. There were times when she would allow herself to wonder if she had failed them, but those times were few. Somehow, nursing that resentment against her parents made her feel better about herself.

Now it was her turn. She found a job in the city, found an apartment that she could afford, and settled down into adulthood. What she quickly realized was that adulthood was even lonelier than childhood. At least in childhood, though she had few friends, she always had people around her. During the day, she had classmates and teachers, and in the evenings, she had her parents and her parents' visiting students. Not that they paid much attention to her, but they were there. They were voices *not* coming from a TV. It was the illusion of being part of a group. Gwen had always known at some level that it was indeed just an illusion but didn't fully admit it to herself until the groups were gone.

Now during the day, Gwen was surrounded by coworkers. She was working at a CPA firm and didn't mind working long hours. Tax season was great—she was expected to work a minimum of ten hours per day. Though she didn't admit it to herself, she liked being part of a group; she could tell herself that she wasn't lonely.

She hadn't had any close friends in years. One of her coping strategies for rejection was to reject the other person first. So in general, Gwen was a class A bitch whenever possible. She purposely came off as arrogant and condescending. After the first few weeks, no one at the CPA firm went out of their way to chat with her. If a group of employees was standing around chatting, as soon as they saw Gwen heading their way, the group quickly dispersed. Gwen pretended not to notice. If she thought too much about this, it was painful, so instead, she found fault with everyone she met. "He's a moron." "She's an airhead." "Those boobs are fake." "She's just a slut." If she didn't like the person, she wouldn't want to make a friend out of them, and if she didn't try to make a friend, she didn't get rejected.

Her bosses quickly realized that she was a great accountant. She got a lot done in record time with perfect accuracy, but she was not a good person to put in front of clients and not a good person to put on a project with colleagues, so Gwen did most of her work alone in her cubicle. She would listen to the voices and conversations around her. She would pretend that she was part of the conversation, and in her mind, she would answer questions or respond with witty comments, making her coworkers laugh, sometimes correcting them when they were wrong but always commanding attention with her brilliance and insight. In Gwen's imagination, she was a beloved and integral part of the firm even as she looked down on and criticized her coworkers at every opportunity.

Evenings, however, were lonely. No one ever came to visit. Actually, the only time another human being had been in her apartment was when her parents helped her move in. Her phone rang once a week, every Thursday evening, 7:00 p.m. sharp, when her mom called to "check in." Every few times, Gwen would just let the phone ring so that her mom would think she was out. Other than that, the phone never rang, and Gwen never picked it up to call anyone either. She had no one to call. Her evenings were spent either watching TV or reading—reading mostly. That made for long evenings, and she started to fill the time by drinking. Cocktail hour started the minute she walked in the door and ended around eleven or twelve when she finally fell asleep.

Eventually, that routine lost its appeal, and Gwen decided to try going out. She lived near Fells Point, a part of Baltimore that had a bar every few steps. She chose one a few blocks away because she had seen an advertisement for it that referred to the pub as a "dimly lit tavern." If the lighting sucked, she could blend in.

As she was preparing to go out, Gwen examined herself in the mirror. There was nothing she could do about her beady eyes; her fat, flat nose; or her nearly nonexistent lips. But her color was pale. Turning her face from side to side, she wondered if she should run to the drugstore first and get some blush, maybe some mascara and lipstick, just to give her face some color.

*****

Gwen thought back to the one time about eight years ago at the age of fourteen when she had purchased makeup. She had noticed the other girls at school wearing makeup and how pretty they looked. She wondered if makeup would make her pretty too. She didn't want to buy the cheap stuff either. She wanted to go to the department store, to the brightly lit counters where beautiful young women let you try different colors and brands, helping you to find just the right one. When Gwen got there, she pretended to be examining merchandise on nearby racks and just watched the ladies working there and the customers they served. They were all pretty. The women sitting in the chairs trying different colors, looking at their altered faces in the small mirrors, they were all pretty. Not one of them was ugly. Gwen felt that if she approached that counter, they would all wonder what she was doing there. She imagined one of them saying, "Oh sweetie, there's nothing we can do for you." Gwen left the department store and walked to the nearest drugstore where she purchased mascara, blush, and lipstick. She remembered buying neutral colors of blush and lipstick. No red for her. She wanted color; she didn't want to stand out.

After her purchase, Gwen had hurriedly walked home. She wanted to get there before her parents got home from work. Entering the house, she ran upstairs and emptied her new cosmetics on her bedroom dresser. She stood looking at them for a bit, unsure how to begin. Her mom didn't wear makeup, so she had never had that mother/daughter experience where the little girl sits and watches her mom primp. It just didn't happen. Gwen decided that the best thing to do was to start with a clean face, so she carefully and thoroughly washed her face. Once it was dry, she started with the blush. She tried to mimic what she saw at the department store and brushed upward along her cheekbone, adding a touch of mauve to each cheek. She stood back and looked. Not happy with the results, she washed her face and tried again. It took a few tries to get the color just right.

Once her cheeks were right, she applied the mascara. She found this to be a bit easier. She had steady hands, and the mascara ended up where it was supposed to go. She did get a dot or two on her eyelid but quickly cleaned that up with a Q-tip. Lipstick went on next. The color was just enough to show that she actually had lips. She stood back and examined her reflection in the mirror. *Not beautiful, but almost pretty*, she thought. She brushed and examined her shoulder-length hair. It was just a mousy brown color, no real highlights. She had bangs, which she brushed to one side that day. She put her hair behind her ears, pulled it out, and put it back, trying to decide which was best. She finally decided that behind her ears showed off the color on her cheeks. Finally content with the results, she sat on her bed and waited for her parents to come home. She was too excited to read or do her homework or watch TV. She imagined her parents commenting on how pretty she was and oohing and aahing over her makeup.

When she heard her parents come through the front door, Gwen waited. She wanted to make her grand entrance at dinner. While waiting, she would look in the mirror every few minutes, excited to see the difference in her face—her cheekbones stood out, her eyes popped a little bit, and her lips looked feminine. She was very excited for her parents' reaction.

When finally called for dinner, she calmly strode into the kitchen and took her place at the table. Dad looked up briefly, but if he noticed anything different about her, he didn't show it. He was rambling on about something that happened that day with a student. As Mom served dinner and listened to her husband, she looked at Gwen, and Gwen could see a look of surprise on her face, but she said nothing for a bit. It wasn't until about halfway through the meal that Mom said, "I see you have makeup on, dear." That was it. There was no "My, don't you look pretty!" or "You did a great job. It really looks nice." Not even a "Don't you think you should wait until you're older?" There was nothing other than an acknowledgment that she was wearing makeup.

"Yes, Mom, I do."

Dad did look a bit more closely at this point, but only muttered a "Hmmmmmm." That was it. Gwen did her best to hide her feelings, to hold back her tears and not show her parents how hurt she was. Immediately after dinner, she ran to the upstairs bathroom, washed her face, and threw away the makeup she'd purchased only a few hours before. She had not bought any since.

*****

Sighing, Gwen shrugged her shoulders at her image in the mirror. *It is what it is*, she thought. She brushed her teeth and hair and was ready to go out.

Gwen exited her apartment and headed to the pub. This was new for her. She didn't know how to act and felt a bit out of place walking among the partying yuppies of Baltimore. She kept her head down and literally plowed her way through groups of people to get to her destination. She was completely immune to the calls of "Hey, watch out, bitch" or the sarcastic "Excuse me" from one particular woman. Gwen had a biting tongue and knew she could bring anyone of these assholes to tears with just a few words, but she didn't really have the energy to retaliate tonight. She was feeling a bit down and just needed company.

Gwen sat at the end of the bar for a good two hours. She did a lot of "people watching" that night, critiquing pretty much everyone else in the place. She noticed a small gaggle of young men who looked her way every once in a while. Finally, the tall one of the group headed her way.

He came up behind her. "Hey, can I buy you a drink?"

Gwen turned and looked up at him, ready to send him packing with a quick insult but was stunned by his good looks. "Sure."

He sat down next to her, ironically enough the only open barstool in the place.

"So what's your name?"

"Gwen."

"Whatcha drinkin'?"

"Bud Light."

Tall and Handsome, as she immediately nicknamed him, ordered them each a new beer, while Gwen took a closer look. He looked like a model—tall, broad shouldered, muscular, clear skin, thick wavy strawberry-blond hair, and bright-blue eyes.

"All these Barbie dolls here, what are you doing talking to me?"

"Why wouldn't I talk to you?" He looked at Gwen with an amused look.

"Please, I have a mirror."

"You sell yourself short, Gwen."

"Bullshit."

Tall and Handsome just laughed and lifted his glass for a toast. Gwen lifted hers as well. Why? This was not her normal response to anyone who spoke to her. Maybe because he was so darned handsome, or maybe because he talked to her like a human being. Either way, they chatted for a bit. He was an insurance agent (though later, she doubted any of what he said had been true), lived outside the city, came from a large family, graduated from Penn State, yada yada. Gwen did more listening than talking.

Finally, after about twenty minutes, T&H said, "Wanna take a walk? I need a smoke."

"Sure," replied Gwen as she slid off her barstool. She followed her new friend out the door. She didn't notice the group of guys who had been with T&H high-fiving one another as the pair exited the bar.

They walked for a bit. He lit up and puffed his cigarette. Gwen didn't smoke and declined his offer to partake. He chatted; she remained silent. Gwen noticed that they were heading toward the parking garage but didn't mention it, though her defenses were immediately raised again. She silently scolded herself for letting them down at all. As he chatted amicably on about who knows what, she considered her options. *Do I go with this guy, or do I tell him to fuck off? Clearly, he's just trying to get in my pants. Do I care?* She took a good look at her companion. *Maybe I just want to get in* his *pants, and then I can tell* him *to fuck off.* That scenario appealed to Gwen. She looked at him again. *What are the chances that he's really into me? Slim to none.* That last thought was accompanied with a slight sigh. Meanwhile, she nodded and smiled at what she hoped were the appropriate times.

The pair entered the garage, and Gwen followed her new friend into the elevator. "Hey, let's go sit in my car a while. It's a bit chilly out here."

How stupid does this guy think I am? she thought, but replied, "Sure."

They rode the elevator in silence. As they got off, he looked around and then said, "Do you get high?"

"Why? Do you need to be high to get in the car with me?"

T&H laughed. "You're a real piece of work, you know that? If you tried being nice once in a while, you may not have to spend your nights sitting alone."

"What makes you think I spend my nights alone?" Gwen glared at him, waiting for a response. Part of her knew he was right. She knew that her social skills sucked, to put it mildly. Usually, she could blame everyone else, but every once in a while, in her weaker moments, she knew it was *her*.

He looked at her a minute, shrugged, and said, "You're right. I just met you. I don't know a thing about you." With that, he pulled out his keys and clicked. The lights on an Audi a few spaces away blinked.

Typical yuppie car, she thought. "Nice car."

"Thanks, I like it. Wanna get in and get a closer look?" He waited for her to respond and could tell she was torn. "I won't bite, I promise." T&H flashed a perfect smile, and Gwen, without answering, headed toward the passenger door. "I'll take that as a yes." He knew he had her.

He didn't follow her and open the door for her, but that was okay. Gwen didn't expect it. They both just silently got in the car and sat looking forward. Gwen made her decision on how to proceed.

T&H turned toward her and said, "Well, what now?" That was when Gwen threw herself at him. She lunged over the center console and planted her lips right on his, grabbing his crotch at the same time. Either he would push her away or take advantage, she wasn't sure which. If he pushed her away, she would apologize, blame it on the alcohol, and hope he understood. If he didn't, then she had the upper hand.

He was definitely shocked, but it only took him a second to get into it. The entire debacle lasted less than ten minutes, and most of that time was spent trying to get into a position that worked.

When it was all over, they both sat back, trying to catch their breath. Gwen waited for him to speak. *He's over there figuring out how to get me out of the car without causing a scene*, she thought.

After a minute or so, he said, "I really should get back."

"Well, that was a disappointment," said Gwen, as she pulled on her pants.

"Excuse me?"

"I don't know." She shrugged. "I just thought that a man your size would be…you know…bigger."

Not knowing how to respond, he just looked at her for a minute. "Are you kidding me? You beady-eyed twat with your pock-marked face, fat ass, and saggy boobs, *you're* complaining about *me*? You should be thanking me for even speaking to you."

And there it was. If she had been surprised at all, she may have broken down at that point, but she wasn't surprised. Disappointed maybe, but not surprised. "Sorry, little dick. I just call 'em as I see 'em." She opened the car door, got out while straightening her clothes, turned back to him, slowly for effect, and said, "Have a nice life." Closing but not slamming the door, she walked away. He did not follow, but as she walked away, he rolled down the window and yelled, "I only talked to you to win a bet, bitch. You just earned me fifty dollars."

Gwen kept walking, lifted her hand in the air, and gave T&H the finger, held that for a few seconds, then changed the gesture to one where her thumb and forefinger were just an inch apart, reminding him of her disappointment.

Once alone in the elevator, Gwen leaned her head against the wall and sobbed. "A bet. A fucking bet! I was just a joke." She stood up straight and wiped her tears before the elevator door opened. "We'll see who the joke is."

She went back to the bar and walked right up to the table of T&H's friends. She stood there looking at them, enjoying the looks of confusion and worry on their faces. Once she knew she had their full attention, she said, "I just wanted to tell you that your friend has the smallest dick I've ever seen. I mean seriously, I couldn't feel a thing." The men all burst out laughing as she turned and left. T&H was on his way in as she was on her way out. Resisting the urge to lash out at him, she simply nodded in his direction and kept on going, enjoying the laughter that continued as the door closed behind her. She knew that now they were laughing at *him*.

That was her last attempt at making friends.

About two months later, Gwen realized she was pregnant. A week after that, she lost her job for cursing at a client over the phone.

Chapter 4

1979

Genetics Are Amazing, but Sometimes They're Just Not Fair

Gwen was eight years old when she began to think of herself as ugly. Like most young kids, she never really thought about her appearance. Up until then, she'd had a pretty normal childhood. She always had a few friends in school and day care. Her parents never really kept her involved by signing her up for activities, and they never arranged playdates, so those were her only two opportunities to be around other kids. But school and day care were sufficient, and thinking back, Gwen remembered those years fondly.

The bullying and teasing began in the third grade. The kids started calling her "fatty," "gerbil eyes Gwen," "tunnel nostrils," and "ape face." Even the girls who had previously been her friends joined in. One boy in their class, Paulie, had started it all that year. Gwen assumed it was because she was smart and he was stupid that he picked her out of the class as his target. As usually happened with kids that age, the "bad" kid was seen as "cool," and the rest of the herd followed his lead.

Several months into the school year, Gwen broke down over dinner and told her parents what was happening.

"Every day, they call me names. Horrible names. They make fun of my clothes. They make fun of my hair. They make fun of how I walk. Everything." Gwen sobbed. "Paulie walks by my desk just to knock stuff off it, and then they all laugh. I hate it there! The teacher doesn't help. She pretends not to notice, but I know she sees it. She hates me too. Please don't make me go back." Gwen looked at her parents with tears in her eyes. "Why do they hate me?"

"They don't hate you, Gueneviere. The kids are just jealous of you because you're so smart."

"What about the teacher? Is she jealous too?" Gwen asked, rolling her eyes.

"Of course not. I'm sure she is not aware of what's happening," answered her mother.

Gwen knew her mother was wrong but didn't respond. She put her head in her hands and listened as her parents both talked.

"Ignore them, Gwen. You're smarter than they are. They're just jealous. Focus on your studies. You don't need them."

These were all true but of little comfort to an eight-year-old. What she wanted to hear was that the things the kids were saying about her were not true, and that was the one thing her parents didn't say. She also wanted them to make it stop, but they didn't.

"You're going to make me go back, aren't you?" Gwen asked her parents.

Her parents looked at each other, and her dad finally answered, "You have to go to school, Gwen."

Gwen nodded, knowing this would be their response. Her parents continued to talk, telling her that things would be okay and that they loved her, but as far as Gwen was concerned, the conversation was over. Gwen finished her dinner as they spoke, asked to be excused, and then went to her room for the rest of the evening.

That night, Gwen got up from bed to use the bathroom. As she walked past her parents' room, she heard them discussing her.

"There's not much we can do about the way she looks," her mother was saying. "She got the worst of both of us. Genetics are amazing. We both know that. But sometimes, they're just not fair."

Her dad replied, "Well, it's not going to get any better for her, I'm afraid. She's in for a lot of years of this nonsense. She'll need to learn how to deal with it. Maybe when she gets older, we can get her nose fixed for her. We'll need to keep an eye on her weight too." He stopped for a minute, and Gwen heard her mom mumble something but couldn't make out the words. Her dad continued, "Look, neither of us was ever going to win any beauty contests either, but we made out okay, right? She will too."

Gwen closed the bathroom door as quietly as she could, barely breathing, and, for the first time in her life that she could remember, examined herself closely in the mirror. Her eyes were small like a gerbil's. Her nostrils were big like tunnels. Her hair was a mess. Tears were running over her fat cheeks. She was fat.

Gwen realized that night that she was ugly. Even her parents thought so. She knew the word, knew what it meant, but had never thought of it in terms of herself. She lay awake all night worrying about where to go from here. Using her eight-year-old brain to decide what to do with this news, how to handle being ugly on a day-to-day basis, and how to protect herself, she decided she would handle it head-on. She decided at the age of eight that ugly people could not trust anyone but themselves. She might be ugly, but she wasn't going to be a target. She wasn't going to be bullied. The teachers wouldn't stop it, and her parents wouldn't stop it, but she would.

The next day in school, during recess, Paulie started again. As Gwen sat on the swings by herself, he yelled to her, "Hey, gerbil eyes! Who punched you in the face and flattened your nose?" He started laughing, and so did the kids around him. Today, Gwen was ready. She quietly but quickly hopped off the swing and walked right toward him. She could see the look of uncertainty in his face as she approached, and that gave her confidence. She could feel the surprise of the other kids but kept her eyes on Paulie. She walked right up to him, hauled off, and punched him squarely on the nose. He dropped to the ground crying, blood spouting from his nose. "I don't know," said Gwen, bending down so he could see her face. "But we all know who punched you." She stood and looked at the kids who had formed a circle around them. "Don't we?"

Gwen spent the rest of that afternoon in the principal's office. Her explanations of why she punched Paulie seemed to be ignored. Her parents were called in for a conference and punished her when they got home. But it was worth it. Nothing they did removed the satisfaction she felt that day for having bested her tormentor.

Paulie tried to get back at her over the next few weeks, but she was just too smart for him. His first goal was to regain the upper hand by proving his physical superiority. At recess a few days later, he started taunting her again but was ready this time when she came toward him. When she got within reach, her grabbed her to throw her to the ground, but he wasn't ready for her knee coming up full force into his groin. Again, Paulie was on the ground crying as Gwen stood over him. "What's wrong, Paulie boy? Got your butt kicked by a *girl* again?" She looked around at the kids staring, jaws dropped at the scene before them, and she enjoyed it. She tried to look each one of them in the eye, but none would meet her gaze. "Wussies," she mumbled as she squared her shoulders and walked away.

Gwen soon found she could beat her foes with words as well. The final straw, the confrontation that finally made Paulie throw in the towel, happened a few months later. Gwen had on a shirt that day that was just a bit too small for her and really accentuated her belly hanging over her pants.

As soon as they were outside that day and out of the teacher's hearing, he started. "Look at fatty Gwen! You look like you're having a baby!"

Gwen turned on him. "Well, I may look like I'm *having* a baby, but you *are* a baby! You still wet your pants. At least I don't come to school smelling like piss every day." She turned and walked away.

At first, there was dead silence as she walked away, but then she heard laughter, and this time, the laughter was directed at Paulie.

The kids now gravitated toward Gwen. She was the "cool" kid now, but she knew she couldn't trust them. She quickly rejected any friendly advances from the other kids. She would scare them away with an insult or just a mean look. She would never let them hurt her again.

Eventually, they all left her alone. Entirely.

Chapter 5

1983

A Fresh and Immediate Target

Gwen remained friendless from third grade through sixth. It was okay, really. She was good at keeping herself busy. She learned not to think about what other kids were doing, to not be hurt when kids at school were all talking about birthday parties they were invited to or what they had done together that past weekend. She listened but pretended not to hear. She pretended not to care, told herself she didn't care, and kept busy with other things.

She did her homework, studied, worked out, and read. She read everything she could get her hands on—history, economics, psychology, biology, politics. She also read newspapers and magazines, not fashion magazines but publications like *Time, Life, National Geographic*, and *The Atlantic*. If she expressed an interest in a subject, her parents made sure she had related reading material. Consequently, she knew more than most of her teachers, more than most adults that she knew. She enjoyed showing that off too, especially to the hoity-toity college students who would come and visit her parents. Gwen suspected that her parents enjoyed this as well.

At the start of seventh grade, there was a new girl in their school, Claire Lambertson. Claire was tiny, unkempt, with frizzy blond hair, and she wore Coke bottle glasses and walked with a slight limp. Claire was a fresh and immediate target for her fellow classmates.

Gwen watched from a distance as Claire's tormenting began. Claire was safe in the classroom, but out in the halls or in the lunchroom, she was fair game. It looked like Claire was pretty good at ignoring the taunts of "Your hair looks like a rat's nest" or "Hey, buy some conditioner!" or "Hey, gimpy!" or "You're in the wrong school. First graders don't go here!" and, of course, the ever-popular "Hey, shorty." Gwen suspected this was not new to Claire.

What was difficult for Claire to ignore was the physical abuse. It started with kids just pushing her in the hallway. It quickly escalated to pushing her hard enough to knock her down. Some of the taller kids would steal her books and then hold them up high enough over her head so that she couldn't reach. Others would simply knock her books out of her hands and then laugh as she knelt down to pick them up. Not only was Claire too meek to defend herself, she was also too small.

By about the fourth week of school, Gwen had enough. She was angered by what she saw, and she pitied this small girl. She had seen kids bullied before and never thought twice about it, but something about Claire pulled at her heart. Every time she saw someone mistreat the girl, she would become infuriated and sad at the same time.

Her first defense of Claire came almost immediately after she had made up her mind to step in. Walking to her next class that day, Gwen came upon Claire being tormented by a boy named Sam. He was holding her books up high, and Claire was trying to pull his arm down to get to them. Gwen couldn't see Claire's face, but she knew how she felt. She knew that Claire was probably close to tears and trying hard not to let them see her cry.

Gwen kept walking until she was even with Sam and Claire. Without looking at anyone or even breaking stride, she switched her books to her left arm and threw an amazing punch with her right arm, catching Sam right in the gut. Gwen kept walking. She never looked back, but based on the sounds that followed, she knew the books had fallen to the ground, and so had Sam. Gwen smiled and continued on to her next class.

Over the next few weeks, Gwen learned Claire's schedule and made sure to hurry to Claire's class at the bell and then follow her to her next class. If anyone laid a hand on the girl, Gwen would wait and then follow them. Once out of Claire's sight, Gwen would find the offender.

Even the bigger kids weren't safe from Gwen. They may have had height and muscle on their side, but Gwen was ruthless, merciless, and fearless, and most of all, she was prepared. She would wait until the bully had his or her locker open and brutally bump into that person from behind, hurling them into the locker. With girls, sometimes, she would follow them into the ladies' room and wait patiently for them to use the stall, and as soon as she heard the latch open on the inward swinging stall door, she pushed against it with all her weight, catching the student by surprise and hurling them backward against the wall or, better yet, the toilet. Sometimes, it was as simple as tripping the bully in the hallway, on the stairs, or, and this was Gwen's particular favorite, in the cafeteria while carrying a tray of food. Some bullies would return to their lockers at the end of the day to find their coats drenched with water or milk. Her attacks were stealthy, quick, and painful, and Gwen would nonchalantly walk away before her victims even knew what happened. But always, later that day, the bully would find a note in his or her locker telling them that if they bothered Claire again, the punishment would be much worse the next time. And Gwen made sure it was.

It didn't take too long for the bullying to stop, but Gwen continued to walk behind Claire every day between every class. If anyone called out to Claire, Gwen stared them down. If anyone even looked at Claire the wrong way, Gwen stared them down. While no one had proven that Gwen was Claire's avenger, it was well-known, and the unassuming, unfortunate-looking, chubby seventh grader inspired fear among her classmates.

She was walking behind Claire one day after things had settled down. The two girls had never spoken, and Gwen didn't think Claire knew the role she played in lessening her torment. But that day, when Claire reached her classroom door, she turned back to Gwen. "I know what you're doing."

"Me?" Gwen said, surprised.

"Yes, you." Claire smiled. "I know you've been protecting me. I don't know how you've done it, but thank you."

"You're welcome." Gwen turned to walk away.

"Hey, wait," Claire called after her. "Do you want to come to my house this afternoon? We can play a game or something."

"I don't know," answered Gwen. She hadn't been invited to anyone's house in years. She had no idea if she wanted to go or not.

"Think about it, okay? I'll see you after class." And with that, Claire entered her classroom.

Oh, crap, Gwen thought. *What do I do now?* She worried as she hurried to her class, and she worried all during class. *I feel bad for this girl, but I don't know if I want to hang out with her.* She sighed. *What else are you going to do this afternoon, Gwen?* she asked herself. In the end, she decided, *I'll go today, and if I don't like it or she even looks like she's going to turn on me, I won't go back.*

Gwen met Claire at the end of class, and this time, for the first time, they walked together. Gwen kept an eye out for any threats, but Claire seemed unaware. They chatted about their classes and teachers. When they made it to Claire's classroom, Gwen said, "I would like to come over today, if that's still okay."

"Great!" said Claire, smiling brightly. "I'll meet you out front, and we can walk there together. Do you have to go home first?"

"No, nobody is home at my house until around six, so I'm good."

"Yeah, nobody's at my house until five today."

"Okay, see you in an hour then," said Gwen as she turned and walked away. She was hoping that she had made the right decision. Her goal was to play a game or two and then hightail it out of there before Claire's parents got home. Making a new friend was enough excitement for one day.

As scheduled, the two girls met in front of the school at the end of the last class. Both were carrying an armload full of books. The burden was not a problem for Gwen, but Claire seemed to be struggling.

"Can I help you carry any of those?" asked Gwen.

"No, thanks. I'm used to it." Claire smiled. "It's not a long walk. I only live a few blocks away. Mom says it helps me build muscle."

Gwen smiled and thought to herself, *Yeah, as long as you don't fall over.*

As they walked, Claire chatted on and on about a lot of things— school, her house, her mom. Gwen listened politely but, inside, was terrified, worrying about how to act and if Claire's family would like her. Before she knew it, they were walking up the sidewalk to Claire's small house. Turned out, Claire only lived two streets over from Gwen. The house was much smaller and the yard completely overgrown with weeds, but it seemed like a nice house. Balancing her books in one arm, Claire fished in her pants pocket with the other to retrieve her key.

"Are you sure you don't want help?"

"I've got it." Claire smiled. "I do it every day. It's easier than putting everything down and having to pick it all up again! It's all about balancing the books just right."

"I can see that," replied Gwen, nodding and smiling. "Impressive."

With that, Claire had the door open, and both girls went inside. Claire led Gwen into her bedroom where they both dumped their books on the bed. Gwen looked around; the room was nothing fancy—a bed, a desk, a dresser, a closet. But Gwen's attention was drawn to one entire wall in Claire's room that was nothing but bookshelves. The top shelf had pictures and knickknacks, and the bottom shelf had games, but the middle two shelves were jam-packed full with books. "Wow!" said Gwen, impressed. "This is awesome. Have you read *all* of those?"

"Yes, the ones I haven't read yet are here," said Claire, opening her closet to reveal a smaller bookcase packed with books. "I love to read."

"So do I," said Gwen, "but I don't think I've read this many books!" Gwen walked down the length of the wall, scanning the titles of the books Claire had read. "Would it be okay if I borrowed one sometime?"

"Sure! Whatever you want, just not from the unread shelf yet." Claire smiled. "I get anxious if I don't have a good selection to choose from."

"I hear ya," agreed Gwen. "I usually go the library for my books, but if you don't mind, this is even better!" Gwen liked the idea of being able to browse shelves of books without having to wait on one of her parents to drive her to the library. Then they had to stand around waiting for her to make her selection. She always felt rushed. "I see you like history."

"I do. Those are probably my favorite, but I like other types too. I like books that are either true or seem like they could be true."

"Me too." Gwen looked at her new friend. She felt comfortable with Claire. "Do you remember most of these after you read them?"

"Yes, especially if I enjoyed them."

Gwen had an idea. "If you pick out a book or two that you liked, I'll read them, and then we can talk about them." She stopped for a second and looked at Claire, worried that she had just said something dumb. "Does that sound stupid? If you think it's stupid, we don't have to."

"I think it's a great idea! Sometimes, I talk about books with my mom, but she doesn't have much time for that anymore." Claire walked to her books and started looking through the titles for what she wanted.

"I hear my mom and dad discussing books or articles, but those are usually science related, new discoveries, stuff like that. I like to read them too, but when I join in, they want me to hear their opinions but aren't really interested in mine."

"Yeah, I guess that kinda takes the fun out of it," Claire replied without judgment. Claire grabbed a paperback. "How about *The Thin Red Line*? Have you read that? It's sad but really good. Takes place during World War II."

"No, I haven't," she said, taking the book from her friend. "Thank you."

"Let's stay with the WWII theme…hmm…here we go, *The Diary of Anne Frank*." Claire looked at Gwen.

"Read that one, really sad too."

"Yeah, it was. Well, we can talk about that one today. How about *The Naked and the Dead*?"

"No, that's on my 'to read' list though! I heard it's really hard to read."

"It is," said Claire, handing Gwen the book. "That gives us three to start with!"

Gwen continued to scan the bookshelves. She noticed a leather case sitting on top of the books on one shelf. "What's that?"

"That's my mah-jongg set."

"Your what?"

"Mah-jongg. It's a Chinese game my mom taught me to play."

"Never heard of it."

"It's fun!" declared Claire. "It takes a while to learn, but once you get the hang of it, it's fun. Old people play it a lot." Claire smiled. "There are a few ladies at the senior center that play. I go down there every once in a while to play with them."

"That's nice," Gwen said doubtfully.

"It's fun. They enjoy it. They give me soda while I'm there, and I think they just like having someone young come in and hang out with them. Maybe you can go with me sometime?"

"I don't know, maybe." Gwen wasn't convinced that it would be much fun. "I need to learn to play first, I guess." Gwen thought that should buy her some time.

"Okay, then let's start today!" Claire pulled the case down and led Gwen out to the kitchen. "Maybe in a few days, once you have the basics, you can go with me and play at the senior center. We can play together as one player, and you can learn while we play. Those ladies are awesome."

"We'll see," said Gwen. She wasn't sure she would like the game yet, and she surely wasn't sure she wanted to play with old ladies.

They sat at Claire's kitchen table, and Claire opened the case and started right in explaining the game. Gwen quickly realized that Claire wasn't kidding when she said it would take time to learn! For one thing, it was a game for four people, so they each played two "hands."

They had been playing for about an hour when Claire's mother came in. Gwen's first impression of Mrs. Lambertson was that she looked so young. She had long blond hair, pretty blue eyes, and a perpetual smile. She was also very short, not much taller than Gwen herself. "I'm home, my love!" she called as she walked in the door.

Claire jumped up from the table and ran to her mother, giving her a big hug. Mrs. Lambertson hugged her daughter back tightly, lifting her off the floor, and kissed her on the top of the head. "How's my angel?" Gwen felt a slight stab of jealousy. Her parents never greeted her like that.

"Good, Mom. Come meet my friend." Gwen broke out in a sweat. She had wanted to be out of here by now.

"Mom, this is Gwen…Gwen…Gee, I don't even know your last name, Gwen!" She laughed.

"Marsh."

"Well, hello, Gwen Marsh," said Claire's mom, reaching out to shake Gwen's hand.

"Hi, Mrs. Lambertson." Gwen wasn't quite sure what to do, so she stood up and shook the woman's hand.

"Please call me Miss Ann. Mrs. Lambertson makes me sound too old." She smiled at Gwen. The smile seemed genuine to Gwen, and she allowed herself to relax a bit.

Gwen sat back down. "So, Gwen, is that short for Gwendolyn?"

"No, ma'am, it's short for Gueneviere." Gwen smiled. "My parents thought that a pretty name would make a pretty child." She shrugged her shoulders.

"Well, they were right!" exclaimed Miss Ann, coming over to Gwen and giving her a quick hug. Gwen stiffened; she was not used to anyone touching her, certainly not someone she had just met.

Sensing Gwen's discomfort, Miss Ann quickly released the hug and changed the subject. "So have you girls been playing mah-jongg all afternoon?"

Claire answered, "Yes, I'm teaching Gwen. She's learning fast too. We also like the same books, so we're going to have a book club. We'll read books and talk about them."

"Awesome!" Miss Ann seemed pleased to hear this. Gwen watched this woman closely as she removed her coat and listened with enjoyment as her daughter talked excitedly. Gwen noticed that she was wearing scrubs.

"Are you a doctor, Miss Ann?"

"A nurse. I work at Saint Joe's Hospital, cardiac care. Do you know what that is?"

Gwen smiled. "Sure, I do. That's for people with heart issues."

"That's right! Aren't you smart?" Miss Ann smiled, and Gwen knew that her comment had no malice, no sarcasm. She was genuinely pleased that Gwen understood. "Well, that's what I do. I help take care of people with heart ailments."

"Do you like it?"

"Most of the time," said Miss Ann. "Sometimes, it can be difficult, but mostly, it's very rewarding."

Gwen nodded and tried to think of something to say. She liked Miss Ann, but she was still nervous. "What does Mr. Lambertson do? Will he be home soon?"

Claire looked at her mom. Miss Ann thought for a second and replied, "Mr. Lambertson passed away two years ago."

"Oh my god, I'm so sorry," Gwen stammered. She had just met these people, and already she was screwing up. Her eyes filled with tears.

Miss Ann walked back to Gwen and hugged her tightly. "It's okay, sweetie. You had no way of knowing. And we like to talk about Dan. So thank you for asking about him! You are such a sweet girl."

Gwen was shocked. She didn't think they would throw her out for asking, but she didn't expect Miss Ann to be so sweet about it. "I am sorry."

Ann stood up. "I know you are, sweetie, but there's no need to be." She smiled brightly. "Now would you like to join us for dinner tonight? I have no idea yet what I'm making, and I don't promise anything special, but we would love to have you."

Gwen was torn. Part of her wanted desperately to stay, but part of her was still terrified. "I would love to, but I have to give my parents notice if I'm not coming home for dinner."

"Okay, then how about tomorrow? You can ask them tonight if tomorrow is fine. How does that sound?"

Claire looked expectantly at Gwen, nodding her head yes.

"That sounds great. Thank you, Miss Ann," replied Gwen, smiling. She was happy because these two people seemed to genuinely want her company and also because she had a full twenty-four hours to prepare herself.

Chapter 6

I've Had Dinner Guests Before, Dear

Gwen's parents were darned near giddy with excitement when she asked them if she could have dinner at Claire's house the next day.

"You made a new friend? That's wonderful, Gueneviere! What's she like?"

"I don't know, Mom. She's like me. She likes to read, and she's teaching me to play mah-jongg."

"Mah-jongg? I've never met anyone who can play mah-jongg," chimed in her dad, for once interested in the conversation.

"Yeah, it's a cool game. Hard. You have to really pay attention and plan out your strategy."

"It's like bridge, right?" asked her dad.

"I think it's more like rummy," corrected her mom. Gwen thought that this would be when they cut her out of the conversation, but Mom turned back to her. "Well, I think this is just wonderful."

"We also want to have a book club. It's only two people, but that's okay because we can talk about books we like. If anyone else joined, they would want to talk about stupid books. We like history and books about real life. Today, while we played, we talked about *The Diary of Anne Frank*. She's read that one too, so we talked about it. Claire has a great memory too. It was fun." Gwen was visibly excited now, talking about her day. "She also lent me two books. Both are World War II era too. We thought we would stay with that theme for a bit. I'm going to start one tonight so we can talk about it tomorrow." Her mom and dad listened and looked at each other, smiling. They were so happy to see their Gwen so happy. They worried so much about their daughter, and it bothered them that she seemed to have no friends. This was a good omen.

"Well, Claire sounds like a wonderful friend," beamed Gwen's mom. "I would like to call her parents though. I don't like you just going to someone's house if we don't know them."

"Okay, Miss Ann figured you would want to talk to her." Gwen reached into her pocket and pulled out the little slip of paper Miss Ann had given her with their number. "And don't ask about Claire's dad. He died."

"I'm sorry to hear that," said Mom.

"Yeah, so don't ask to talk to her dad, please."

"I got it. Anything else?"

"No," answered Gwen. "Yes, please don't make a big deal over this. I don't want them to think I've never been to a friend's house before."

"Got it. What is Miss Ann's last name?"

"Lambertson, but she prefers Miss Ann."

"That's fine, but the first time you speak to someone, you should be respectful, so I will call her Mrs. Lambertson."

Gwen rolled her eyes. "She asked me to call her Miss Ann."

Gwen's dad joined the conversation again. "Well, I just think this is wonderful! I'm so happy for you, Gwen."

"I'm not getting married, Dad. It's just a new friend." Gwen rolled her eyes, but inside, she was happy too. She smiled at her dad to soften the eye roll. This was all new to her, and she didn't know how to act.

As Gwen cleared the table, her mom picked up the kitchen phone to call Miss Ann. Gwen hung around so she could hear her mom's end of the conversation.

"Hello, Mrs. Lambertson? This is Dr. Marsh, Gueneviere's mom…Okay, Ann, and you can call me Madeline…Well, thank you. She is a sweetheart." Gwen smiled. She knew Miss Ann had just said something nice about her. "Gwen had wonderful things to say about

Claire as well…I am too. The girls seem to have a lot in common… Yes, Gwen mentioned that you had invited her to dinner. That was very kind…No, she has no allergies and is not a picky eater at all… Well, thank you so much for having her over. We would love to have Claire visit with us soon as well. If you don't mind, I would like to pick Gwen up after dinner tomorrow so you and I have a chance to meet…That sounds wonderful. Thank you again."

When her mom hung up, Gwen immediately said, "Why did you have to do that?"

"What?" Gwen's mom started rinsing the dishes and placing them into the dishwasher.

"Say you wanted to come and pick me up. It sounds like you don't trust her!"

"Gueneviere." She stopped what she was doing and turned toward her daughter. "If I didn't trust her, I would not let you go there in the first place, which you did today without giving me a chance to make their acquaintance, I might add."

"Sorry, it was spur-of-the-moment, and I didn't think you would mind." Gwen knew she was supposed to ask permission before doing anything after school but seldom did anything, so she hadn't even thought about it.

Returning her attention to the dishes, Madeline responded, "From now on, if you go anyplace after school, please find a phone and call me."

"You're never in your office, Mom," said Gwen, still trying to defend herself.

"Actually I am, but I also have a secretary. You know that. Leave a message with Mrs. Connor." Madeline looked at her daughter. "I'm your mother, Gwen. I need to know where you are."

Gwen rolled her eyes. "Okay."

"Be sure to invite Claire here for dinner soon, okay?" Madeline thought for a second and knew that Gwen would not do as she asked. She closed the dishwasher and continued as she dried her hands. "Actually let's plan on this coming Tuesday, okay? I can come home a bit early that day and make a nice dinner. How does that sound?"

"That sounds great, Mom. But I want you and Dad to relax, okay? Please don't make a big deal in front of Claire."

Now it was Madeline's turn to roll her eyes. "I've had dinner guests before, dear. I know how to behave."

Chapter 7

The Toe-Thumb

Gwen and Claire resumed the mah-jongg lessons the following afternoon as they waited for Miss Ann to get home. Gwen was picking up the game and was really starting to enjoy it. While they played, they also discussed the books they had read, so it was a combo mah-jongg /book club. Claire made them each a cup of tea, and they felt very grown up.

For the first time, Gwen noticed that Claire sometimes had trouble picking up the mah-jongg tiles with her right hand. She looked more closely and noticed that there was some scarring on Claire's right thumb knuckle, and her right thumb was noticeably shorter than her left. It was also shaped a bit differently. Claire caught her staring.

"I lost my thumb when I was about three. It got caught on an escalator. I was picking something up off the stair of the escalator just as it got to the top, and my thumb got pulled in." She said this as though she was telling a story about losing a shoe.

"Oh my god! That's awful," cried Gwen. "Did it hurt?" *Of course it hurt, you idiot. What a dumb thing to ask*, Gwen scolded herself.

"Honestly, I don't remember, but my mom said I screamed bloody murder. Someone shut down the escalator and called an ambulance. Mom says a maintenance guy took apart the escalator to free my hand."

The game forgotten, Gwen stared at her friend in disbelief. "That's awful. I guess the doctors were able to sew it back on?"

"Well, the thumb didn't actually come off in the escalator, but it was so damaged that it had to be removed." Claire held up her right thumb. "They replaced it with my toe." She smiled when she saw Gwen's eyes widen.

"Okay, now you're just trying to fool me," Gwen said suspiciously, sitting back and crossing her arms.

"No, it's true," answered Claire. "Look, I'll show you." Claire bent down to remove her right tennis shoe. "Prepare yourself. This isn't pretty, but it's not nearly as bad as it was right after it happened. Mom says the surgeons did a great job, and it looks like I was just born this way."

Gwen watched with fascination as Claire pulled off her sock, revealing a little foot with just four toes. No big toe, just an empty space there. Gwen leaned over and examined the foot more closely. Miss Ann was right. It looked like maybe Claire had been born that way. You really had to look to see the scarring.

"That's amazing. I had no idea they could do that. Does it hurt?"

"Not anymore. It did at first, and for a while, I remember that much." Claire smiled. "I had to learn to get my balance, which doesn't sound hard, but the big toe must help us balance because it was weird. That's why I walk a little funny now. And I had to learn how to use my new thumb. I went to physical therapy for a while for that. But really I hardly ever think about it now." Claire started to put her sock and shoe back on. "Unless, of course, someone *stares* at it," she added, smiling.

"Sorry. That might be the coolest thing I have ever seen," said Gwen, still awed by what she now would always think of as the toe-thumb.

Claire laughed. "Yeah, I guess it is pretty cool."

Gwen stared at her friend's thumb for a few seconds more, then turning back to the game, she teased, "By the way, your feet stink." Both girls laughed.

Gwen had a new sense of respect for her friend. She had been through a lot but didn't make a big deal out of it. She could have shown the bullies at school her missing toe when they made fun of her walk, but she didn't. Gwen would bet that Claire was being completely honest when she said she hardly ever thought about it. "You're a lot tougher than you look."

Claire laughed again. "I don't know about that, but thank you."

The girls went back to their game and book discussion as though they had not just discussed a very traumatic event in Claire's life.

As scheduled, Gwen had dinner that evening with Claire and Miss Ann. Ann prepared spaghetti and meatballs. What kid doesn't like spaghetti and meatballs? Ann knew she had chosen well as she watched Gwen eat.

During dinner, the three of them talked about the books the girls were reading. Ann tried to read most of what Claire read but only vaguely remembered reading what they discussed. She held her own though and really enjoyed having a "literary" discussion with the girls.

The girls enjoyed it too. Gwen loved how Miss Ann would ask her opinion about something and then actually listen to the answer. It was obvious that they were all part of the discussion, and Gwen responded by opening up. She felt completely comfortable in the Lambertson house. She could be herself, and never once during her time there did she wonder what her friend and Miss Ann thought when they looked at her. She didn't worry about her nose or her eyes or her hair or her weight. None of it mattered.

As they were having dessert, a really yummy chocolate cake that Miss Ann had picked up today, Ann said to Gwen, "I understand that you have been a big help to Claire in school. Thank you for taking up for her."

"You're welcome. I was happy to do it," replied Gwen, thinking back with satisfaction to how she had handled some of Claire's bullies. She hoped Miss Ann didn't know all of it.

"It was very brave of you. Kids your age can be so mean."

"I know what it's like to be picked on," said Gwen. "I wanted to stop it."

"I'm sorry that you've had to deal with that too, sweetie," said Miss Ann sympathetically.

Thinking about how Claire dealt with having a toe-thumb and the awful experience leading up to that, Gwen replied, "It's no big deal. I learned how to deal with it."

"You're a sweet girl, Gwen. There are probably three hundred students at that school, not to mention a few dozen adults, and you were the only one to stand up for my girl. I will never forget it."

Gwen smiled, a bit embarrassed now. She just nodded her head and held Miss Ann's gaze. After a few seconds, they both smiled and went back to their cake. Miss Ann knew that Gwen understood how much she was appreciated, and Gwen knew that Miss Ann truly meant what she said.

To change the subject and lighten the mood a bit and to remind them both that she was sitting right there, Claire said, "I showed Gwen my foot today and told her about my thumb. She thinks it's pretty cool."

Gwen responded, "It *is* cool! Who knew you could replace a finger with a toe?"

"I guess it is pretty cool," said Miss Ann doubtfully. "It wasn't cool when it happened, but it is…unique. Your mom is a doctor. You should ask her if she's ever seen that."

"Oh, she's not that kind of doctor. She has a PhD in biochemistry. So does my dad. So they *are* doctors, but not doctors like you work with."

"Oh, I misunderstood. Do they do research?"

"Some, but mostly they teach, both at the Dulaney U."

"Wow, that's pretty neat. They both must be very smart," said Miss Ann, impressed.

"I guess so," replied Gwen. She had never really thought much about it. She knew *she* was smart but hadn't considered just where that had come from.

When they had finished dessert, Gwen and Claire helped clear the table and then headed back to Claire's room to do their homework.

"Can I ask you a question?" asked Claire.

"Sure."

"The first time I saw you was when you punched Sam in the stomach. Thanks for that, by the way." Claire smiled at Gwen. "Where did you learn to punch like that? He went down like he'd been hit by Muhammad Ali!"

Gwen laughed. "Good, I didn't stay around to watch, and I didn't think anyone saw that it was me."

"I did."

"Well, I learned in the third grade that I had to take care of myself. I could either accept the abuse of all the bullies I would come across in school, or I could learn to defend myself. So I learned to defend myself. I do push-ups every night. I have weights that I lift daily, not heavy but enough to build muscle. And I started punching. First, I would set up my mattress on its side, against the wall, and punch that, then I used my allowance to buy a punching bag. It's in our basement. I punch on that a few times a week. I thought about taking some kickboxing classes, but my parents are *non-violent*." Gwen added air quotes to show just what she thought about that. "So that would be hard to get past them." Gwen smiled.

"Don't they care about the punching bag?"

"I told them I needed it for exercise. They weren't happy, but they wanted me to keep my weight down, so they allowed it." Gwen stopped and gave Claire a conspiratorial smile. "If they had any idea that I used it to prepare for punching Sam in the gut, they would die."

"Mum's the word," said Claire, smiling. "It's our secret. Is he the only person you have ever punched?"

"No, but he was the first in a long time. I had to punch a few kids back in third grade to get my nonbullying message across, but between then and Sam, I had no reason." She looked at Claire. "I'm not a bully, but I will defend myself, and I wanted to defend you."

"And boy am I glad you did!" exclaimed Claire. "I never thought you were a bully! Just a nice person who stepped up to help me, and now my best friend." She smiled at Gwen.

Gwen didn't know how to respond to that. She had never been anybody's best friend before. She wanted to say thank you but was afraid to speak. She was afraid that if she opened her mouth, she would cry. Claire seemed to sense that and went back to her home-work. So did Gwen.

It wasn't long after that when they heard a knock at the door. Gwen's heart sank a bit; she knew it was time to go home.

Claire ran to open the door, anxious to meet Gwen's mother. Swinging open the door, she said, "Hi! I'm Claire. Come in."

Dr. Marsh entered the house. "Hi, Claire, I'm Dr. Marsh."

Gwen spoke up immediately, "You can call her Miss Madeline." She wanted Claire to be as comfortable with her parents as she was with Miss Ann.

Madeline looked sharply at her daughter but didn't contradict her.

Miss Ann came out of the kitchen, wiping her hands on a dish towel. "Hi, Madeline, so nice to meet you," she said, reaching out her hand.

Shaking hands, Madeline replied, "Very nice to meet you too. Thank you so much for having Gwen to dinner."

"You're very welcome. She is delightful!"

Madeline smiled at her daughter, proud to hear that she had been a good dinner guest. "We would like to have Claire for dinner on Tuesday, if that's okay with you. We live only two streets over. They can come to our house after school, and then I'd be happy to run her home for you after dinner."

"Thank you. I'm sure Claire would love that." The girls smiled at each other. Neither failed to notice that they hadn't been con-sulted, but that was okay. "I can pick her up though. No reason for you to have to run out."

"That's fine. If you change your mind, just call. It's no prob-lem." Arrangements for Tuesday being made, Madeline motioned for her daughter to grab her things. "Thank Mrs....Miss Ann for dinner, dear."

"Thank you for dinner, Miss Ann. It was great!" Madeline was a bit surprised when Ann gave Gwen a big hug.

"Thank you for joining us! You are welcome anytime."

The girls said their goodbyes, and Gwen left with her mom.

And so it began that each day after school, the two girls went to one house or the other. Usually, it was Claire's, but maybe once a week, it was Gwen's. Gwen's parents did pretty well too. They engaged Claire over dinner, enjoyed learning mah-jongg, and taught the girls how to play bridge. There were no hugs though; Dr. and Dr. Marsh, or Miss Madeline and Mr. Carl as they allowed for Claire only, were just not the hugging type.

The weekends were the same. The days were spent together, and they even spent a few hours each Saturday at the senior center, playing mah-jongg with "the ladies." To Gwen's surprise, Claire was right, it *was* fun! And once the ladies learned that the girls could play bridge, they would alternate games. Also, as there were three ladies and two girls, Gwen and Claire took turns each hand. It worked out well.

The girls were inseparable all through seventh and eighth grades.

Chapter 8

1985

What About Me?

Life changed for Gwen again toward the end of eighth grade.

It was early spring, and Gwen noticed that Claire was very quiet in school and on the walk home to Claire's house.

"Is something wrong?" she asked.

"Yes," replied Claire but not looking at Gwen. "We have to move."

Gwen was shocked and immediately panicked. "Why? Why do you have to move?"

"My nana, my mom's mom, is sick, and we have to go live in Ohio so Mom can take care of her."

Gwen didn't respond. She knew she should, but her mind was racing. *What about me?* she thought, immediately knowing that she was selfish but not really caring. *What about me?* In the ten minutes between getting this blow and reaching Claire's house, Gwen thought through the possibility of moving with the Lambertsons to Ohio but discounted that idea when she realized her parents would never allow it. If she was eighteen, she could do it, but not at thirteen. She considered offering to have Claire live with them until graduation but knew that Claire would not want to stay here without her mom. By the time they reached Claire's front door, Gwen had accepted the fact that her best friend, her only friend, was moving away. Her heart felt heavy, and as she waited for Claire to open the front door, she wanted to cry and scream and pound her fists on something, but she stood silently, trying just to breathe.

When they were finally in the house, the girls just sat on Claire's bed.

"When did you find out?"

"Last night. We knew Nana was sick, but earlier this week, she was diagnosed with cancer. Mom wants to take care of her. I would want to do that for my mom too."

"But you'll come back after…" Gwen realized what she was saying. "I'm sorry. I hope your grandmother is okay, but do you think you'll come back here someday?"

"I don't know."

The girls sat in silence for quite a while. Eventually, Claire spoke, "Remember that time we were playing mah-jongg with the ladies, and Mrs. Benson farted? It was *so* loud and *so* smelly, but they kept playing like nothing happened?"

Both girls cracked up. "That was *so* funny! I didn't know what to do. I wanted to hold my nose, but no one else was doing anything!"

"Me too!" replied Claire, still laughing. "I did catch Mrs. Truitt smiling though."

"You did? She *is* the cool one in the group."

The girls' laughter broke their solemn mood, and they spent the next two hours reminiscing. They relived one funny story after another. Their favorites were the day Gwen learned about Claire's toe-thumb and the time Gwen punched Sam in the gut and kept walking like nothing had happened. Claire's description of Sam's face after getting punched had them both in tears. Neither of them had heard Miss Ann get home.

"What's so funny?" asked Miss Ann, sticking her head into Claire's room.

"We're just telling funny stories, Mom, reliving our best moments!" She threw her arm around Gwen.

Miss Ann smiled. "Well, I will let you continue then." She started to back out of the room and then added, "Are you staying for dinner, Gwen?"

"Not tonight. I have a paper due, and Mom said I need to be home by six. Thank you, though."

"You're welcome, sweetie."

The girls continued their walk down memory lane until it was time for Gwen to go. She grabbed her stuff and headed toward the door. As she said goodbye, Miss Ann gave her a big hug. Gwen held on tight for a minute, knowing she was going to miss this almost as much as she was going to miss Claire. "See you tomorrow," she said as she left.

Gwen walked slowly home. That night over dinner, she told her parents that Claire was moving, and for the first time since she was eight, she let her mom hold her while she cried.

The next few weeks went by quickly. The girls continued to spend every afternoon and weekend together. Miss Ann had to fly to Ohio a few times to help prepare her mom's house and to find a job, and Claire stayed with the Marshes during those trips.

So their schedule was unchanged, but a cloud hung over them. Gwen couldn't help but notice the ever-increasing number of packed boxes at Claire's house, and with each box, Gwen's anxiety grew. They didn't talk about it much, but every once in a while, one of them would say, "I'm really going to miss you," or "We have to write each other *at least* once a week." And they planned out how they could continue their book discussions via letter. They agreed to both save their money so that they could fly out to visit each other and agreed that once they could drive, they would spend time together again on the weekends—that was only three years away. But otherwise, they tried not to think too much about it.

Four weeks to the day after Gwen learned that her friend was moving, she stood in Claire's driveway, next to their packed car. The moving van had already come and gone. It was time to say goodbye. Miss Ann gave Gwen a big hug. She held her tightly. "I love you, sweetie. Thank you for being such a good friend to Claire, and please come and visit us."

With tears in her eyes, Gwen held on tight. "I love you too. I will. I'll miss you so much."

Finally, Miss Ann had to let go. She gave Gwen one last kiss on the cheek. "Stay sweet, my love." She turned and got in the car.

Gwen turned to Claire, her best and only friend in the world. She threw her arms around the tiny girl. "I love you, and I'm going to miss you more than you can know." She began to openly cry.

"I love you, and I do know because I'm going to miss you that much too."

The girls held on tight for a long time. Finally, Gwen let go. "You'd better go. You need to get on the road."

"Okay. I'll write you as soon as we're there."

"You'd better! Don't let that toe-thumb ever keep you from writing me," she teased, smiling.

Claire laughed. "I won't! And you try not to punch anybody," she teased back.

They both laughed and gave each other one more quick hug, and Claire got in the car.

Gwen stood in the driveway and waved until the car was out of sight and then walked home. When she got to her house, she went directly up to her room, lay down on her bed, and cried. When her parents called her down for dinner that evening, she told them she wasn't feeling well and stayed in her room for the rest of the night.

Morning in school the next day was uneventful, but that all changed at lunch. Gwen went through the line, got her lunch, and headed to the table where she and Claire normally sat. She knew she would sit alone now. Again. She was prepared and had a book to read. As she passed a table of boys on her way, she heard Sam say to his buddies, "Oh, lezbo Gwen is sad. Her girlfriend moved away. Her wittle wover is gone." The boys all cracked up, but Gwen acted as though she hadn't heard and continued to her table, her rage building with each step.

She silently took all the food off the tray and placed it on the table. She adjusted her backpack, held onto the tray, and walked back to the table of boys. Standing behind Sam, she said, "Hey, Sam."

"What?" he answered, turning.

As he turned, she swung the tray with all her strength. Her timing couldn't have been any better. The sound of the tray slamming against Sam's face was followed by loud gasps all around the table. Then there was a second of absolute silence as Gwen turned and stormed out of the cafeteria. When she was a few steps away, she could hear Sam cry, "She broke my nose!" Gwen smiled.

Chapter 9

My Heart Is Broken

"What were you thinking, Gueneviere? You hit him with a tray? In the face?" Gwen was sitting on the couch in the living room, prepared for a verbal beating from her parents who sat directly across from her in two armchairs.

She looked at her mom and defended her actions. "He made fun of me and Claire. He called us lesbians."

"And you felt this justified hitting him in the face with a lunch tray?"

"Yes, I did," replied Gwen, looking her mom in the eye. It was immediately clear to Gwen that her parents would not understand. She looked at her dad sitting across from her with his head in his hands. No, they would not understand.

"Do you even know what a lesbian is?"

Gwen gave her mom the "duh" look. "Of course I do, Mom. And it wasn't even *what* he called us. It was that he was making fun of us. He was making fun of Claire." It was also that he was saying out loud exactly what Gwen thought—she was alone again. If she were honest, this was what made her so mad, but she kept that to herself.

"I don't care what he said or how badly he made fun of you or Claire. You cannot resolve that by hitting him in the face!" Madeline was leaning across the coffee table, toward her daughter, hoping to break through Gwen's calm demeanor.

"Oh? Well, then tell me, Mom, how *do* you resolve it?" She looked at her mom, eyebrows raised, waiting for an answer.

Madeline was taken aback by her daughter's question. She sat back in her chair. How indeed? "You ignore it. You rise above it. Nothing he says matters, Gwen."

"And if I hadn't put a stop to it then and there, do you think he would have 'gotten bored with it' and left me alone? Do you really think that, Mom? No, he wouldn't have. He would have continued, and it would have gotten worse and worse. So please don't tell me to ignore bullies. That didn't work when I was eight, and it won't work now." Gwen sat unmoved, arms and legs crossed, gaze fixed on her parents.

Madeline took a deep breath. "Watch how you talk to me, Gueneviere. You don't have to agree with me, but I am your mother, and you will listen and be respectful." She took a breath. "You'll probably get expelled. Do you know that? And what if that boy's nose is broken. You realize that his family will probably sue us, right?"

Gwen jumped to her feet. "I hope his nose *is* broken, and I hope I *am* expelled. I hate that school anyway. Do you even care how *I* feel in all this? Do you even care that my heart is broken? Do you even care how Sam made *me* feel today? What about me, Mom? You care about everybody else so much and how this will make *you* look, but what about me??"

Madeline stood and reached for her daughter, but Gwen pulled away. "Of course we care about you, dear. But you still can't hit people. We can talk about your feelings, but you need to control your behavior."

"I don't want to talk about my feelings, and I'm not going back to that school. Ever!" yelled Gwen.

Her dad spoke up, "Gwen, please go upstairs and let your mother and I talk for a bit." Gwen looked as though she was about to say something, and he continued, "Please. This will be okay. I promise you." Gwen turned and stormed up the steps to her room.

Her parents sat in stunned silence for a moment, and then Madeline looked over at her husband and said sarcastically, "Thanks for your help with that, Carl."

Carl looked up. "What did you want me to say that you didn't say already?"

"You could have backed me up," she snapped back. "I don't know what to do with her. Things were looking up for a while, but now it seems they're worse than ever."

"Maybe she really *was* being picked on, dear. Maybe this kid deserved to be hit in the face."

"Really, Carl? *Nothing* warrants violence! If he was that bad, Gwen should have reported him to a teacher or to the principal."

"I don't recall the school staff being very helpful when she was bullied in elementary school," replied Carl.

Madeline thought for a minute and then answered, "No they weren't, were they? And were we? Things did seem to get better after a bit." They both sat, thinking their own thoughts.

"Maybe the best thing is to pull her from that school," said Carl after a few minutes. "We can afford private school. Let's see if we can get her into Our Lady of Sorrows."

"We may have no choice," added Madeline. "Chances are, she'll be expelled anyway."

After planning out their course of action, Madeline went upstairs to tell her daughter their decision. She knocked on Gwen's door, but after receiving no response, she walked in. Gwen was on her bed reading. "Why didn't you answer me when I knocked?" Madeline asked, hand on her hip.

"I didn't hear you," lied Gwen, not looking up from her book.

"Put your book down, Gueneviere." Madeline chose to ignore the obvious lie. Gwen put down the book and looked at her mother impatiently. "Your father and I have decided to pull you out of that school and enroll you at OLS. You can stay home for the rest of this week, and Dad and I will work out the details. OLS may want an interview, but we'll see." She waited for her daughter to respond, to say thank you, to show some excitement or some appreciation, but there was nothing.

"Okay." Mother and daughter looked at each other for a moment, one hoping to see some sign of emotion and the other just waiting to have the room to herself again.

"Okay then, we'll start making arrangements tomorrow." Madeline sighed as she turned and left the room, quietly closing the door behind her.

Gwen picked up her book and went back to her reading. She was glad that she didn't have to go back to that school but still mad at her parents for not taking her side.

Gwen had the next few days off while her parents took care of everything. They notified the public school that Gwen would not be coming back. No one seemed too bothered by this, and an agreement was reached to not add the recent altercation to any of Gwen's records sent to other schools. Madeline picked up Gwen's transcripts and went to OLS to see if she could enroll her daughter. Gwen's transcripts were great; she was a straight A student, and of course, there was no mention of Gwen's handling of stressful situations. OLS was happy to have her. Madeline and Gwen went shopping for school uniforms, and by Monday morning, Gwen was ready to go to a new school.

Gwen spent the next four and a half years at OLS completely isolating herself from the other girls in school. At first, a few girls tried to make friends but soon gave up. Some tried bullying her but quickly learned that didn't work out well for them. So they left her alone, and she left them alone.

Chapter 10

Most of the Girls Are Snobs

Dear Claire,

Well, as it turns out, I only spent one more day at Ridgely Middle School than you did. To make a long story short, Sam said something I didn't like in the lunchroom, and I hit him in the face with my tray. Hard. Trust me, he deserved it! Grrrrrrr.

Needless to say, my mother was called in, and I was subjected to another lecture on the "evils of violence." I wanted to remind my parents that if the world hadn't reacted to Hitler with violence, we would all be speaking German, but I didn't think that would go over well. She was not happy. Dr. and Dr. are both worried that they're going to be sued by Sam's parents. I'm not worried about it. He'll never admit to his parents that a *girl* did that to him. Hahahahaha.

Mom was worried that I would be kicked out of school, so she pulled me out, and Monday I start at OLS. It's a Catholic all-girls school.

It's going to be torture! I really wish I could just graduate already and be done with it.

Anyway, so that happened the day after you left. I had the rest of the week off, so I was able to read a lot.

I'll probably head down to the senior center after I mail this letter. The ladies and I will miss you. It just won't be the same.

Onto a happier topic, I've picked out our next books! The Kent Family Chronicles! The first book is called *The Bastard*, so I'm going to have to hide my copy from Dr. and Dr., but I bet your mom will be open-minded! I'll probably have to hide my copy from the nuns at my new school too! Can you imagine? Oy. Anyway, in my next letter, I'll include a page with thoughts and questions on *The Bastard*. I think I just like saying, "The bastard."

Well, I have to go. Mom wants to take me to the store for school uniforms. Ugh. Uniforms. I'm sure they're ugly.

I love you, and I miss you. Please hug your mom for me. I miss her too.

Love,

Gwen

PS. I hope your grandmother is doing well.

Dear Claire,

OLS isn't too bad, but the uniforms *are* ugly. The classes are hard, but I like that. Being the new girl though made me a target for the school bullies. I quickly put a stop to that. I did have to punch one girl to get my point across, but that was it. Most of the girls are snobs, so I stay away from them. They talk incessantly about boys, clothes, and parties, like there is nothing more important in the world. Ugh. I really miss you. I wish you were at OLS with me.

The teachers are okay for the most part. Two of my teachers are nuns! That's a bit weird. They seem nice though, just like anybody else actually. There's one priest here too. I don't think he teaches, but I see him in the hall all the time. I don't know *what* he does. Other than the janitor, he's the only man in the building. Poor guy.

No, I haven't made any friends yet, so don't ask. When I find someone like you, I will.

Dr. and Dr. seem to be happy now that I'm in a new school. Nothing came of me breaking Sam's nose, no court summons, no letters from a lawyer, no nuthin'. I'm sure my parents are still waiting for the other shoe to drop, but I think it's over and done with.

Glad to hear that you like your new school. Have you found anyone who plays mah-jongg? I've only played once since you left. The second Saturday that I went to see the ladies, I found out that Mrs. Truitt died. She was our favorite. I just can't bear to go back. Maybe when I can think about her and our games together without crying, I'll try again.

How are you enjoying *The Bastard?* I have my part of the discussion enclosed in this letter. My mother was "appalled" at the title when she saw my book but didn't take it from me.

Take care of that toe-thumb. Hahahahaha.

Xoxoxo. Please hug your mom for me. I miss her almost as much as I miss you.

Love,

Gwen

Chapter 11

1987

A High and Strong Wall

Gwen's years at OLS would have been quickly forgotten had it not been for Sister Mary Francis. Because she turned in outstanding work and lived up to her academic potential, the staff didn't worry too much about Gwen's social discomfort. One teacher, however, Gwen's sophomore lit teacher, Sister Mary Francis, noticed, and it broke her heart.

She took note of Gwen on the first day of Gwen's sophomore year. Sister had learned over the years that the girls who came into class first, day after day, were those having trouble making friends. Most girls took their time getting from class to class, stopping to chat with their friends in the halls, loitering by their lockers to gossip, laughing over some absurdity. But those who came in first on a routine basis did not get involved in all that. So when she saw this short, sad, somewhat odd-looking girl enter her class first that day, she took note and decided to keep an eye on her.

Turned out, her intuitions were correct. Gwen continued to be the first girl to class day after day. Sister Mary Francis noticed also that Gwen was the last to leave after class. If this held true for all her classes, that meant that Gwen simply made a beeline from class to class. She had to if she was consistently last out and first in.

At the end of her classes with Gwen, Sister would step out into the hallway ahead of the girls and stand by her classroom door. She wanted to watch Gwen's interactions as she left class. What she found was that there was no interaction. Gwen simply put her head down and plowed through to her next destination. Sometimes, she would dodge the other girls, and sometimes, she would push her way through the groups. She also noticed that most of the other students, if they saw Gwen coming, would step aside. Sometimes, the girls would look knowingly at one another after Gwen passed, but never did one tease her, call out after her, or in any way try to stop her.

After a few weeks of observing Gwen in her classroom and in the hallways, Sister decided to visit the lunchroom to see how Gwen was faring there. What she saw completely broke her heart. Gwen was sitting at a table for ten completely alone, reading. Girls were squeezed in at other tables, happy to sit shoulder to shoulder rather than join Gwen.

Sister Mary Francis did not approach Gwen that day but instead went up to a tableful of other sophomore girls. She tapped one of her better students, Juli, on the shoulder. Juli turned. "Hi, Sister Mary Fran!"

"Julianna, can you come to my classroom today after school? I'd like to speak with you."

"Sure, Sister...am I in trouble?" Being approached by a teacher during lunch was unusual.

"No." Sister smiled. "I just have something I would like to discuss with you."

That afternoon, Juli tentatively knocked on Sister's classroom door. "Come in, Juli. Thank you for coming."

"Hi, Sister."

"Close the door, please."

Juli closed the door and slowly entered the room, still unsure as to why she was there.

"Have a seat, please."

Juli obediently took a seat close to the Sister's desk and waited.

"I wanted to speak with you confidentially. This means I would like you to keep what we discuss just between us. Can you do that?"

"Yes, Sister." This was really weird. Sister Mary Francis was a favorite at OLS. She was young, not much older than her students really, so she understood them in a way that the other teachers didn't. She could communicate with her students on their level. And she truly loved each and every one of them. The kids, including Juli, could feel this and responded by opening up to the young nun. But this was odd; never once had Sister seemed so serious.

"Okay, with that in mind, and with your agreement and promise to keep this between us," Sister waited for Juli to tentatively nod her agreement, "I would like to talk to you about Gwen Marsh."

"Oh, her." Juli immediately relaxed. She wasn't in trouble, and she didn't know enough about that weirdo to make any difference.

"Why do you say, 'Oh, her,' like that? How do you feel about Gwen?"

"She's just really odd. I'm sure if *you* talk to her, she's all polite and sweet, but if one of us tries to talk to her—and when she first transferred here, we did—she looks at us like she wants to kill us. And if she does respond to us, it's with an insult. She uses names that I won't repeat in front of you, Sister."

Sister Mary Francis smiled. "Well, I appreciate that, Juli. I'll just use my imagination there."

"So we all stopped trying." Juli thought for a minute as Sister patiently waited. "I don't want to get anyone in trouble, but I'm sure you know that we have a few bullies here at OLS."

"Yes, I know that."

"Well, shortly after Gwen came here, one of those bullies decided to pick on her. She followed Gwen into the bathroom and, from what I hear, started to push her and ask her why she was so weird. Gwen took it for about five seconds and then punched this other girl right in the face. Gwen then went into a stall, used the bathroom, came out, washed her hands, and left as though nothing happened. Meanwhile, the other girl was on the floor bleeding, and everyone else just stood watching, in shock. I wasn't there. This is just what I heard. I do know that when Shar..."—Juli caught herself—"the other girl, came out of the bathroom, her nose was still bleeding, and she had two black eyes the next day."

Sister nodded her head. "I remember that. I remember the nurse having to send someone home who claimed to have run into a door. We all assumed the door story was a ruse."

"Please don't tell anyone. I don't want to get anyone in trouble."

"When I said the conversation was between us, I meant that anything you said here was also safe." Sister smiled. "I will keep my word."

"I will too, Sister."

"Is there anything else you can tell me?"

"No, Sister. We just all decided it was safer to stay away from Gwen. She never punched anyone else that I know of, but her insults can be just as painful and embarrassing. So we just leave her alone. That seems to suit everyone just fine."

Sister Mary Francis stood, indicating that the meeting was over. "Thank you so much, Juli. I appreciate your insight."

"You're welcome, Sister. I'm glad I could help." Juli stood and walked toward the door. With her hand on the doorknob, she turned back. "We did try, Sister."

"I know you did." Sister nodded, smiling. Juli left and shut the door behind her.

Sister sat and thought for a bit. Apparently, Gwen was not easy to befriend. This meant that the child had erected a high and strong wall around herself. The question was why?

The following day, at the end of Gwen's lit class, Sister Mary Francis waited until the other girls left the classroom. As Gwen slowly made her way out, Sister stopped her.

"Gwen, I'd like to speak with you today. Would you mind bringing your lunch back to my classroom? We can talk over lunch."

"Yes, Sister." Gwen nodded and left. It was unusual that the child didn't ask why or express any concern about being asked to return to talk to her teacher. But Gwen was not a typical teenage girl.

As promised, Gwen was back in Sister's classroom for lunch. She carried her lunch bag and a bottle of water.

"Hi, Gwen. Thank you for coming. Take a seat."

Gwen selected her normal seat right in front of Sister's desk. She sat silently and waited.

Sister Mary Francis opened her own lunch. "Go ahead and start your lunch. We can talk while we eat." She smiled at Gwen, trying to put her at ease.

Gwen opened her lunch and started on her sandwich. She waited patiently to find out why she was there. She watched her teacher. *The nun didn't seem upset, so I'm probably not in trouble*, thought Gwen. Actually, Sister looked pretty much like she always did—calm with a slight smile and sweet, soft eyes. Gwen was at a loss as to why they were having lunch together. As she chewed, she thought over her recent work, none of which she thought was subpar, certainly nothing that required a "talking to."

"You're one of my best students, Gwen," started Sister. "I really enjoy reading your papers. Your insight into the literature we have covered so far is well beyond your years."

"Thank you, Sister. I love to read, always have."

"Me too. Is there a particular genre that you enjoy?"

"Historical fiction mostly, but I'll read just about anything. Well, I don't particularly care for sci-fi though. I prefer stories that are, or could be, real."

"I agree. There may have been a few exceptions over the years, but mostly, I stay away from sci-fi too." Sister smiled at Gwen, hoping to get a return smile, but Gwen just continued to eat. So Sister went back to her salad. Her hope was that the silence would be uncomfortable for Gwen and encourage her to speak. It was not and did not.

Finishing her salad, Sister finally spoke again. "Gwen, I want you to know that anything you and I say in this room when we are alone remains between us. Nothing you say will go any further than this room."

"Okay." Gwen wanted to say, "Like confession?" but kept that to herself.

"I hope that you will offer me the same courtesy and keep anything I say to yourself."

"Okay."

Sister smiled. "Okay then. Well, I didn't ask you here to talk literature, though we can do that another time."

Gwen nodded, sat back, and folded her hands on her lap. "I assumed as much."

"I'm concerned about what appears to be your inability to make friends here at OLS. Do you mind talking about that?"

Gwen took a deep breath. "There's really not much to discuss, Sister. I learned at an early age that people don't like me."

Sister Mary Francis frowned. "I'm sure that's not true, Gwen. I like you." Sister smiled.

"With all due respect, Sister, teachers don't count." Gwen smiled to soften the statement.

Sister laughed. "Well, I have to say I'm disappointed to hear that!"

"What I mean is that teachers have a different perspective. You like me because I'm a good literature student. I'm sure Mrs. Armacost likes me because I'm an excellent math student. My fellow students don't care about that."

Sister nodded. "What do they care about?"

"They care about looks. Notice how the pretty girls are also the popular girls? They care about parties and boys and gossip and clothes and going to the mall and…just fitting in."

"And you don't care about those things?"

"No."

"Do you really think that a student here has to be pretty to be liked?"

"It doesn't hurt, and before you tell me that I'm pretty, please don't. I have a mirror, and nuns are not supposed to lie."

Sister chuckled. "No one is supposed to lie. But you're right. Nuns should be known for their honesty. So with that in mind, you are not what most would call beautiful, but that doesn't mean that you are not pretty or that you are not worthy of friendship. And a person's appearance is not what is important."

"Well, that's what everyone *says*, but what I see is just the opposite."

"I'm disappointed to hear that, Gwen." Sister remained quiet for a moment, thinking about how she could get through to this child. "Is there anyone in this school that you consider your friend?"

"No, ma'am."

"Is there anyone outside this school that you consider to be your friend?"

"Yes, I have a friend, Claire, but she had to move to Ohio when we were in eighth grade. We write though."

"How did you and Claire become friends?"

Gwen gave Sister a brief history of how she and Claire became friends.

"So you became friends because you had sympathy for her when she was bullied, and you stepped in to help, which was very brave. But how did you stay friends?"

"We liked the same things. We discussed books that we read. She taught me to play mah-jongg, and my parents and I taught her to play bridge. We spent every day together. She never made fun of me. I knew she would never betray me to make points with the cool crowd." Gwen stopped, and her eyes filled up with tears. "I miss her very much."

"I'm sure you do, Gwen. Have you tried to make another friend since?"

"Before Claire moved, we would go to the senior center on Saturdays to play mah-jongg and bridge with a group of older ladies. I did want to keep going after she moved, so I thought of them as my friends."

"And do you still see those ladies?"

"No." Gwen shook her head. "Two weeks or so after Claire moved, I went there one Saturday, and Mrs. Truitt wasn't there. The other ladies just looked at me when I got there. Then Mrs. Singer got up, came over, and put her arms around me and told me that Mrs. Truitt had died that week. Mrs. Truitt was my favorite. I ran out and never went back. I just couldn't be there without Claire *and* Mrs. Truitt. Since then, I've been alone, and I'm okay with it. It's less painful," finished Gwen, straightening her shoulders.

"Ohhhh, I'm so sorry, Gwen. I'm sure that was a very painful time for you."

"It was, but I was expected to just go on. No one understood. No one ever understood."

The Sister nodded; she understood. "Have you tried since then?"

"No."

"Why not?"

Gwen thought for a moment and decided just to be direct. "Sister, I started getting bullied in third grade. I learned to protect myself and put a stop to it. I also learned that most people can't be trusted. The friends I had before third grade joined in when others started to make fun of me. Claire was an exception. I can't change my size or my face, but I can protect myself, and I do."

"But do you think that you protect yourself too much? You're not in third grade anymore. People change. People grow. It's not good to use your experience as an eight-year-old to make decisions and guide your behavior today."

Gwen thought for a minute. "Maybe. Probably. But I'm okay with things as they are."

"Don't you think you should try again though? Though there is sometimes pain, the joy we get from relationships overall outweighs the pain."

"That has not been my experience, Sister." Gwen appreciated her teacher's concern and wanted to put her mind at ease. "I write to Claire. I read a *lot*. When someone has to miss my parents' bridge group, they ask me to substitute, and I focus on school. So I stay busy. I'm okay, Sister. I really am."

"Well, I'm glad you are okay," replied Sister. Wanting to dig a bit deeper, Sister changed her line of questioning. "So what brought you to OLS? Why leave the school you were in?"

Gwen was not sure she wanted to answer that question. "What I say here stays between us?"

"Yes. That is my promise to you, and nuns are not allowed to lie," Sister added with a twinkle in her eye.

"Okay, but this might change the way you think about me."

"Perhaps, but that's unlikely."

"Okay, well, the day after Claire moved, a kid named Sam started making fun of me and Claire. He called us lezbos. So I hit him in the face with my lunch tray." Gwen said this very matter-of-factly.

"Oh my," replied Sister, trying to sound surprised, but after learning of how Gwen handled being bullied here at OLS, she was not. "Did Sam learn his lesson? And more importantly, how did you feel about what happened?"

"I don't know about Sam. That was my last day at that school. Mom and Dad decided to pull me out. And I felt okay about it. If you don't stop a bully right away, they get worse. Most adults would say that if you ignore a bully, he will get bored and move on to something else. That's bullsh—" Gwen caught herself. "That's not true. They just get worse. If you don't respond, you give them the power they need to continue. So I respond quickly and firmly."

"I see." Sister Mary Francis wasn't quite sure how to handle this. "Have you ever tried handling bullies another way?"

Gwen thought for a moment. "No, I guess I haven't, Sister. But I've seen kids get bullied all my life, and it's always the same."

"I'm sorry that you went through that, Gwen." She wanted to help this child, but she really didn't know how. She knew the bell signaling the end of lunch would be sounding any minute. "Would you like to have lunch with me once a week? Nuns get lonely too. Not too many people feel comfortable hanging out with a nun." She smiled at Gwen.

"I would like that, Sister, but can we please not talk about my social status each time?"

Sister laughed. "Agreed. Not each time, but from time to time, I may ask a question or two. Otherwise, I think it would be fun to discuss books, and maybe you can teach me to play mah-jongg."

"Deal," said Gwen, sticking out her hand to the nun. Sister Mary Francis reached out and shook Gwen's hand.

"Good, let's meet for lunch, here, every Wednesday."

"Okay."

"Thank you for coming today, Gwen."

"Thank you, Sister." And with that, Gwen left the classroom and headed to her locker to grab her afternoon books. Her first thought was that she could write Claire and tell her that she made a friend. She knew that news would make Claire happy.

As Gwen walked to her locker, Sister Mary Francis sat back down to think. She decided that at some point, when the time was right, she would introduce another student to their Wednesday lunches, hoping to help Gwen form a friendship.

From that day until she graduated, Gwen spent lunch every Wednesday with Sister Mary Francis. It turned out that mah-jongg proved not to be a game that the Sister enjoyed, so for the most part, they discussed literature, current events, and whatever else came up. They seldom discussed Gwen's social life after that first day. The nun quickly realized that Gwen was truly okay with things the way they were, and to force her to "mix" with the other students would just be painful for her, so she never invited anyone else to join them.

On the last day of Gwen's senior year, after her very last class, she rushed to Sister Mary Francis's classroom. She saw her friend sitting at her desk, making notes in her grade book. Gwen knocked on the door.

Sister looked up. "Gwen! Come in. So nice of you to stop by to see me before you left today."

"Hi, Sister. I wanted to thank you. Thank you for all the time you took with me. I'm sure there were better things that you could have been doing, but you had lunch with me every week. Thank you."

"Oh, Gwen, I was doing exactly what I wanted to do." Sister smiled and stood and opened her arms to Gwen. Gwen rushed into her arms, and they held on tightly to each other. Gwen had not had a hug like that since Miss Ann and Claire moved; she didn't want to let go.

After a minute or so, Sister let go slightly and pulled back to look at Gwen. "I have enjoyed our time together, Gwen. You are truly a remarkable young lady. Best of luck to you at college, my young friend."

Gwen wiped the tears from her eyes. "Thank you, Sister. I will never forget you. Can I write to you?"

"Of course. You must!" Sister gave Gwen one last quick hug, and Gwen hurried off. The two kept in touch until Gwen got pregnant. She was too embarrassed to let Sister know what had happened and so had stopped writing. Sister Mary Francis didn't know what had happened to her young friend until more than two decades later when she read about her in the paper.

Chapter 12

1989

We Just Want What's Best for You

For her college education, Gwen decided to attend Dulaney University. There were two reasons for that. One, since both of her parents taught there, they got quite a break on Gwen's tuition. Two, Gwen could commute. This started a large argument with her parents. Dr. and Dr. Marsh thought that living on campus would be a good experience for their daughter. Gwen thought it would be anything but.

After trying to reason with her parents on the topic for a few weeks, Gwen finally resorted to emotional manipulation. "Are you in that much of a hurry to get me out of your house? Because if that's the case, I can get an apartment off campus for the next few years. I won't be in your way then."

Madeline looked up from the paper she was reading. "Oh, for Pete's sake, Gueneviere, you know that's not true. Your father and I just think it's an important experience, a good experience, for college students to have."

"Mom, when has throwing me in with a group of my peers *ever* been a good experience?"

"At some point, you need to learn to get along with others, Gwen. Don't you think it's time?"

"I get along fine with others, but I refuse to spend time with people who treat me like crap, like a second-class citizen. Why do you want to subject me to that?"

Madeline sighed. "We don't want to subject you to anything, dear. We just want what's best for you."

"Well, what's best for me is to commute. Okay?"

"Fine, we can try that for your freshman year, and then we'll revisit this topic next summer. We're not buying you a car though. You'll need to ride with me and your father each day."

"I can get a job and get my own car."

Madeline chuckled. "You think it's that easy?" She thought for a moment. "Actually, I think that's a great idea. I think you should get a job, save up some money, and purchase a car." A job would be a good thing for her daughter.

And so the decision was made that Gwen would commute to college. The summer before her freshman year, Gwen started job hunting. She did this by thinking about all the businesses in her area, trying to think of one that held even the remotest interest for her. Anything in the mall was out. Restaurants were out; no way she could be nice to difficult customers. Fast food was just gross. Mini-marts were too dangerous, not to mention the clientele that one would need to deal with. Maybe her mother was right; finding a job was not going to be so easy.

A few weeks after the job discussion, Gwen was at the local library, stocking up on reading material. She had an armload of books but had another twenty minutes before her mother would pick her up. Gwen sat down at an empty table and pulled a book off her pile to start reading while she waited, but she didn't open the book. She happened to notice a young man going up and down the aisles of books, pulling a cart behind him. He would stop in each aisle, pull out a few books from his cart, put them on the shelves, and move on. She also noticed him opening a book every now and again to read the inside cover.

Gwen got up and walked to the main desk. "Excuse me."

"Hi, are you ready to check out?"

"Yes, but actually, I wanted to see if you had any job openings here."

"I don't know, but I can give you an application. Just fill it out and leave it with me. I'll make sure the head librarian gets it. I know we have people come and go all the time." She pulled open a drawer, pulled out an application, and handed it to Gwen.

"Thank you. Would you also happen to have a pen?" Gwen smiled. "I wasn't anticipating filling out forms today."

The librarian reopened the drawer, pulled out a pen, and handed it to Gwen.

Gwen went back to her table, quickly filled out the application, and returned it to the librarian as she checked out her books. There was another woman at the desk who noticed Gwen handing over the form. "I've seen you here a lot." She reached over the counter to shake Gwen's hand. "I'm the head librarian, Mrs. Patel. You're interested in a job?"

"Yes, ma'am, I am."

"We need someone in the children's section. Could you commit to a few afternoons as well as Saturday each week during the school year?"

"Yes, no problem."

"Why do you want to work in a library?"

"I love to read, and I love the atmosphere here."

"You don't get to read while you work." Mrs. Patel smiled at Gwen. "In the children's section, you'll spend most of your time putting books back on shelves, cleaning up trash, putting toys back in place, arranging for story readers, and finding lost parents. Does that sound like something that would interest you?"

Gwen wasn't so sure but answered, "Yes, ma'am, it would. I know that I wouldn't be able to read while I'm working, but I just love to be around books. And I do like kids." That last part was a lie; Gwen hadn't been around kids since *she* was a kid.

Mrs. Patel and Gwen discussed scheduling. Gwen would work nearly full-time during the summer and then, once school started, three afternoons during the week and all day on Saturday. This was assuming that things went well during the summer. It was made clear to Gwen that not showing up or not showing up on time or not doing the job was not tolerated. This did not concern her.

"Great, then we'll see you tomorrow morning, nine a.m. sharp. You'll need to bring your own lunch, but we do have a refrigerator and microwave for you to use."

"Thank you, Mrs. Patel. I'm looking forward to it." And she was. But even more than looking forward to her new job, Gwen was looking forward to telling her mother that she had a job. She picked up her books, checked out, and went out to the parking lot to see her mother already pulled up to the curb, waiting for her.

"Hi, Mom," she said brightly as she got into the car.

"Hi." Madeline didn't fail to notice that her daughter was in a good mood. "How was the library? Find some good books?"

"Yes, I did. And I got a job." She looked at her mother to see her reaction.

"You did?" Madeline smiled brightly and looked at her daughter. "At the library? How did that happen? I didn't even know you had put in any applications."

"I hadn't. I thought of it while I was in there, asked for an application, talked to the head librarian, and voila, your daughter has a job." Gwen was smiling for ear to ear. "I think it's going to be great. What better place for me to work than a library? I'm here every week anyway."

"That's terrific, Gueneviere. I'm so proud of you! When do you start? What will you be doing? How much will you get paid?"

"I start tomorrow, nine a.m. Please tell me you can drive me here, Mom. I'm going to work Monday through Friday throughout the summer, nine to five. Then when school starts, I'll work three afternoons a week and all day on Saturday. I'll start off in the kids' section, which should be fun, I hope." Gwen smiled. "But I think that will be temporary. They'll see how good I am and will move me up quickly."

Madeline laughed. "Confidence is good. What is the pay rate?"

Gwen sighed. "I never asked."

"That's okay." Madeline didn't want to ruin Gwen's good mood. "It has to be at least $3.35 an hour."

"Right. I doubt they pay more than minimum for new employees." Gwen thought for a minute. "So if I work forty hours a week for the next ten weeks, that's four hundred hours. That's $1,340. How much do you think a used car would be?"

"I don't know. We'll have to ask your father to look into that. But you have to take taxes into consideration, Gwen. You're not going to have $1,340 at the end of ten weeks. You have to figure 15 percent for federal taxes, 7.5 percent social security, and maybe 5 percent Maryland."

"Oh, crap! *Ugh*. Okay, so now I'm left with about $970. Jeez."

"Welcome to adulthood."

"I should go into politics. This is bullsh——. Sorry, this is just wrong."

Madeline smiled. "Perhaps, but taxes are a part of life, sorry to say."

"Okay, so once I'm back in school, I'll probably work twenty hours a week, so that means…ugh, only about fifty dollars a week after taxes. It might take me longer than I thought to get a car."

"Well, let me talk to your father. I like that you're taking the initiative here, and I think I can talk your dad into splitting the cost of the car. That would help. So you would have to save half the purchase price, plus car insurance, which should not be too much for you, estimate two hundred dollars per year. Once you buy the car, you should have no problem covering gas and insurance. You don't have any other expenses."

"Right. Thanks, Mom." Gwen allowed herself to become excited about the prospect of having a job, owning a car, and yes, even paying taxes. She couldn't wait to get home to write Claire.

"You're welcome, Gueneviere. Just remember one thing please—school comes first. If your grades suffer at Dulaney, you'll need to cut back on your hours."

"Please, Mom." Gwen rolled her eyes. "I think I'll be fine."

"College is different than high school, dear. I just want to make sure we're clear on priorities." They pulled into the driveway. "I'm sure you will do just fine, but school comes first, okay."

"Deal. And thanks for talking to Dad." She felt a closeness to her mom right now that she didn't feel very often. Gwen wondered about that. Her parents were good at practical help; it was emotional help where they were pretty useless. Maybe it wasn't their fault. Maybe this was all they were capable of. She smiled at her mom. "Thank you for everything, Mom."

Madeline looked at her daughter, a bit taken aback by her gratitude. "You're very welcome, Gueneviere. We're happy to help and very proud of you."

Mother and daughter looked at each other for a moment, neither knowing what to say next. Madeline smiled. "Let's go tell your dad the good news!"

It was Christmas before Gwen had enough for a car. Together with her parents, she purchased a used Mustang. The only time in her life that she ever felt "cool" was driving that car. And as it turned out, she *was* good with kids. The kids who visited the library loved her. The number of kids who came for weekly book reading sessions grew to capacity, and most weeks, Gwen was the reader. Parents learned quickly to stay away from her, but they tolerated her because of the kids.

Mrs. Patel quickly found that Gwen was a huge help at the library. In addition to her duties in the children's section, Gwen helped with paperwork, took over making calls for late books, kept the periodical section neat, and helped with the setup of the new computer system. As long as they could keep her away from adult visitors, Gwen was indispensable. It was a job she kept throughout college.

Chapter 13

1991

The Semester of David

College years for Gwen went by quickly. Between school and work, she was too busy to worry about much else. One semester was different though. That was what she would always remember as the semester of David.

She and David met in a Latin class her junior year. She had seen him around campus before but hadn't paid any more attention to him than she had anyone else. She could tell that life had been tough on him too. Like her, he was short and heavy. He was already balding, wore thick glasses, and walked like a duck. He dressed oddly, too, for a college student, always in dress slacks that were a bit baggy and a dress shirt. She didn't have to be there to know that he had probably been bullied his entire life.

One day after class during the first week of the semester, David approached her. "Hi, I'm David Goldfeder."

"Hi," responded Gwen with suspicion.

"We have an exam coming up, and I couldn't help but notice that you always ace your exams while I barely squeak out a C. Would you be willing to help me study?"

Gwen sighed and looked at David, ready to tell him that she didn't have time to tutor his sorry ass, but when she looked in his eyes, she saw something. It could have been fear or desperation or just hope, but it softened her heart. "Sure, but I don't have a lot of free time. Only Tuesday and Friday afternoons and the occasional Sunday."

"Today is Tuesday. Could we meet this afternoon? We could use one of the library study rooms."

Ugh, thought Gwen. *I set myself up for that.* Then she answered, "Sure, I'll meet you in front of the library at three. Don't be late, and make sure you have your books." With that, she picked up her stuff and left. David stood still for a few minutes, then smiled and headed out of the room.

He was already waiting in the designated spot when Gwen arrived at three. He waved as she approached. "Thank you so much for coming. I wasn't sure you actually would."

Gwen rolled her eyes. "I said I would be here."

"Thank you," repeated David, smiling. He just stood there staring at Gwen until she finally raised her eyebrows in a questioning manner. "Oh yeah, let's go inside and get a study room." He took her books from her. "I'll carry those."

She let him take her books but said, "I'm capable of carrying my own books."

"I know, but you're doing me a favor by being here, and I'm a gentleman."

Gwen just shook her head and followed his balding head inside.

They found a quiet room on the study floor and sat across from each other at an empty table. Gwen immediately pulled out her Latin books and started to grill David. When he didn't know the correct response, she would patiently explain and then move on, but she always remembered to come back and ask the questions he missed several times again to make sure he got it. This went on for about an hour, when Gwen began to gather her things, indicating their tutoring session was at an end.

"You should be a teacher," David told her.

"Nah, an hour with one person is fine, but I wouldn't have the patience to deal with a whole room of people."

"You were very patient with me."

"Well, you actually knew the material pretty well, and when you didn't, you listened and picked it up. Honestly, I don't think you really need any more help."

"To be honest, Gwen, I just wanted to meet you."

Gwen stopped and look at him. She set her books back down on the table. "Why?"

"I noticed that you are always alone. I am always alone. I thought we might hang out together."

"I don't *hang out*."

"Do you eat?"

"Of course I eat." Gwen rolled her eyes again.

"Good, so do I. Can we go eat dinner together?"

Gwen looked down. She had never been asked out to dinner before. Ever. Her first inclination was to say no and get the hell out of there. But this did give her an opportunity to tell her parents that she had plans and wouldn't be home for dinner. They bugged her incessantly about not having friends, about getting out. This one meal might hold them at bay for a bit. She decided to try to catch David off guard. "Okay, I'm hungry now."

Hoping he would hesitate and give her an out, Gwen was disappointed when David's face lit, and he said, "Great! Do you like Mexican?"

"Yeah, it's okay." The only Mexican she had ever had were the tacos her mom made occasionally.

"Well, there's a little Mexican place a short walk from here. You'll love it. Once you eat here, you'll never be able to eat Taco Bell again." David smiled, obviously excited at the prospect of introducing her to his find.

"Okay then, lead the way."

They left the library, and David dropped off their books in his dorm room. Though she was invited up to see his room, Gwen simply said no and waited outside. They then walked in relative silence; David tried to make conversation but quickly gave up as Gwen would respond with just a nod or a one-word answer.

As promised, the restaurant was just a short walk, no more than seven or eight blocks, from the school. She had probably driven by it a few hundred times but had never noticed it. It was just a small yellowish building with no parking lot. The small sign in the window read, Mesa de Guac. *Oh, jeez,* thought Gwen as they approached the building, *this place looks like a dump.*

David held the door for her, and Gwen walked in. Once inside the door, she just stopped and looked. The restaurant was like nothing she had ever seen. So much color! The tables were simple, but every chair was an explosion of color. They were high-back chairs covered with parrots and flowers and Mexican sombreros. The walls were covered with frescos of the same bright colors.

"It looks like a party," whispered Gwen.

"Yeah, that's exactly it! It looks like a party." David smiled, pleased with Gwen's first impression of the restaurant. Gwen didn't look at him or respond. She just continued to scan the restaurant.

"Two?" asked a young woman.

Gwen didn't respond, but David nodded yes, and the hostess led them to a small table for two in the middle of the restaurant. Gwen didn't immediately follow, so David gently grabbed her elbow and escorted her.

Once seated, David asked, "You like it?"

Gwen smiled, the first honest smile from her that David had seen. "Yes, I do."

"Wait until you taste the food," promised David as he handed her a menu. "Everything is good, but my favorite is the Texas fajitas."

Gwen looked at the menu. She didn't know a fajita from a quesadilla, to be honest. She had no idea what she wanted. "Texas fajitas sound good to me."

David nodded. "And let's start with some freshly made guac, okay?"

Gwen thought, *I have no idea what that is,* but said, "Sure, that sounds good."

A young Latino man in an apron approached their table. "Señor David, welcome!"

David offered his hand to the waiter. "Mauricio, how you doin'?"

"I'm doing great, living the dream." Mauricio laughed as the two shook hands.

"Meet my friend and Latin tutor, Gwen," David said, introducing his dinner partner.

Mauricio bowed slightly in Gwen's direction. "Señorita, very nice to meet you."

"Nice to meet you too," replied Gwen, very quietly. This whole scene was *way* outside her comfort zone.

David seemed to sense her discomfort and ordered for them both. "We'll start off with some fresh guacamole, and then we'll both have the Texas fajitas. I'll have an iced tea, and Gwen will have…," he looked at Gwen, and she nodded slightly, "an iced tea as well."

"You got it, señor."

Once the waiter walked away, Gwen said, "He doesn't sound Mexican."

"He's from Jersey." David smiled. "I'm not convinced that his name is really Mauricio, but he's a great guy. No matter where I sit now, he's my waiter."

"You must tip well," quipped Gwen.

"I do." David nodded, taken aback by Gwen's comment. "But I don't think that's why. When it's slow, Mauricio will sit and chat with me while I eat. He has a great sense of humor, and I like his company. I'm from Jersey too, so we talk about home a lot."

Gwen just nodded. She had lost interest in the David/Mauricio connection already and was more concerned about what she and David could possibly talk about while they waited for their food.

"So I never see you on campus in the evenings. Do you commute?" asked David.

"Yes." She paused and then realized that she would need to offer more than one-syllable answers if this dinner was going to be even mildly comfortable. "I live in Towson. My parents actually both teach here. If you take a biochem class, chances are, likely, you will have one of the Dr. Marshes."

"I did! I guess I had your father last year."

"How'd you do in his class?"

"C."

Gwen smiled. "That's pretty standard, unless you're majoring in biochem. Dad assumes that *everyone* should be as into his subject as he is."

"Yeah, I gathered that. I liked the class, but I'm just not scientist material."

"So what's your major?"

"Economics with a minor in finance. You?"

"Accounting."

"Plan on being a CPA?"

"Sure do."

"Were your parents disappointed that you didn't select a science major?"

"Yes, they were!" Gwen chuckled. "They envisioned me getting my PhD and then going into research or teaching. I think I disappointed them."

"I doubt they're disappointed. Most kids don't follow in their parents' footsteps."

"What do your parents do?"

"Dad's an oncologist, and Mom is a trophy wife."

Gwen laughed. "I've never heard anyone refer to their mother as a trophy wife."

"Yeah, well, it applies here. She is your typical JAP, Jewish American princess."

"Jewish American princess?"

"Yeah, she was raised in luxury, married my dad, and continued in luxury. Never worked a day in her life. Dad spoils her rotten." David smiled. "But don't get me wrong. She's a great mother. So I guess that's what she does. She 'mothers.' She was home every day and took care of me and my brother. Still does when we're home."

"That sounds wonderful. I never had that." The pitying look on David's face made her immediately sorry she said that. Thankfully, before he could respond, a woman approached their table, pushing a cart.

The cart was expertly parked next to their table, and Gwen watched, fascinated as the little woman made a bowl of fresh guacamole for them. She had tasted guacamole before, but it was store-bought. She hadn't given much thought to what was in it. To her, it was just something to dip nachos in. Once done, the woman placed a huge stone bowl full of fresh guac on their table and then a bowl of tortilla chips. David tipped her a few dollars, and off she went to the next table.

"You first," offered David nodding toward the bowls.

Gwen tentatively grabbed a chip and dipped it into the guac. She dug in deep, wanting to get a heap of it on her chip, and then ate it. David could see her eyes light up as she chewed. Mouth still full, "This is great!"

"Isn't it?"

"If you had asked me ten minutes ago if I liked guacamole, I would have said, 'Yeah, it's okay,' but now, this is just delicious!"

"I'm glad you like it," David smiled as he dug in too.

They enjoyed the guac in relative silence, only looking at each other to smile or if they both dug in at the same time. It didn't take too long for them to empty out the bowls.

"I take it you didn't like the guac?" Mauricio was standing by their table, smiling.

"It was awful, as usual," answered David, smiling.

"Then let me get these bowls off your table. I'll be bringing out your meal in just a minute."

As Mauricio was clearing the table, David asked Gwen if she would like a frozen margarita. "Trust me," he said, "you'll love it."

Gwen knew she should say no as she was not yet twenty-one but nodded, and David ordered two.

The couple enjoyed the rest of their meal together. David was truly funny and had Gwen laughing until tears rolled down her eyes. He told stories about his family, things he and his brother had done together, and lots of stories about what it was like to grow up Jewish. Gwen hadn't laughed like this since Claire moved away. She also hadn't felt this relaxed around another human being since Claire left. When the meal was done and the conversation had come to a lull, she smiled at David. "Thank you. I really enjoyed this."

"You're very welcome." David smiled back. "Let's get some coffee before we go. I want to make sure you're okay to drive."

Gwen didn't reply. She was not used to someone being this concerned for her. Her brain ran through several scenarios as to what his ulterior motive was but nodded yes.

"Sorry, I didn't mean to offend you. I'm not saying you're drunk off one margarita."

"No, it's okay. I am just…impressed, I guess, that you would think about me driving."

Unsure of how to respond, David just smiled. He motioned to Mauricio and then ordered two coffees.

The couple continued their conversation as they sipped their coffee.

"Tell me another funny story," asked Gwen.

David noticed a touch of sadness in her voice and in her eyes, so he selected a story that his family relived nearly every time they were all together.

"My family was vacationing in New England somewhere. I was nine, my brother, Alan, ten. My mother thought a hike would be a good idea. She was always trying to make her *men* exercise. She was the only one excited by the hike, but like I said, Dad did whatever Mom wanted, so he checked with the hotel concierge, got info on a nearby trail, and off we went."

David chuckled. "I often wonder what people thought as we walked through the lobby, heading out on our hike. It was like the great Jewish migration out of the Concord Hilton." He shook his head. Gwen smiled. "So we go hiking. I didn't weigh much less then than I do now, so you can imagine that I was out of breath pretty quickly. Alan and Dad, though both thin, weren't faring much better, but we followed Mom. Do you have brothers or sisters?"

"No," answered Gwen.

"Then as an only child, you are probably unfamiliar with the ongoing competition that exists between siblings. Alan and I competed constantly—games, school, our parent's affection. It was all a competition. Still is actually. The only competition I was sure to win was wrestling. If I could get on top of him, he was rendered helpless." David chuckled.

"Anyway, as we're walking along the trail, we come to a ravine with a small wooden bridge that crossed it. The ravine was probably six feet across and six to eight feet deep. The sides of the ravine were pretty much straight down, and you could see roots and stones in the dirt. There was only a few inches of water at the bottom.

"So Alan looks at me and says, 'I bet you can't jump across that.' And of course, being an idiot nine-year-old, I replied, 'I bet I can.' So the conversation went on like that for a few rounds. By this time, our parents were on the bridge and had stopped to see why we weren't right behind them. Also, by this time, I'm determined to prove myself to my brother. I knew *he* couldn't make that jump, but I was so sure that *I* could.

"I turned and walked about ten feet back away from the ravine. I faced my target. Out of the corner of my eyes, I could see Alan watching. I could see my parents standing on the bridge, my mother with her hands on her hips and my dad trying to figure out what moronic thing his youngest son was up to. I took a deep breath and ran toward the ravine as fast as I could go. Now one look at me will tell that that was not very fast." He smiled and looked at Gwen, who was watching him and listening intently.

"So I ran at not much more than a trot but what I felt like was at a lightning speed to the end of the ravine, where I took off in flight over my target." He stopped.

Gwen waited a second. "And? Did you make it?"

"Well, imagine this is the far wall of the ravine." David raised his left hand and held it straight up and down. "And imagine this is me." He held up his right hand, holding it straight up and down across from his left. He quickly moved his right hand and slapped it against his left and then slowly slid himself down the side of the ravine.

Gwen's eyes widened, and her hand came to her mouth, "Oh no."

"Oh yes." David nodded. "I flew smack into the wall of the ravine and then just slid down into the mud and water."

Gwen tried hard to suppress laughter. "Were you hurt?'

"Just my ego, along with some cuts and scrapes," David shook his head and laughed. Gwen joined him. "You should hear my brother tell the story. He draws it out as much as possible, describes my face, my sliding down the wall of dirt. It was a great day for Alan."

Gwen laughed. "You'll have to get him to tell me some day."

"I will," promised David.

Gwen looked down at her now-empty cup of coffee. "We'd better get going."

David agreed and motioned to Mauricio to bring the check. Gwen offered to split the check, but David refused. "Consider this payment for today's tutoring session."

As they walked back to the campus, David asked Gwen for her phone number. She could hardly believe her ears—no one, *no one*, had asked for her phone number since Miss Ann. She recited her number for him and then said, "I'll write it down for you when I get my stuff."

"No need. I'll remember it. I'm pretty good with numbers."

When they reached David's dorm, he ran up to his room to grab Gwen's books and then walked her to the car. He opened the car door for her, and as she went to get in, he quickly kissed her. She was too shocked to respond. She simply said "Good night," started her car, and drove off.

And just like that, Gwen had a boyfriend.

Chapter 14

Play It Cool

Claire,

I have a boyfriend! You would love him. His name is David, and we met in Latin class. Actually, he asked me for help, and then we had dinner, which was awesome, and then he walked me to my car, opened my car door for me, and then kissed me! Yikes! I didn't know what to do, so I didn't do anything. I just drove away. Hahahahaha.

That was a few weeks ago. Since then, on the days I don't work, we hang out after classes. We go to the campus library to study, then out to get something to eat. Sometimes, we just walk around campus holding hands. I had never really noticed before, but Dulaney really has a nice campus.

He introduced me to this local Mexican restaurant. The food is amazing, really amazing. I've probably put on ten pounds since we started dating because we eat really well! We also found a nice place to get ice cream. Fortunately, he enjoys eating as much as I do!

You can imagine the twenty million questions I've gotten from Dr. and Dr. *Ugh*. The first night, you would have thought I had done something miraculous. They were just ecstatic that I had gone out to dinner with someone. It was embarrassing. Then when my dad found out that David had taken one of his classes, he was over the moon. He remembered David and liked him. Asked about David's major, econ with a minor in finance; asked about his family, parents and a brother; asked where he's from, New Jersey, etc., etc., etc.

You would love David. He's *so* smart. He's more of a numbers person than history, so we don't really discuss books we've read, but he is really interesting. And *funny*. He makes me laugh like we used to laugh about stupid stuff. He even stopped by the library a few times while I'm working to help me out. One day, when it was reading time, he offered to read to the kids, and they *loved* him. He used different voices and accents for each character in the book, and the kids were loving it.

He's perfect for me, and I think I'm perfect for him too. I know it's early to say that after just a few weeks, but it's true. Other than you and your mom, I have never felt so comfortable with another person.

I know it's crazy that I'm nearly twenty years old and this excited about a boyfriend, but it's my first. Around here, I just play it cool, like it's nothing special. But you understand. I *never* thought I would have a boyfriend at all, and yet, here I am. Girlfriend to an awesome guy.

I'd tell you about my classes, job, and everything else, but that's boring in comparison.

Love,

Gwen

Chapter 15

Cocky, Aren't You?

As November approached, walking around campus hand in hand lost its allure. Walking hand in hand is fun when the weather is warm, or cool and crisp, but when your breath starts freezing, not so much. So the couple would spend a bit more time in the library studying and continuing the Latin tutoring, but inevitably, they would end up laughing uncontrollably about something or another and then would quickly leave before being asked to do so. Gwen had never been so happy.

Finally, one day in early November, after having to run out of the library, David turned to Gwen. "Look, this is nuts. The weather is only going to get colder. It's obvious that we can't hang in the library all the time, and it's also obvious that you are *never* going to invite me to your house, so…would you like to come up to my room? I promise I will not attack you. My roommate is hardly ever there. Honestly, I don't know why he has a room on campus. He goes home for dinner every night and spends every weekend at home. So you don't have to worry about making conversation with someone you don't know. We can study, we can talk, and you can teach me how to play mah-jongg. I'll even read a book you like so we can talk about it." He smiled at Gwen, hopefully.

She thought, *He remembered when I talked about what Claire and I used to do. He was listening.* Gwen took a deep breath. "Okay."

David smiled and took her hand. "Thank you. I don't do well in the cold."

They walked silently for a bit, and then Gwen said, "I'm sorry I haven't invited you over yet. I just know that my parents will embarrass me."

"What do you think they'll do? Do they throw food or dance on the table?"

Gwen chuckled and gave David a little push. "No. But they will ask you at least two million questions. And most of those will be about Judaism."

"It's okay. I can deal with that. You know I like to talk, and after all my years at Torah school, I can answer pretty much any question they can throw at me about being a Jew." He shrugged. "I'm like a professional Jew."

Gwen smiled and nodded. "Okay, plan on coming to dinner Sunday then."

"Don't you think you should ask your parents if Sunday is okay first?"

Gwen rolled her eyes. "Are you kidding me? They have been haunting me about you coming for dinner since the day we met. I don't care what they have planned. They'll change their plans at a chance to interrogate you."

"Then Sunday it is." David smiled, squeezing Gwen's hand.

"Let me warn you though, Dr. and Dr. Marsh are very serious people. Don't expect them to smile, laugh, or understand any jokes."

"I'll make them laugh."

"Wanna bet?"

"Sure, let's make it twenty dollars."

"It's a bet. You may as well bring that with you Sunday because I'll expect payment before you leave."

David smiled. "Cocky, aren't you?"

"I know my parents."

"I've never met a person I couldn't make laugh. Even the kids who used to torment me in elementary school. Being able to make them laugh saved my ass on a number of occasions."

Gwen smiled but thought, *My way of handling them was more satisfying.*

The couple reached David's dorm, and he opened the door for Gwen. As an upperclassman, David was in one of the newer dormitories, and the lobby was pretty nice. Gwen had never been in any of the dorms at Dulaney. There were chairs and coffee tables arranged in groups, like a half dozen little living rooms in one big room. There were a few snack and drink machines along the back wall and even what appeared to be an ice machine. There were a few people hanging out in the lobby, but for the most part, it was empty. "This is nice," Gwen observed. She assumed they would sit in the lobby and actually felt a bit relieved at this, but David headed toward the elevators. She remained quiet as they waited for the elevator and then took it to the fourth floor. David then led her about halfway down a hallway with doors on each side. It reminded her of a condo building she had visited once. Some of the doors were open, and Gwen could see inside. The rooms were incredibly messy—unmade beds, clothes thrown all over the room, take-out boxes covering the desks. *Oh jeez,* she thought, *I hope David's room isn't a pigsty.* She didn't know if she could date someone who lived like a pig.

"It's quiet up here. Where is everybody?"

"Class, dinner, sporting events. It doesn't get loud here until nine or ten p.m., and then again in the morning."

David pulled a key out of his pocket and stopped at room 411. He let go of Gwen's hand and unlocked his door. "Welcome to my humble abode," he said as he stood aside so Gwen could enter.

Gwen's first thought was, *Thank God,* as she looked around a very neat and tidy dorm room. Both beds were made, no clothes thrown around the room. No bad smells. "Very neat," she commented, nodding her approval.

"Thanks." He pointed to a door on the right side of the room, "Bathroom is this way if you need it. It's also clean," he said, smiling.

Gwen didn't need to use the bathroom but took a peek inside anyway. It *was* clean. Again, she nodded her approval. "So who's the neat freak, you or your roommate?"

"Both of us," confessed David. "Aaron and I are both *fussy.*" David used air quotes around the word *fussy.* "Must be a Jew thing." He smiled.

"I'm not Jewish, and I'm a neat freak too. I just like order."

"Yeah, I think that's really what it is with me too. I like order." He looked into Gwen's eyes for a moment, and she could tell he was nervous. She wondered if he was going to kiss her now—not the little pecks he would give her at her car but a real kiss. She was feeling a bit nervous about that herself. Finally, David looked away and said, "Well, I guess we should finish studying." He motioned to Aaron's desk. "I'm sure Aaron won't mind if you use his desk."

Gwen started to walk to the desk and then turned back to David. "Kiss me."

"What?"

"Kiss me. I want you to kiss me." Part of her truly just wanted to kiss him, and part of her was testing him. If he was really into her, he wouldn't hesitate.

"I thought you would never ask." David put his hands on Gwen's face and smiled. He kissed her, only this time, he didn't plant a quick smack and then move away. This time, he moved in closer so that the full length of their bodies were touching. Gwen slowly put her arms around his neck as David moved his down around her waist. Their tongues found each other and played together for a bit. It was the most wonderful feeling that Gwen had ever experienced.

After a moment, David pulled back so he could look into Gwen's eyes. They both smiled, and Gwen put her hand behind David's head and pulled him back into her. Eventually, they made their way to David's bed and sat down, never letting go of each other. They continued to make out and run their hands up and down each other's back. Neither really knew what to do next, but neither wanted to stop. They were two people starved for physical contact.

At one point, David started to lie down and pull Gwen with him. She immediately pulled away. "No, not yet." He didn't question her, just nodded. He reached up and touched her breast. When she didn't pull away, he gently cupped her breast and squeezed. Gwen moaned and moved in closer to him. He did the same now on the other side and squeezed both breasts at the same time.

"Oh my god." She moaned.

David started to lift her shirt. "No, not yet."

"Okay," he answered breathlessly. "Then we'd better stop." He pulled back and smiled. "That was amazing, Gwen."

Gwen smiled, truly happy. "It was. I'm sorry I said no."

"Don't apologize. We won't ever do anything you don't want to do. Ever."

"I love you, David." She did. She really loved him. Other than her parents, no one, *no one*, had cared what she wanted since the day the Lambertsons moved.

"I love you too, Gwen."

She believed him. He loved her. "I want to get out of here before the other guys in this building start coming back, okay?" David nodded. He didn't look happy about it, but he nodded. "But I have an idea." She smiled slyly. "I'll take off Friday, and after classes, we'll grab a quick dinner and then come up here. Aaron will be gone for the weekend by then, right?" David nodded. "So we'll come here, and if it's okay with you, I'll stay the night." David's face lit up. "I just want to be out of here really early in the morning, so I can sneak out without anyone seeing me."

"You don't have to sneak out, Gwen. Women spend the night in this dorm all the time."

"I know, but…I'd rather just not run into anyone here."

"Why?"

"I can't explain why, David." Gwen didn't like to be questioned. "That's just how I feel. I don't want them looking at me, imagining what we've been doing, okay?"

"Okay, it's okay." David rubbed her back. "Whatever you want. C'mon, I'll walk you to your car."

"You're not mad at me?" she asked.

"Of course not. More than anything, Gwen, I want you to be comfortable and happy when you're with me."

She smiled at him. "I am."

David grabbed Gwen's books as she put on her jacket, and they left his room. Gwen was thankful that the dorm was still quiet. When they reached the lobby, there were a number of students there, but they were all busy talking and laughing, and no one paid them any attention. They walked to her car in silence, holding hands. Gwen couldn't remember ever feeling this happy and contented. She looked at David, walking beside her. "I don't think I've ever had that much fun."

David laughed. "Me neither!"

He kissed her goodbye as she got into her car. "Don't forget our bet either."

"Oh, I won't. Plan on coming to dinner Sunday and make sure you bring your twenty dollars."

"Nah, I won't need it," he said as he shut her door for her.

Gwen smiled and drove off.

At dinner that evening, she did two things. First, she lied to her parents and said that she was going to a party on campus Friday and would stay in the dorm with her friend Cara. There was no Cara, and her parents were surprised that Gwen was going to a party and that she had a friend that she would stay over with. They were very excited for her. Then she asked if David could come to dinner on Sunday. "And can we *please* not make a big deal about this?"

"Sunday is fine. We look forward to meeting him." Madeline looked at her husband, and he nodded agreement.

Chapter 16

Some Things You Just Keep to Yourself

Claire,

David and I spent all afternoon yesterday *making out*! It was unbelievable. I love him, Claire. I really do. He is just amazing, so caring and thoughtful. He wanted to go further, but I said no, and he stopped. He wasn't bothered by that either! He said he wanted me to be comfortable and happy. Can you believe that? Someone cares that much about me! I mean, besides my parents and you and your mom. I never thought a man would care about me this much. I am so happy, Claire. The only way I could be happier would be if you still lived here!

Anyway, David is coming for dinner on Sunday. Pray that my parents don't embarrass me. Please. David and I have a bet. He says he can make them laugh; I say he can't. We bet $20. I think it's a sure thing for me. Hahaha. Do you ever remember seeing my parents laugh? I don't. Hmmm, I think I'd better clarify the rules with

David. A chuckle doesn't count. He needs to make them *laugh*! Good luck with that, right?

Love you,

Gwen

Gwen thought about telling her friend about her plans to spend the night with David but decided against it. Some things you just keep to yourself.

Chapter 17

Oh, We're Doing It Again

Gwen was a nervous wreck all day that Friday. She was excited, and she was scared. She hoped David knew what he was doing because she sure as hell didn't.

The pair met at their usual spot in front of the library after classes. Both were visibly nervous, and David, trying to get them past that, said, "Look, let's forget about studying today. We'll go to Mesa de Guac, get some dinner, have a drink, and just calm down, okay?" He smiled at Gwen. "And if you decide you don't want to come back to my room tonight, it's okay. I'll understand."

And this is why I love this guy so much, she thought to herself. "Thank you. Dinner and a drink sound great."

David grabbed her hand, and they walked silently to "their" restaurant. Once seated, he started to tell her about his day and, as always, put a humorous spin on every single event. By the time Mauricio served their appetizer, Gwen was laughing and again felt that familiar sense of comfort she enjoyed with David.

As they finished dinner, Gwen asked, "Do you think it's safe?"

"I do. Let's go." David paid the tab, held out his hand to Gwen, and together they walked back to his dorm. The lobby was empty, and they took the stairs to David's floor. He peeked out into the hallway to confirm it was empty, and then they walked to his room. As he shut the door behind them, he chuckled. "I feel like James Bond."

Gwen didn't laugh. "I've never done this before."

David grabbed her hand. "Neither have I, Gwen."

"Really?"

"Really." He moved closer and took her other hand. "I'm glad my first time is with you."

"Me too." Gwen leaned into David and kissed him. She then pulled back just a bit and began to unbutton his shirt and then gently remove it. Then she unbuckled his belt and helped him off with his jeans. There he stood in his boxers, very, very erect. She leaned in to kiss him again, and she slid her hand into his shorts. She felt him inhale sharply as she gently grabbed his penis. Her first thought was how soft it felt. She gently trailed her fingers up and down the length of it, then she cupped her hand around his testicles, squeezing gently, just wanting to explore.

"Oh my god." David pulled away slightly. "You're gonna make me finish too quickly." He gently removed her hand from his pants. "That was unbelievable." He took a deep breath. "Let's get you undressed."

"Can we turn out the lights first?"

"Well, that hardly seems fair!" David smiled.

"I know. I'm sorry."

"It's okay. I want you to feel comfortable." David turned out the lights and made sure the blinds were completely drawn.

"And you're sure Aaron won't be back tonight?"

"Positive." David found Gwen in the dark and kissed her. He helped her get her shirt off and then gently turned her around so he could undo her bra. This he then slipped off over her shoulders. He turned her back to him and cupped both her breasts in his hands. He kneaded them gently, then bent and kissed each one. "You're shaking." He observed.

"I'm terrified."

"Don't be. Any time you want me to stop, you say the word, I stop."

Gwen nodded her head. She undid her pants and stepped out of them, keeping on her panties. David ran his hands up and down her mostly naked body. "You are beautiful," he whispered. She pulled his head toward her and kissed him as deeply as she could. No one, not even her parents, had ever told her that she was beautiful. She didn't even care if he was lying. She felt like her heart would explode. She gently took his right hand and placed it between her legs. He lightly ran his fingers back and forth over her panties. Finding her clitoris, he gently traced circles around it.

Gwen could barely breathe. She pushed him back a bit and removed her panties. "Let's get into bed."

David led Gwen by the hand to his bed, pulled back the covers, and let her get in first. He slid in beside her and covered them both. She turned toward him and they lay side by side, the full length of their bodies touching, caressing each other and kissing. Gwen pulled pack and again gently grabbed him in her hand. This time though, she squeezed a bit and rubbed back and forth. He began to explore between her legs. She began to move her hips and press against his hand.

"Take me now," she whispered. "I don't think I can wait any more."

"Are you sure?"

"Positive," she said as she rolled on her back.

Gwen let out a little gasp of pain when he first entered her, but the pain was quickly replaced by a sense of joy and excitement that she had never known or expected to know. She was just figuring out her lover's rhythm when she felt him shudder and murmur, "Oh my god. I love you, Gwen." She assumed he had orgasmed.

"I love you too. That was amazing." She ran her hands along his back. She could feel him shrinking inside her.

"Did you orgasm?"

"No, at least I don't think so, but that's okay. Next time."

"It's not okay." David rolled off her and used his fingers to tease Gwen's clitoris. She spread her legs for him and moved her hips back and forth, moaning. As the feeling intensified, she pulled the pillow from under her head and put it over her mouth, afraid that she would scream. Her orgasm was like an explosion. Her head came up, and she forced the pillow into her mouth, stifling any noise she might make. Her entire body shuddered. Finally, as her body settled down, she gasped for air.

"That was...I don't even know how to describe it. Amazing isn't sufficient." She looked at him. "If this is your first time, how did you know how to do that?"

"I listen when the guys talk." He smiled. "I'm glad you enjoyed it."

"Enjoyed it is an understatement."

"I enjoyed watching you. You are beautiful." He kissed her.

"No, I'm not." Gwen reached for the covers, which had been kicked off at some point.

"Don't, please." David grabbed her hand. "I don't know who told you that you're not beautiful, but you are."

She let her hand drop. "Thank you. You make me feel beautiful." She smiled at David. "Can we do it again?"

He laughed. "Oh, we're doing it again. Don't you worry. I just need to rest a bit."

They made love two more times that night, and David brought her to orgasm with his hands another three. Neither slept, and the covers stayed off.

At about 4:00 a.m., they both got dressed and snuck out of the dorm. As David walked Gwen to her car, he said, "You can't show up at your house at this hour. How will you explain that?"

"Yeah, I was just thinking that. I think I'll go to the Dunkin' Donuts, get some coffee, and read until a reasonable hour. I have to work at nine, so they won't be surprised if I show up home around seven."

"I'll go with you. I don't want you sitting there by yourself."

And so they sat in the local Dunkin' Donuts until around 7:00 a.m., holding hands and enjoying being in love. Gwen had never been so happy in her entire life.

Chapter 18

David Is the Man!

Gwen had never seen her parents laugh so hard. Her mother had tears rolling down her cheeks, and her dad's face was red from laughing. Gwen glared at David as he continued on with his story of when he jumped the ravine. He looked her way a few times to make sure she knew he had won the bet but continued on. He regaled her parents with one funny story after another. By the end of the meal, Gwen was sure that her parents loved David as much as she did.

As Madeline cleared the table and Carl prepared coffee and dessert, David smiled at Gwen. "You owe me twenty dollars."

"I can't believe you made them laugh like that. They *never* laugh."

"They just never met anyone funny before."

She slapped his arm playfully, reached into her pocket, and pulled out a twenty. "I was ready just in case. Didn't think I'd need it, but I was ready."

David made a show of taking the money and putting it in his wallet. "That will teach you to doubt me."

"Unbelievable. And if that's not enough, they let you call them by their first names. I only remember one other time they allowed someone to refer to them as anything other than Dr. Marsh and Dr. Marsh." Gwen shook her head. "And really, that other time, I didn't leave them much choice."

"Parents love me, what can I say?"

Over dessert, her parents began pummeling David with questions about his family, where he grew up, his classes, his Jewish faith, his future.

"Mom, Dad, please, enough with the twenty questions," Gwen interjected, trying to save her boyfriend from getting the third degree.

David reached over and gently grabbed Gwen's hand. "It's okay, really. They just want to know who's dating their daughter. I understand that." Gwen gave his hand a squeeze, silently thanking him for understanding; she knew that understanding came from love.

The question and answer session took so long that by the time the last question was answered, it was late and time for David to go. Gwen drove him back to his dorm. "Well, I think that was a success."

Indeed it was, and for the next five or six weeks, David was a regular Sunday dinner guest. The couple spent as much time together as their classes and Gwen's job allowed, and Gwen spent every Friday and Saturday night in David's dorm room. She suspected that her parents knew what she was up to, but she didn't care. David had Thanksgiving with the Marshes, and Gwen planned to spend Hanukkah with the Goldfeders. Gwen had never been this happy.

Two weeks after Thanksgiving, David and Gwen woke up late on Sunday morning. "Shit!" growled Gwen, waking up her lover.

"What?"

"It's seven! Dammit."

David, still half asleep, responded nonchalantly, "It's okay. I doubt anyone is up yet. They're probably all hung over. There was a game last night."

Gwen wasn't listening. She was up and getting dressed. "Well, hurry up then. I need to get out of here."

Wide awake now, David sat up. "I don't understand why you're so afraid of being seen. *Everybody* in this dorm has had female overnight guests."

"Just get ready, please, and check the hallway."

David sighed. "Okay, okay." He threw on some clothes and peeked out into the hallway. "All clear."

They tiptoed down the hall to the elevator and waited, Gwen nervously, David calmly. Gwen silently thanked God when the elevator doors opened, and it was empty. They silently rode down to the first floor. David wanted to say something, maybe lighten the mood a bit, but thought better of it.

When the doors opened in the lobby, there were two guys standing there. David grabbed Gwen's hand and began to walk.

"David, my man! Scored last night!"

The other joined in. "David is the man, getting a little action!"

David lowered his head and pulled Gwen past the two taunters, but Gwen stared them both in the eyes.

"Whoa! David, you'd better hold your dog back. It looks like she's gonna bite somebody."

"Fuck you, assholes," David replied as he continued to pull Gwen through the lobby.

"How the hell do they fuck?" asked one, loud enough for the couple to hear. "Seriously, how can they get close enough with those two guts in the way?"

David finally pulled Gwen out the front door, but not before she heard the two guys laughing hilariously at the thought of her and David making love. The most beautiful thing she had ever experienced was a joke. Shaking with fury, she let go of David's hand and started to run toward her car.

"Hey, wait up!"

She stopped and turned on David. "Wait up? Wait up? You want me to *wait up*? Like nothing happened? Like I wasn't...we weren't just humiliated in there?"

"Who cares what they say, Gwen? They're assholes."

"Yes, they are, and what did you do? Did you defend me? You let that *asshole* call me a dog. You let them make fun of us."

"What did you want me to do, Gwen? Fight them? Look at me! I would have gotten my ass kicked."

"You should have stood up to them." Gwen turned and walked to her car, got in, and drove away without looking back.

David gave her an hour or so to cool off and then called her at home. "Gwen..."

"Don't call me again and don't come to dinner. We're done." She hung up the phone, went back up to her room, and cried for hours.

She didn't leave her room for two days. When she went back to the campus, she avoided seeing David as much as possible. When she did see him, he looked like a lost and abused puppy, and if she allowed herself to feel, her heart broke for him. But she would remember how he let those two assholes make fun of her, and she would turn and walk away.

Her parents questioned her, asked about David, and asked what happened, but she would just reply, "We broke up. End of story."

When she next wrote Claire, she ended her letter with this, "David and I broke up. I don't want to talk about it." That was it. Claire knew better than to ask, and so she didn't, and Gwen never talked about her experience or her feelings with anyone. She protected her anger, and she nursed it.

She directed that anger, that unbridled hate bubbling up inside her, at the two assholes. She thought of them as Asshole 1 and Asshole 2. They had to pay for what they had done, and she would see to it. Gwen started following Asshole 1. She wanted to find out what he loved, what meant a lot to him. It was pretty quickly evident to her that his car was his most prized possession. It was a red Nissan 300ZX, and Gwen could tell that Asshole 1 was very proud of that car. He would park it in the far corner of the lot, away from other cars, so his doors wouldn't get hit. Once a week, he took it to the local car wash where he washed it and vacuumed out the interior. The car always shone.

About two weeks after the incident in the dorm, Gwen was ready. When she went to bed that Wednesday night, she set her alarm for 1:00 a.m., but she didn't really need it. She tossed and turned all night, looking at the clock every ten or fifteen minutes. At 1:00 a.m., she got out of bed, dressed in black pants and a black sweatshirt, and left the house as silently as she could. She drove to the campus, parked about a half mile from David's dorm, and then walked to the parking lot. The streets were empty at this hour, but Gwen kept her eyes and ears open for any activity around her. There was none. Even so, when she reached the parking lot, she ducked behind a car and just waited for about five minutes, making sure that no one else was around. She pulled out her keys and walked quickly to the red Nissan in the corner. Using her key, she scratched up the passenger side of the car, then calmly walked around to the other side and repeated her destruction. She stood back and admired her work in the dim light. Happy with what she saw, she walked calmly back to her car and drove home.

The next morning, on her way into class, Gwen drove by the dorm parking lot to see if her work had been discovered. She smiled when she saw a group of young men standing around the Nissan. Asshole 1 was stomping around the car, cursing and threatening to "kill the son of a bitch who did this." She pretended not to notice the group and drove past. She felt good, but she wasn't done with Asshole 1 just yet. She just needed to wait for him to get his car fixed, and she would strike again, which she did until Asshole 1 stopped bringing his car on campus.

Chapter 19

Pay Dirt!

Now it was Asshole 2's turn. With just a little stalking, Gwen learned that he had a longtime girlfriend, Stacey. Asshole 2 was a different person around Stacey. Around his friends, he was a typical frat boy, well deserving of Gwen's nickname for him. But around his girlfriend, he was kind, gentle, and considerate. It was obvious he cared for her. From what Gwen could gather, as she would walk behind whenever she could or sit near them when possible, his name was Russell, though Stacey often called him Russ, and they had been dating since high school. She even heard them talk about getting married and having kids. This was perfect.

Gwen took her time. She didn't take any action before spring break, but she didn't forget either. During the entire break, she thought about how she would destroy Asshole 2's relationship, how his heart would be broken, and how sad he would be. She wanted him to feel just like she did.

On her days off, she continued stalking Asshole 2. This required Gwen to stay on campus well into the evening, which had the added benefit of giving credence to her lies when she told her parents she had plans to be out. They had been "worried" about Gwen since David stopped coming around and were always asking questions about her social life. Gwen's evening absences seemed to satisfy them.

Russ and Stacey had a pretty standard schedule. During the week, they would eat dinner together every day in the school cafeteria and then go to either her dorm or his. Sometimes, they would hang out in the student center with other students. Wherever they were, Gwen would also be, watching and waiting. She took to having her dinner in the school cafeteria and spent a lot of time just walking on campus, waiting for the couple to come out from wherever they were and head to the next location. After a few weeks, Gwen could pretty well anticipate when and where the couple would be and would move her car to a location where she could watch without having to stand outside, lurking behind trees and buildings. She didn't go home until Russ entered his dorm for the night, alone.

Weekends were a bit trickier as the couple had no set pattern, but Gwen did her best to trail them from location to location, and this was where she hit pay dirt. One Friday night, a few weeks into her stalking, the couple went to a frat party at the Phi Psi house. Gwen didn't dare enter the house, knowing that could not possibly end well—she would stand out like a sore thumb—but waited about a block away in her car. She was surprised when the couple came out of the house at about 11:00 p.m. and started walking back to the dorms. Gwen got out of her car as quietly as she could and followed them at a distance. They headed straight to Stacey's dorm where they kissed goodnight, and Stacey went in. Gwen thought this was odd as this was pretty early for the couple to part ways on a Saturday night. As expected, though, Russell headed back toward his dorm. When he got to the dorm, however, rather than go inside, he headed toward the parking lot and got into his car. "Damn it!" cursed Gwen under her breath. She was a few blocks from her car, which was still parked near the frat house; she was going to lose him.

She headed back to her car as quickly as she could and was surprised to see Russell's car parked now in front of the frat house. She got into her car and waited, catching her breath. A few minutes later, Russell came out of the house again, this time with another male student.

Gwen assumed that maybe Russ was giving this guy a ride home or, better for her, maybe they were going downtown to a strip club or a bar. Surely, Stacey wouldn't know about that. Gwen discreetly followed the car, staying back as far as she could without losing sight of them.

She followed the car down York Road and then onto Dulaney Valley Road. At one point, she saw Russell reach over and rub the other guy's neck, not typical frat boy behavior. Maybe this was Russ's little brother, she thought. Just then, Russell turned off the road and headed down to the fishing center at Loch Raven Reservoir. Gwen pulled over on Dulaney Valley. She knew exactly where she was; her dad had taken her here to go fishing when she was younger. The road led down to the water where there was a parking lot and a few piers. There was a thin beach-like area along the water where a few dozen rowboats were lined up, waiting for renters. The place would be deserted this time of night. Gwen turned off her car, got out, and quietly walked down the access road to the fishing center. There were no lights, and Gwen was a bit scared, but her curiosity kept her moving forward.

After a few minutes, she was close enough to hear the water lapping against the shore, and then she heard the two men, whispering and laughing. There was a chain at the end of the access road, blocking cars from entering the parking area, and this was where she found Russell's car. She stopped and listened, until again she heard them laughing, and the sound was coming from down by the water. Gwen went around the chain and into the wooded area that surrounded the parking lot. Staying hidden, she got as close to the beach as she could. It was dark, but she could see well enough to know that the two men had laid a towel or something on the beach and were sitting side by side, making out. *Oh my god!* thought Gwen. She continued to watch as the men began to undress each other, then she slowly backed away. She didn't want to watch these two men have sex. She wanted proof that they were having sex, and for that, she would have to wait.

As Gwen drove home, she thought out her plan. First thing she needed to do was find her dad's camera. He had bought a nice one years ago, with plans on taking up photography. That lasted a few months, and Gwen hadn't seen the camera since. She would find that camera and keep it in her car. Then she would continue to follow Russell to figure out how often he and his lover came out here, and then, finally, she would be waiting for them.

Chapter 20

She Drowned Herself in It

For the next few weeks, Gwen continued to stalk Russell, or Asshole 2 as she still preferred to call him. The day of the week that Russ would meet up with his lover varied, but the scenario was always the same. Russell would walk Stacey back to her dorm a bit earlier than usual, kiss her good night, and then go get his car. The first few times, the sky was too cloudy, and therefore, the night too dark to get any good shots or the weather just too cold. But finally one night, there was nearly a full moon. The sky was clear, and Russell walked Stacey back to her dorm early. Gwen headed for her car.

She drove directly toward the fishing center but pulled off Dulaney Valley Road a few blocks before the access road. She hurried through the trees to the parking lot and then to the thin stretch of beach. She laid down on her stomach between two of the rowboats parked in a line on the beach. She pulled the fronts of those boats as close together as she could to keep her hidden but leaving enough space for her camera to get a good shot. She worried about the clicking sound her camera would make, so she took off her jacket and wrapped it around the camera, leaving only the lens exposed, hoping that would block any sounds. And then she laid as still and as quietly as possible. Her feet were getting wet, and the water was cold, but she remained in place, motionless. She waited for what seemed like an eternity.

After about fifteen minutes, as Gwen began to wonder if this was really worth it, she heard a car pull up on the access road. She pictured this asshole laughing at the thought of her and David making love. She decided then that yes, it was worth it.

She watched as the two men walked toward her. She watched as Russell laid a blanket on the ground. She watched as they embraced. She started taking pictures when the men started to kiss. She took pictures as they undressed, and she took pictures as they made love. She stopped only when she ran out of film. Then she continued to lie still and quiet as she hoped she got some good shots. By the time the men left the beach, Gwen had been lying there for about two hours. Her legs were soaked, and she was shivering, but she stayed in place until she heard the car drive back down the access road and away from the fishing center. Then she got up, put her jacket back on, and hurried to her car. She was almost there. Russell had helped ruin one of the only good things in her life, and now he was going to pay. Gwen smiled as she drove home.

The next day after classes, Gwen headed toward the mall. She had seen signs for the Ritz Camera store there that promised one-hour film developing. When she entered the store, it was empty except for one young man behind the counter.

"Can I help you?"

"Hi, I would like to get this developed," said Gwen, placing her roll of film onto the counter. "Can you do it in an hour?"

"Sure can."

"And listen, the pictures are pretty personal. I'm doing a favor for a friend."

"Don't worry about it. You wouldn't believe the pictures I see. I stopped being shocked, or even interested, a long time ago."

"Thanks. I'll be back in an hour."

Gwen hung out in the food court for the next hour, enjoying pizza and a Coke and reading a book she had brought along. Her pictures were waiting for her when she returned to the camera store. She quickly paid for them, put them in her purse, and headed home.

She didn't look at the pictures until she was home and in her room with the door shut. There were a few shots that were nearly

117

perfect. The best were when the men were still standing as they were kissing and undressing each other. You could clearly see Russell's face, and you could clearly see that these were two men. Gwen selected one. The pictures from when the men were having sex were not as clear. Their feet were pointing toward the camera, so it was hard to tell who it was exactly. She selected one of Russell kneeling over his partner. You couldn't see his face, but he would be recognizable to anyone who knew him.

Gwen wanted copies of these two pictures but didn't trust any photo shop to do that without asking questions. She decided to take the two pictures to work with her that weekend and try the color copier. The copies weren't perfect, but they would work. She made twenty of each.

Gwen set her alarm for 3:00 a.m. but again slept fitfully as she checked the clock frequently. At about 2:45, she got up, got dressed, grabbed her books, her photocopies, and some tape and quietly left the house. As she drove to the campus, she briefly wondered if this was such a good idea. She knew that what she was about to do could ruin someone's life. It wasn't like scratching up a car; this was personal. But then again, it was personal when this asshole helped ruin her life. She had been happy, and those two assholes had ruined it. She decided that in reality, she had let Asshole 1 off too easily. Asshole 2 was getting what he deserved. Gwen was feeling angry and justified by the time she pulled into Dulaney University. She parked her car in the first lot she came to and got out of the car. Her first stop was David's dorm where she posted one of her pictures on the inside of the door. She taped another one to the front of one of the snack machines. She walked across campus to Stacey's dorm, where she taped a picture on the door. Gwen did feel a stab of pity for Stacey, knowing how hurt this young woman would be, but decided that she was really doing Stacey a favor by showing her the real man she was in love with.

Within thirty minutes of parking her car, all of Gwen's pictures were gone. After the dorms, Gwen hit the dining hall, the library, a few of the buildings where she knew Asshole 2 had classes, and the gym. She was confident that within a few hours, everybody who knew Russell would have seen one of these pictures. Gwen walked back to her car, then headed to the Dunkin' Donuts to wait out the next few hours.

At 7:30, Gwen headed back to the campus, and as she parked her car near the main dining hall, she saw a group of people huddled near the front door, near where she had taped up one of her pictures. She got out of her car and leaned against it to watch. Within a few minutes, she saw Russell running from his dorm to the dining hall, clutching crumpled-up papers in his hand. He pushed his way through the crowd and ripped down the pictures. No one spoke to him; the other students looked away guiltily. Gwen heard noise to her right and turned to see Stacey walking toward the dining hall, surrounded by a group of girls. Stacey was clearly upset and was also holding crumpled papers in her hand. Russell also saw Stacey and ran toward her, yelling, "You don't understand. Let me explain, please." But Stacey just held up her hand to stop him. She looked at him for a second without speaking and then walked past him.

As Gwen watched Stacey continue on to the dining hall, she noticed David standing there, watching her. He started to walk toward her. Gwen smiled and thought, *I think I can forgive him now. We can get past this.* "Hi," she said.

"Please tell me that you didn't do this. Please tell me that the woman I loved is not capable of something this horrid."

Her smile gone, Gwen responded, "I don't know what you're talking about." She immediately knew there was no chance of her and David getting past anything.

"I hope not, Gwen." And with that, David turned and walked away from her forever. She never spoke to him again, and she never saw Russell again after that morning. She was once again completely alone, and she drowned herself in it.

Chapter 21

2013

My Daughter's Death Will Not Go Unanswered

Gwen could hear the footsteps and voices of people entering the room. She looked down on her daughter for another minute and then turned to take her place at the head of the casket, ready to accept the hugs, handshakes, and words of condolence from a long line of people she didn't know. Her goal for this evening was to get through the next two hours without crying and without being "rude." She reminded herself that she could not embarrass Leah tonight.

So she put herself on autopilot. She'd respond to the hug or the handshake appropriately, shake her head when appropriate, and say "Thank you so much" or "Thank you for coming" when appropriate. No one would expect her to smile; no one would expect her to make conversation. Good thing because she just wasn't capable of it, not today, not even for Leah. It was just too much.

She did her best to ignore the looks of surprise when visitors realized who she was. Today, she would let that go. She would not look into the eyes of Leah's friends, trying to find the son of bitch who gave her that last dose of heroin. It was all of them. All of Leah's friends were to blame for the path Leah had taken; they were all to blame for her death. Today, she would let that go. For Leah's sake.

She knew who was with Leah the night she choked to death on her own vomit, but she would deal with her later.

As she performed for Leah's friends, she thought back over her life with her daughter.

Leah had been a great kid, the only joy of Gwen's life. Early in her pregnancy, Gwen had gone through jobs at two other CPA firms, both jobs gotten quickly and then lost quickly. After losing the third job, it was impossible for Gwen to even get an interview at a local CPA firm, so she started her own bookkeeping business. Before going in to make her pitch to each potential customer, she reminded herself that she really needed the business, that it wouldn't be just her anymore. So she kept her cool; maintained a polite, professional manner; and let her potential customer know that they were getting more than just a bookkeeper with her. She was a licensed CPA and could help answer tax and GAAP-related questions. They weren't getting a bookkeeper; they were getting an accountant at bookkeeper prices.

By the time Leah was born, Gwen had built up a nice little business. She was making enough to move from the city out to an apartment in Timonium. The apartment was in a nice little complex. There was a pool for the summer and a nice playground for when the baby grew. There were plenty of kids in the area, and the schools were considered good. All in all, it seemed like a good place to raise a child.

A home-based business worked perfectly for the new single parent. Leah was such an easy baby. From the day Gwen brought her home, she slept well, and when she was awake, she was just a happy baby.

Gwen was prepared financially and logistically, but she was not prepared for just how much she would love this baby. She knew she would love her. She fell in love with her before she was born, but in no way was she prepared for the overwhelming feeling she experienced when she first looked into the face of her daughter. She knew at that moment that her life was forever changed. This baby, her daughter, was the single most important thing in the world. Scratch that, she was the *only* important thing in the world. Gwen knew she would do anything to take care of and protect this child. And she did.

Dr. and Dr. Marsh offered to help with the baby. They offered to watch Leah in the evening so Gwen could work or get out for a bit, but Gwen refused. She worked when the baby slept. When Leah was awake, Gwen would feed her, change her, bathe her, and play with her. She didn't want to miss or waste any of that time, and she seldom put Leah down. When Leah slept, Gwen got her work done, working into the night because she knew she needed to keep every single client.

As Leah grew, Gwen realized that she needed to get her daughter around other people and so would take her to the library, sign her up for toddler-type classes, whatever she could find. But there were never playdates, and mother and daughter were never apart.

These first five years of Leah's life were the happiest years of Gwen's life. Gwen loved her daughter with all her heart, and her daughter loved her back. Never had Gwen had someone look at her with such pure love. Never had anyone depended on Gwen so completely. Never had anyone thrown their arms around her and hugged her for no reason other than because they loved her. Gwen was truly content; she needed nothing else in her life.

Gwen's saddest day, up until Leah's death, was Leah's first day of kindergarten. This was even worse than the day Claire moved. Gwen knew things would change. Her daughter would make friends, start asking for playdates, and come to love other people—all good things for a growing child, but devastating to Gwen. She knew that as of that day, she would slowly lose her daughter.

Sure enough, she had. Leah turned out to be a very popular little girl, and that followed her throughout her school years and beyond. With each passing year, Gwen spent less and less time with her daughter. With each passing year, Leah needed her less and less. It didn't matter that this was the way things were supposed to be; it was painful. Gwen did her best to remain the most important person in Leah's life, and this involved giving her daughter anything she wanted. This involved doing for Leah anything that Leah asked.

Eventually, Leah ran the show. She told Gwen what she wanted, and Gwen made sure she had it. She told Gwen how to behave, and Gwen complied. Leah had quickly learned how to manipulate her mother as well. She'd set her own curfew by saying, "I'm going to a party tonight. It ends at one, and so-and-so is driving me home, so I think if we say I'll be home by two a.m., that would work." Gwen would agree. She even had Gwen write absence notes to school when she didn't feel like going. "You know it's not going to kill me to miss one day, Mom. Tell them I'm sick".

Gwen started covering for Leah's behavior at a young age. In exchange for control, Leah gave her mother love. It wasn't unconditional love, but it was love. Gwen knew this; she wasn't blind, and she wasn't stupid. But where Leah was concerned, she was weak. *No* was not part of her vocabulary with her daughter.

Gwen could see that Leah was getting out of control and was doing some dangerous things, but she always felt that it would all turn out okay. Leah was smart and beautiful; she would be okay. How wrong she had been.

She had no idea how many people she hugged that night or how many hands she shook. She didn't know how many thank-yous she had mumbled, but all of sudden, the room was empty again, except for her and her daughter. She leaned over and kissed Leah on the forehead. "I'm sorry, baby. I'm so sorry." Wiping away tears, she stood up straight. "I'll be back tomorrow, my love, first thing in the morning."

And she was. Somehow, she got through the funeral, shook more hands, accepted more hugs, and mumbled more thank-yous. And at the very end, she said goodbye to her daughter, again promising to be back.

Gwen went from her daughter's grave site to a local gun shop/ firing range. She got the information she needed to get a gun license. She filled out and filed the paperwork that very day.

Six weeks later, she had a gun license and went back to the gun store to purchase a small firearm. She then became a regular at the firing range, going there to practice several times a week. It wasn't long before she was a great shot, consistently hitting her target.

Her next goal was to get a rifle. She did a lot of research on which rifle to purchase and how she could modify that weapon to be a sniper rifle. She didn't rush the process; she wanted to get things just right. She eventually ended up purchasing two .308-caliber rifles. She was pleased to learn that rifles did not have to be registered in the state of Maryland, but she registered one. At different stores, she also purchased a scope and a tripod.

She found an outdoor gun range where she could practice with the rifle. It only took six months from the day she buried her daughter for Gwen to become a crack shot with a revolver and a rifle. She was ready.

When she determined she was ready, she went back to Leah's grave site. It was the first time she had been back since the funeral. She explained to Leah why she hadn't visited. She explained how she was prepared to avenge her death, to make things right, to make up for failing her as a mother.

Gwen then went home and emailed Claire.

She and Claire had only seen each other a few times since the day Claire moved to Ohio. Gwen and her mom had flown to Ohio forthe funeral of Claire's grandmother. After that, there had been opportunities, but Gwen always found a reason to back out. The girls sent each other their annual school pictures, and while Gwen got heavier, got acne, and never made friends, Claire got prettier, became quite popular, and seemed very happy. Gwen just could not face her friend and tried to maintain the relationship via letter only.

However, a week after coming home from the hospital with her daughter, Gwen was pleasantly surprised to find Claire standing at her door one morning. "Don't think for a minute that I wouldn't come and see my best friend's new baby!"

Gwen threw her arms around her friend and cried. They both just stood in the doorway, holding on to each other, crying. Gwen didn't say a word until they let go.

"I am so happy you're here! Come in. Why didn't you tell me you were coming?"

"Because you would have told me not to come."

Gwen nodded. "Probably, but it's not because I don't want to see you."

"Then why?"

"Because I'm embarrassed. Look at me, Claire."

"I am looking, and I see my best friend, the *only* person in the world other than my mother who stood up for me when I needed it. I think you're perfect."

The young women hugged again, then Gwen quietly took Claire into Leah's room to see the sleeping baby. Claire stayed for three days, and the young women enjoyed their time. It was just like old times really—they played mah-jongg, discussed books, and relived their childhood. The only difference was that on this visit, they took turns holding Leah.

When it was time for Claire to leave, the two women hugged again, both sobbing. Claire didn't ask her friend to come out and visit; she knew that she would not. But they both promised to keep writing and to call frequently. Since then, they had seen each other for Claire's wedding and the funerals of Gwen's parents.

Gwen started typing.

Dear Claire,

I'm so sorry that I haven't been in touch for so long. I don't know how to do this gently, so I'll just say it. Leah passed away six months ago. As you can imagine, it's been a really tough time for me. I am not coping well. Life without her is just…just…I don't have words for it. The grief is overwhelming.

Leah made some bad decisions in her life but didn't deserve to die because of them. She had gotten into drugs and died after passing out. She choked to death on her own vomit—her own vomit! There was someone there with her, a friend of hers, who didn't help her. I can't forgive that, Claire. I think about it day and night. I saw

this person once, the day Leah died. I could tell by
looking at her that she could have helped my girl
but didn't. The hate I feel is also overwhelming.

I still don't know who sold my child the
heroin, but I intend to find out. My daughter's
death will not go unanswered.

I would call, but I am still unable to talk
about this without crying hysterically.

I love you and always miss you. Please give
my love to your mom.

Love,

Gwen

Chapter 22

Deep, Never-Ending Emotional Pain

Gwen's first target was Donna, the friend who had been with Leah when she died. The person who had been with Leah as she drank and drugged herself into unconsciousness. The person who had not called for help when Leah passed out. The person who did nothing to help as Leah choked to death. Yes, Donna needed to pay for what she had done.

Donna and Leah had worked together at a chic salon not far from Donna's place, and Leah hung out there often. There were a few times when Gwen had to drive to Donna's place in the city to pick up her daughter because her car had been towed, or she had left it someplace else and needed a ride to pick it up. So Gwen knew just where she could find Donna.

Gwen started hanging out across the street from Donna's building. Stalking was not new to her, but she had watched enough TV over the years to know that cameras were everywhere now, so she wore a hoodie and did her best to hide her face as much as possible. She changed locations often and did a lot of walking around the block, going in and out of buildings, trying hard not to look conspicuous. And of course, she parked a mile or so away so that her car was not seen in the area.

On her walks, she noted several corners in the area that appeared to be occupied by local drug dealers. Wondering which dealer her daughter had used, she made sure to keep an eye on them as well and learn their schedules. If she noticed these dealers without even trying, why didn't the police see them and put a stop to it? This question bugged Gwen. How could the people whom we pay to protect us allow this to happen?

As she stewed over this question, she continued to watch Donna for a few weeks, changing up days and times, to get an idea of her schedule and, once, when Donna stumbled home, even followed her into the building to make sure she knew which apartment was hers.

The next day, when she knew Donna would be at work, Gwen went back to the apartment to see if she could break in. Once in the apartment building, Gwen pulled out a pair of gloves and put them on. She kept her hoodie up over her face. She didn't see any cameras but was still concerned about being seen. She had never done anything like this before and had no idea how she was going to get in, but it turned out to be pretty easy. There were two locks on the apartment door, the one in the doorknob and a dead bolt. Today, the doorknob lock was locked, but the dead bolt was not. Gwen slipped her credit card up and down between the door and the doorjamb and was able to quickly open the door.

Gwen entered the apartment and shut the door behind her. The first thing she noticed was the horrible smell of the place. Wrinkling her nose at the smell, Gwen wondered how her daughter could stand coming here.

She took her time walking through Donna's apartment. The place was a mess, not that there was stuff lying around, but it was just filthy. In the living room, there were four pieces of furniture—a couch under the window with a scratched-up coffee table in front of it. Gwen looked at the couch for a few moments and then ran her hand along the seat cushions. This was the spot where her most precious possession had perished. She pictured her daughter choking to death in this very spot. The thought made her want to scream.

Pulling herself together, Gwen turned away from the sofa, across from which was a chair, and next to the chair an end table with a lamp. The cord to the lamp hung uselessly to the floor. Gwen shook her head. Every piece of furniture was covered with stains over which lay a thick layer of dust. There were no curtains on the window, but that was no problem; the windows hadn't been cleaned in decades by the look of it. She couldn't see clearly looking out, and she knew no one could see in. That was good.

The kitchen was tiny and was just off the living room. Gwen opened the refrigerator to find it completely empty. The sink was empty and looked like it hadn't been used in quite a while. A half-empty roll of paper towels hung over the sink. There were a few dishes in the cupboards and some dirty silverware in the drawers. The trash can was overflowing, and Gwen assumed this was the source of the terrible odor. The only decent thing in the kitchen was a butcher block knife set. It seemed so out of place here. This interested Gwen; why would someone who obviously never used their kitchen have such a nice knife set? She looked more closely and noticed that the wood was engraved—"The Muellers." Donna must have been married at one time, and this must have been a gift from someone special. She shrugged her shoulders and walked back out into the living room.

Off the living room, directly across from the front door, was the bedroom. Gwen walked in and stood in the doorway for a moment. The bed was unmade, and there was a chair in the corner covered with dirty clothes. No dresser. A TV table served as a nightstand and had one empty glass and an overflowing ashtray on it. *This chick is a pig*, thought Gwen, shaking her head. The window in this room didn't have curtains either, but it did have thick blinds which were closed. Good.

Gwen peeked into the bathroom, which turned out to be the most disgusting part of the house. Mold covered the floor around the toilet; the sink was covered with toothpaste spit and makeup. The toilet looked like something you would find in a gas station men's room. Gwen shivered with disgust.

Turning from the bathroom, she walked to the closet and opened the door. This part of the house was fairly neat. She could tell by the plastic bags that Donna had her clothes dry-cleaned. She had nice stuff. Underwear and stockings were thrown on the closet shelf, but the clothes that were hanging were lined up neatly, most still in the dry-cleaner bags. Nice shoes lined the floor underneath. Gwen resisted temptation to pull out those nice clothes and tear them all to shreds. She wanted to pick up those nice shoes and place them in that disgusting toilet. She stood for a moment, enjoying the thought of that, and then closed the closet door.

Leaving the bedroom, she counted the number of steps from the bed to the chair so that in the dark, she would know when to turn a bit right to avoid tripping over the crappy furniture. She repeated the process a few times at different paces and then a few times with her eyes shut.

Next, she needed to figure out how she could get in here tonight when Donna was home. She couldn't assume that the dead bolt would be unlocked, and she doubted her credit card technique would work against a dead bolt.

Gwen went back into the kitchen and grabbed a paper towel. She dampened one a bit, being careful not to allow water past the towel and into the dry sink and fit it into the dead bolt, hoping that it would be enough to keep the lock from working.

That done, she locked the doorknob from the inside and left. She went home and caught up on her client work that afternoon and into the evening. As she did each day now, she changed her system date and time so that if anyone ever looked, it would appear as though she had been working at the same time she was actually stalking. Any emails that she composed to her customers in the evenings would be scheduled to send the following day, when she was out. If her customers were ever questioned, they could honestly say that Gwen had been in communication with them during these hours.

When work was done, she pulled out a book and waited. Donna usually returned home from the bars between midnight and 2:00 a.m. At 11:00 p.m., Gwen called for a cab to take her downtown. She met the cab about a mile from her apartment.

Exiting the cab, Gwen walked several blocks to Donna's building and took up watch at her usual location. She wondered briefly if this would be a problem. The police would certainly question the locals tomorrow, and someone was sure to have noticed this strange little woman hanging around lately. This was, however, Baltimore

City, and it was unlikely the locals would be too helpful when questioned. She'd take her chances.

Donna got home that night shortly before 2:00 a.m. Gwen was pleased to see her stumbling and struggling to climb the few steps to her building; this meant she was either drunk or high and should fall asleep quickly and soundly. She waited a full hour, giving Donna plenty of time, before entering the building. She quietly took the stairs to Donna's floor and stood by the door listening. All was quiet.

She put on gloves and pulled out a credit card and, as quietly as she could, unlocked the door. She breathed a sigh of relief when she realized that the dead bolt had not been locked. She entered the apartment and silently shut the door behind her. She remained motionless for a few minutes to make sure Donna hadn't heard her come in. Eventually, she made her way to the bedroom and looked down on this young woman whom she hated so deeply. There was just enough light coming in through the blinds for her to see the girl's face. As expected, Donna was in a deep, drunken slumber.

Deep in thought, Gwen stood over the unconscious young woman. She thought back to the morning she learned of Leah's death. Gwen had just completed the awful task of identifying the corpse of her only child. All she knew at that point was that her daughter was dead. She didn't know how; she didn't know why. A young policeman, Officer Mandato, was guiding Gwen into the police station to a quiet place where he could explain what they knew. As soon they entered the lobby, Gwen saw Donna sitting on a bench, sobbing.

Seeing Gwen, Donna jumped up. "I'm so sorry, Miss Gwen. I'm so sorry. I just don't know what happened." She walked toward Gwen with her arms out, pleading, face contorted with pain and covered with running mascara. Officer Mandato held out his arm to block Donna, which was a good thing because Gwen's first thought was that she wanted to strangle the girl right there in front of the entire police department. Instead, she just looked at Donna briefly, and then right through her, as she allowed herself to be escorted by the officer. Sounds of Donna weeping and repeating "I'm so sorry" over and over again followed them until they entered a small office, and the door quietly closed.

In a very soothing voice, it was explained to Gwen that Donna had called 911 at 8:00 a.m. that morning to report that her friend was unresponsive. EMTs arrived within ten minutes and found Leah lying on her back on the sofa in Donna's apartment. There was nothing they could do. They would need to wait for the autopsy report, but they suspected Leah had been dead for several hours before help arrived.

Still standing over Donna, Gwen thought for a minute. Her plan had been to shoot Donna in the knees. Gwen had considered killing her but rejected that plan. Killing this girl was too easy, too easy for Donna. She wanted this woman to suffer, but as she looked at Donna's beautiful face, she changed her mind. Shooting her in the knees would indeed cause Donna pain probably for the rest of her life, but she wanted Donna to suffer emotional pain—deep, never-ending emotional pain. Like most of the beautiful women Gwen had known throughout her life, she was sure that Donna was vain, that Donna used her beauty to get what she wanted, that she depended on that beauty.

Gwen went out into the kitchen and grabbed the small paring knife from the butcher block. She smiled at the thought that Donna's suffering would come from something she seemed to treasure. This was appropriate.

Knife in hand, Gwen went back into the bedroom. She had to do this just right. She figured she would only have a few seconds from the first cut until Donna started screaming. She was wrong.

Leaning over Donna, Gwen stuck the knife into Donna's face, just over her left cheekbone, and cut down to the woman's mouth. Donna barely flinched. Gwen then repeated the procedure on the other side of that beautiful, disgusting face. Blood was pouring from Donna's face onto the pillow. Gwen calmly wiped the knife on the bedsheet and laid it next to her victim. She picked up the phone, dialed 911, put the phone in Donna's hand, and left the apartment, being sure to lock the door on her way out.

Gwen exited the building at a normal pace and walked about twenty blocks. She heard sirens a few times but couldn't tell if they were coming from the right direction. She would just have to trust that the EMTs reached Donna in time. She wasn't overly concerned. When she felt she was a safe enough distance away, she hailed a cab. She gave the driver an address a few blocks from her apartment, just in case he was questioned about that night's fares. While riding home, she looked down at her hands, surprised that they were not shaking. She wondered at how calm she was. She knew she had just done something that, if caught, could land her jail for the rest of her life. She didn't care. She was glad she had done it. She was glad that the little bitch would suffer for the rest of her life. No more getting by on a pretty face. Gwen smiled. Her only regret was that Donna would not know why she was suffering.

Chapter 23

There Are a Lot of Short Fat Women

Gwen waited all night for a knock on her door. She put her clothes in the washing machine and wiped her shoes down with cleaner. Just before dawn, she hopped in the shower. As she was drying herself off, Gwen took a good long look at herself in the mirror. She noticed that she had lost quite a bit of weight. All that walking in the city and meals missed when she was stalking had made a big change in her physique. She knew her clothes were looser but had not realized the extent of her weight loss. She didn't own a scale, never wanted one in her home, but she guessed she was down a good twenty pounds. Gwen smiled to herself. "Stalking has its benefits. Who knew?"

Gwen knew this could be helpful to her, so she found clothes that fit her tightly, showing off her new slimmer physique. When the police came, she didn't want them to see a fat woman.

The sun was finally up. Gwen ate and sat at her desk to start working.

The first knock came at 10:00 a.m. Gwen went to the door, took a deep breath, and opened, fully expecting to see the police. She was shocked when she saw Claire standing there. They looked at each other for a second, and then Claire threw her arms around her friend.

"I am so very sorry, Gwen. I wish I had been here with you."

Gwen couldn't answer. She just held on tight, and as they had twenty-two years or so before, they stood in Gwen's doorway for a good five minutes, just holding each other and crying. When they pulled apart, Gwen helped Claire bring her suitcase into the apartment.

"I can get a hotel, but I wanted to come and see you first."

"You're not getting a hotel. You can stay here. Do you mind staying in Leah's room?"

"Not at all. Do *you* mind?"

"No. I don't know that I could let anyone other than you stay in there though."

Gwen put the suitcase in Leah's room and made Claire a cup of tea. They sat in the living room together, and Gwen retold the story of her daughter's death. Claire knew the details from Gwen's email, but she listened as she held Gwen's hand.

When she finished, Gwen said, "I'm sorry I didn't let you know sooner. I just couldn't talk about it. I wasn't fit to be around anybody."

"I understand." Claire didn't really understand, but that was okay. She was here now and would try to help her friend as best she could.

The second knock on the door didn't come until midafternoon. Gwen slowly walked to the door, took a deep breath, and opened it to see two police officers. One was Officer Mandato, and he was with a female officer.

Gwen didn't wait for preliminary greetings. "Officers," she nodded, "you have more news on my daughter's death?"

"No, ma'am," responded Officer Mandato, "not directly. But we would like to come in and talk to you, if that's okay."

Gwen stood aside and motioned them in. "Have a seat. This is my friend Claire Lambertson...sorry Adams. Can I get you anything?"

Both officers responded, "No, thank you."

Gwen sat next to Claire, across from the officers, and waited expectantly. She could feel Claire's anxiety and confusion but focused on the other two people in the room.

Mandato started, "I'm Detective Mandato with the City PD. I'm sure you remember me." Gwen nodded. "And this is Detective Davis. Can we talk privately?"

135

Gwen nodded at the female detective. Looking back at Detective Mandato, she said, "Claire is family. I have no problem with her being here."

Detective Mandato nodded.

"When was the last time you saw Donna Mueller?" asked Davis.

Gwen looked her directly in the eye. "The day my daughter died."

"You haven't been to her apartment or around her apartment building since that day?"

"No. I have no desire to see her."

"Do you hold Miss Mueller responsible for your daughter's death?"

"Yes. She was with Leah. She should have called for help. She did not."

"I see," replied Davis, thinking. "Have you ever thought about approaching Miss Mueller about that?"

"No."

"Why not?" asked Mandato.

"I would end up in jail. I don't want to talk to her, Detective. I want to strangle her." Gwen shrugged. "So I stay away." Gwen sat silent for a second, watching the detectives, who were watching her. "Why all these questions all of a sudden? My daughter has been dead for over six months, and this is the first time anyone has come to talk to me. Have you found her dealer? Has anyone been arrested?"

"No, ma'am," answered Detective Mandato, at least having the decency to bow his head a bit when admitting to that. "Miss Mueller was assaulted last night."

"I see, but that doesn't explain why you are here."

"Someone matching your description has been seen in the area lately."

"There are a lot of short fat women in Baltimore," Gwen responded. She could feel Claire's eyes on her.

"Not many have it out for our victim. You do."

"I have not contacted Donna or gone near her since the day Leah died." Gwen snorted. "She didn't even have the decency to show up at Leah's funeral. I care nothing about her and hope I never see her again. That's all I can tell you."

"Where were you last night, Miss Marsh?"

"Right here. I did some work in the evening, read, and was in bed by midnight."

"What kind of work do you do?"

"Bookkeeping for local small businesses."

"You do that here?"

"Yes, I do."

"Can anyone confirm that you were here all evening?"

"I live alone, Detective." Then remembering that Claire was here with her, she said, "Claire did not arrive from Ohio until this morning." Claire silently nodded assent.

Gwen looked from one detective to the other. "Anything else?"

The detectives both stood. "No. We'll get back to you if we have any more questions."

As Gwen led them to the door, Detective Davis turned and said, "You haven't asked about the assault or if Miss Mueller is okay."

"That's because I don't care. Have a nice day, detectives."

After closing the door, Gwen turned to find Claire looking at her. "I don't want to talk about it." Claire nodded and thought that when her friend was ready, she would talk about it. Claire stayed for three days, and they never discussed the visit from the police.

Once in the car, Detective Davis said, "That is one cold woman, but I believe her."

"I'm not so sure. I saw the look of hate in her eyes that morning at the station. She wanted to kill that girl, and she didn't even know the circumstances of her daughter's death yet."

"I didn't say she didn't hate the victim. She clearly does. I just don't think she did anything about it. She was not nervous at all speaking to us but was very matter-of-fact, and she didn't hide the fact that she hated this woman, even said she wanted to strangle her. I say we keep looking but hold on to this information in case we want to revisit Miss Marsh. If we do, we come back with a warrant to have a look at her computer."

As they drove off, Detective Mandato still wasn't buying it. Miss Marsh needed more looking into. He decided to keep her file on his desk and dig into her a bit more as he had time. Problem was, though, when you're a Baltimore City cop, you don't get a lot of downtime. Assaults take a back seat to murders, and the file on Donna Mueller and Gwen Marsh was quickly buried under higher-priority cases.

Chapter 24

Paid for with Pain and Suffering

Gwen's next target was Leah's drug dealer. This proved a bit more difficult because she had no idea who this was. What she did have though was her daughter's phone, and she went through all of her contacts and recent calls. She recognized most names and made a list of contacts and called numbers that she didn't recognize.

She then started on text messages. Starting at the top, she would open a message and then go back as far as the thread would allow, reading every word. This process took days, so Gwen kept meticulous notes on where she left off each day and anything she found that might lead her to her target. Leah did a lot of texting, paid for by her mother, so there was plenty to read through. For the next few weeks, Gwen did her client work during the day and her text reading at night. She was determined and persistent, sometimes reading entire threads over and over.

Finally, after about two weeks, Gwen was reading through a thread with someone named Cass. Deep in the thread, she found this:

From Cass: "I need to get hooked up."

From Leah: "My guy is at the corner of Shipley and West Fayette, every night, 7–11. Tell him I sent you. He'll take care of you."

From Cass: "Thx"

That was it. Gwen's heart rate sped as she read and reread the messages. This was it. Gwen noted the corner and best times and then began to plan. The first step in her plan was to get back to the firing range. She needed to hit her target the first time. So she carved out an hour each day to get to the gun range and practice with her rifle. She was good too. If she missed her target even once and even by an inch, she paid for more time and more ammo and kept at it. She seldom missed though.

Every night between 7:00 and 11:00 p.m., she would drive downtown past "that corner" as she thought of it, keeping an eye on who was there and what cars were there. After a few trips, she noted that the same SUV was parked near the corner every time, and there were always two people sitting in the car. She wasn't sure which of the two people was actually the dealer, but did it matter? She would gladly shoot them both. She also noted, with interest, that technically, the car was parked illegally, with the driver's side along the sidewalk.

Once she was comfortable that she had found her target, she needed to plan out her attack, so on the next few trips around, she looked for local places where she could set up out of sight but with a clear view of the dealer. On the same side of the street where the SUV was always parked was a small mini-mart, a pub, a check-cashing place, and a nail salon. On the other side of the street were some boarded-up buildings and what might be a few apartments. There were also a few homeless people camped out on the other side of the street. Gwen assumed that they slept in the boarded-up buildings. If she came down this street during the day, it was nearly empty, but in the evening and at night, there was plenty of activity.

Gwen's next task was to purchase a few burner phones. Once she had a few phones, she did some online searching for apartment rentals in the area of "that corner." Using a new phone, she contacted a landlord—slumlord—who owned the building across from the dealer's hangout. He currently had no vacancies but offered to call Gwen back when something opened up.

"Thanks, but I'll check back in with you." And she did once a week.

In the meantime, she needed another way to keep an eye on this piece of shit. So each evening, she would pack a pair of torn jeans, a hoodie, and a baggy old coat into her backpack; walk to a shopping area near her home; call a cab; get dropped off in different locations around the area; find a secluded spot to quickly put on her "homeless" clothes; and go hang out near that corner. The first night, she tried to stay out of sight, away from everyone else. She stood with her back up against the wall of a building down the other end of the block from the SUV. She was carrying as usual, so she wasn't too concerned about being out there alone, but she kept her eyes and ears open while she watched the goings-on around the SUV.

There seemed to be a steady stream of people who would go up to the driver's window of the SUV. There would be a brief discussion, a hand would come out of the window, an exchange was made, and the customer would walk away. At first, Gwen assumed that the guy she wanted was the driver, but then she noted that when the driver got out of the car and walked into the mini-mart, assumingly to use the bathroom, the passenger didn't move. She could hear the driver lock the doors as he walked away and unlock them only when he was within reach of the handle. However, when the passenger exited the car, the driver got out first, walked around to the passenger door, opened it, and walked with this boss to the mini-mart, where he then waited outside for his boss to return, walked him back to the passenger door, opened it, waited for the boss to get in, closed it, and then walked back around to the driver's side to get in the vehicle. This happened at least once or twice a night.

Not wanting to be noticed and having the basic information she needed, Gwen cut her visits back to once or twice a week.

She continued to call the slumlord regularly, every Thursday at 7:00 p.m. Even if she switched phones, the slumlord knew it was her and would sometimes just pick up the phone and say, "Nothin' open yet," and hang up. Some people would be offended by that, but not Gwen. That was what she wanted to know. She was not interested in pleasantries.

One night after a few weeks of surveillance, Gwen was standing in her usual spot when a homeless woman who hung out up the street walked by. The two women nodded to each other as she passed.

The woman, whom Gwen took to be in her fifties, took a few steps farther, stopped for a second, then turned around and came back.

Speaking to Gwen, "I see you around here a few times lately."

Gwen nodded.

"You should come up the street a bit and hang with the rest of us."

Gwen wasn't quite sure what to do. If she said no, it might draw attention, but if she said yes, then every one of those people would know her face.

"We don't bite, I promise," said the woman, smiling knowingly.

Gwen chuckled. "I've heard that before."

"We all have." The woman laughed. "I'm Meg."

"I'm Madeline."

Meg nodded her head toward the group. "C'mon, no need for you to be standing by yourself."

Gwen followed her new friend up the block. As they approached the small group, a big guy who considered himself the leader and protector of his little group approached. "Who dis?"

"This my new friend, Madeline. She cool," responded Meg, walking right past the big dude. The big dude didn't look convinced, but he let them both pass.

The two ladies stood up against the building. "You're welcome to sleep in our place tonight," Meg offered.

"I have a place a few blocks away. If I don't go back, the others there get worried," lied Gwen.

"Yeah, then why are you hanging here by yourself?"

"Those people get on my nerves after a bit." Gwen laughed.

"I hear that!"

They chitchatted for a bit about not much, while Gwen kept her eye on the SUV. She saw the driver, whom she nicknamed Fat Eddie, get out and walk around to the passenger side. She knew this meant that the dealer, whom she referred to as POS, was headed to the head.

"Hey, I hit the jackpot earlier today. I'm going to buy coffee. I'll bring some back for everybody."

"Want help?" asked Meg.

"Nah, they see two of us come through that door, they might get worried." They both laughed as Gwen watched POS enter the mini-mart. "Be right back."

She headed across the street and walked right past Fat Eddie guarding the door. He looked her over with what she was sure he considered an intimidating stare, but she kept right on going. Once in, she went up to the counter and ordered six medium coffees to go. As she was waiting on the coffee, POS came out of the men's room. He seemed surprised to see someone else in the mart. She quickly looked him over without appearing too interested. He was your typical thug POS, nothing special to look at, though he dressed nicely and appeared well-groomed. She wondered how he would look writhing in pain. He ignored her and quickly headed out the door. She could see him and Fat Eddie having a tense conversation as they made their way to the passenger door. Apparently, POS didn't like other people in the mart when he was taking a piss. Too bad.

The guy behind the counter put four coffees in a cardboard tray. "Do you need two trays?"

"No, I can make due with one." She paid for her coffee, picked up the tray, balanced a fifth coffee on top, and held the sixth in her other hand. Smiling, she remembered watching Claire trying to balance her books all those years ago. She pushed open the door with her back and headed back across the street, not looking toward the SUV at all, though she could feel their eyes on her.

Her new group of friends were happy to relieve her of her coffees. One or two said thank you, but she could tell they all appreciated the drink. Mostly because it was warm. The big dude even nodded at her and said, "Yeah, you okay," as he took his.

It made Gwen's heart hurt to watch this small group struggle to stay warm while Fat Eddie and POS sat in a warm car. Those two thugs who ruined people's lives sat comfortably in a car paid for with pain and suffering. She briefly considered walking over to that car right now, pulling out her pistol, and blowing both of those sons of bitches away. Why wait? But as she considered the prospect, she determined that Fat Eddie might just be quick enough to kill her first. No, she would stick to the original plan.

And so she did. She would visit her new friends weekly to keep an eye on things as she waited for a call from the slumlord. She only had to wait a few more weeks.

Chapter 25

Trash!

Gwen met her new landlord on a Friday morning directly across from the mini-mart. He was waiting for her in front of his building as she approached. "Hi, I'm Madeline Kahn," she said, putting out her hand. Gwen had padded her clothing to appear much heavier than she was. She had also purchased a gray wig and used Leah's cosmetics to make herself look older than she was.

The slumlord took her hand. "I'm Joey Keene, and you are one persistent lady."

"That I am," agreed Gwen. "Whatcha got for me?"

"I'll show you." He led Gwen into the building and up to the third floor. She followed him down the hall a bit, where he unlocked the door to apartment 303. Gwen breathed a sigh of relief that it was a front-facing unit.

The apartment wasn't much—a living room, kitchenette, bedroom, and a tiny bathroom. The bedroom had a decent-sized closet with shelving. Everything was old and grungy looking, not that it mattered much to Gwen. She wasn't interested in the accommodations, just in the view of her target. She looked around and then sauntered over to the front window, which provided a clear view of the mini-mart. She would have to come back at night to see if anything would block her shot as he walked from the SUV to the door of the mart.

"I'll take it."

"Good," replied Joey, placing a folder on the small kitchen counter, "We can go over the paperwork here. I'll need to see your ID."

"I don't have an ID."

He looked at her, looked at his forms, and checked the box for Maryland driver's license. "I'm supposed to see your ID, but you can show me that later."

"No problem."

"Uh-huh. Okay, I need you to sign the lease, and I'll need a month's rent as a deposit plus your first month's rent."

Gwen pulled a money order out of her pocket, handed it over, and signed the agreement.

"I like the way you do business, Miss Kahn. You obviously have my number, so call me if you have any problems. I expect rent on the first of every month." He handed her the keys.

"No problem." Gwen hoped she wouldn't still need this place by the first of next month.

They both walked out, and Gwen locked the door. "Any problem if I start moving in my things today?"

"Nope, it's all yours. Have at it."

Once out of the building, Gwen walked a few blocks and hailed a cab.

As soon as she got home, she hopped into her own car and went shopping. She had a few things to get for her new apartment and a few things to get for another project. When she came out, she had an overflowing cart, the contents of which she then crammed into her car. Back home and car unloaded, she then caught up on her customer workload.

The next day, she pulled out her new, extra-large duffel bag. On the bottom, she put a layer of Leah's clothes; on top of that her rifle and attachments, new locks, and tools to install them; and on top of that, the few towels she had purchased. She also threw in the toothbrush, soap, etc. that she had bought. Lastly, she put in her laptop, portable Wi-Fi, a few items of clothing, and a backpack. Putting on her coat, she made sure she had her pistol safely tucked into the deep pocket. She then summoned an Uber, grabbed her fully packed duffle and the folding lawn chair she had purchased, and headed out.

She only had to wait a few minutes before the car pulled up in front of her and the driver hopped out. "Let me help you with that." He grabbed the chair and the duffel and put them in the trunk as Gwen got into the car.

"That bag was heavy!" commented the driver as he got in. "You look too small to lift it!"

"Oh, I'm stronger than I look." She told him where she was headed.

"Why would a nice lady like you go to this part of town?"

"I met a homeless person a few weeks ago when I got lost driving downtown. I am bringing her some supplies."

"This is very nice of you." Gwen could detect an accent, maybe West Africa. If he only knew, she doubted he would think she was very nice.

"Thank you. If we can help just one person, right?"

"Right! If everyone did that, perhaps all the problems would be solved." He smiled at her through the rearview mirror.

"Maybe."

As they neared Gwen's destination, she said, "You can just drop me off at the next corner, please."

"Sure, would you like me to wait for you?"

"No, I plan to spend some time there. Thank you though."

They were a few blocks from the apartment. Not as far as she thought was safe, but the bag *was* heavy. The driver removed her things from the trunk. "Can I carry these for you?"

"Thank you, but I've got it from here."

He looked doubtful but said, "Okay then, I will leave you here." In addition to the tip she added on the app, she handed the driver a nice cash tip.

"Thanks for the ride." She smiled as he got back into the car.

She hoisted the duffel bag over her shoulder and grabbed the folding chair and headed off. She got a few looks as she walked the few blocks, but other than that, it was an uneventful stroll. She ducked into an alley on the way to put on her wig. The makeup would have to wait, so she kept her head down as she walked.

Her first job once she was in her apartment was to change out the lock on the door. She didn't want slumlord to have easy access whenever he wanted. Being a single parent makes you learn to also be handy around the house. *Good thing*, she thought. She added the keys to her key ring, then went into the bedroom and opened the closet. She placed her rifle on the top shelf, put the accessories next to it, and then piled her towels and clothes in front. Not a great hiding place, but it would do for now.

She then checked her wig and put on her makeup and padding, recreating the older fat woman she needed.

Leaving the apartment, she locked the door and began to scope out the building. She needed to have an escape route. Her building was on the corner, so if she could find a way out the back, she might be able to get away unnoticed when the time came. The only access, however, seemed to be the front door. She exited the building and walked around the corner. There were windows on the first-level rear-facing apartments. She would need to figure out how to make use of those; there was no other option.

Gwen went back into the building and went to the door of one of the first-floor units. She listened quietly for a moment and then knocked. An elderly woman answered the door. "So sorry, ma'am. I must have the wrong unit."

"Who are you looking for?" the old woman snarled back.

"My friend."

"That hooker next door? Don't bother knocking. She's asleep. She's out all night and sleeps all day. Trash!" And with that, she slammed the door in Gwen's face.

Gwen smiled and went back up to her new apartment. She hummed the tune to "Movin' On Up" as she climbed the stairs.

In the apartment, she set up her Wi-Fi and computer, made herself comfortable on the lawn chair, and went to work. Technology had progressed since she started this business, and most of what she did now involved little to no face-to-face with her clients. They emailed her what she needed, and she put everything into the system and emailed statements back to the client. There were some clients who had her pay their vendors for them, and she used online banking for that. This made her extracurricular activities that much easier.

She worked for a bit and then decided to take a walk. If she wanted to be out and back before the sun started to set, she needed to get a move on.

She walked a few blocks until she found another mini-mart. She bought a few bottles of water; a few bottles of iced tea; a ready-made wrapped sandwich, which she thought she might regret later; some chips; and some hostess cupcakes. *I'll eat healthy tomorrow,* she thought. As she was leaving, she noticed that the store had a small produce area. She stopped and perused the fruit. *Not quite Giant quality,* she thought but grabbed a plastic bag and took a few oranges and apples. After paying for her produce, she finally headed back "home."

Pedestrian traffic had picked up in that short time. Night was coming. She silently scolded herself for this second bag. Moving that bag to her left hand with the other bag, she put her right hand in her pocket, firmly gripping her pistol. Just in case. However, no one bothered her. She got a few looks that raised her awareness levels, but she kept her eyes forward and plowed on. Giving dirty looks to the population here would only anger them. This was not the place to assert herself.

Once inside her building, she breathed a sigh of relief, then put the bag of produce down in front of the old woman's door on the first floor, knocked, and then hurried up the steps before the woman could answer. As she unlocked her own door, she could hear the old lady cursing. "I can buy my own damned food!" She stood and listened for the sound of the lady picking up the bag and then entered her own unit, quietly closing and locking the door behind her.

Gwen ate and then waited for night to fully descend. Just before 9:00 p.m., she turned out all the lights in her unit and set herself up in front of the window. The scope was on the rifle, and the rifle was in her lap as she watched the happenings on the street below. She saw Meg walk by at one point and would have liked to have invited her in to warm up, but that wasn't possible. At around 10:00 p.m., a scantily clad woman exited her building. Gwen guessed this was the hooker downstairs. If the POS left at eleven like Leah's text predicted, that gave Gwen an hour to shoot and run. She waited for POS to need to pee; that wait was about twenty minutes. As Fat Eddie got out of the car, Gwen positioned her rifle and looked through the scope. She noted that there was a brief window of time after POS exited the vehicle, while Fat Eddie closed the door, that she had a clear shot. She kept watching as the two thugs went through the entire production that was required for POS to take a piss. There might be a few other opportunities to shoot, but Gwen determined that when he exited the car was her best shot.

She put the rifle back into its hiding place, grabbed her credit card, pulled up her hood, and left the apartment, locking the door behind her. As quietly as possible, she descended the stairs and then stood at the hooker's door, listening. After a few moments of complete silence, she slid her card between the door and the doorframe, praying that the lock would open. It took a few tries, but it worked. Gwen was amazed at how careless people were. She entered the apartment stood quietly inside the door, pistol out just in case. The light over the kitchen sink had been left on, so Gwen had no problem seeing. No one was home. She went to the back window and looked out. There was a small alleyway between this building and the back of the building on the next block. She could hop out this window, run down the alley to the corner, and then head to the nearest bar. She struggled to open the window. It probably had not been opened in years, but eventually, she was able to open it just enough where she thought she could squeeze through. Satisfied, she closed the window and exited the apartment. She went back to her unit, locked herself inside, made herself a bed of towels on the floor, and slept.

She didn't wake until ten the following morning. Gwen couldn't remember the last time she had slept that late—probably when she was pregnant with Leah. She could really sleep back then. Getting up off the floor wasn't easy, and Gwen prayed that she wouldn't need to sleep here again. Throwing the computer equipment into the backpack, she headed out, locking the door firmly behind her. This morning, she walked about thirty blocks before summoning a cab for her ride back to Timonium. She would stay home tonight, get a good night's sleep, and return tomorrow.

The next morning, Gwen put on her wig and old-lady makeup. It was going to be warmer today, and the hoodie *and* coat would be too much. She selected a thin hoodie, torn jeans, and slip-on sneakers. She stuffed clothing under her hoodie to make her look as fat as possible. For this trip downtown, she left her computer equipment behind. Other than her keys, wallet, and pistol, she took nothing with her. This time, she called a cab from the Towson Town Center, which required a few miles' walk, and had it drop her off on Baltimore Street. This left her with a second long walk, but that was okay. It was still early in the afternoon. She had plenty of time and plenty of nervous energy. She didn't get to the apartment until around three in the afternoon. Grabbing one of her iced teas from the fridge, she sat and waited for night.

As soon as the sun went down, she pulled Leah's clothes from the closet. Holding them to her face, she breathed deeply, relishing in the faint smell of her daughter that lingered on the garments. She put them in the duffel bag and left the towels in the closet. She wanted to keep the bag as light as possible. She took out the rifle and laid it on the floor in front of the window, set up the chair, and laid the duffel bag right next to the chair, wide open, wanting to be able to quickly throw the rifle in when it was time to run. She checked her wig and makeup, put her fat padding back in place, made sure her pistol and credit card were easily accessible, and took up her position in front of the window. She picked up her rifle and positioned it so she was comfortable. Adjusting the scope, she was now ready. She snacked on the cupcakes as she watched the street below.

The hooker left a bit earlier tonight, a little before nine. This time, she headed toward the SUV. She blew a kiss at POS as she walked in front of the vehicle and then went to the driver's side to do business. Fat Eddie made a trip into the mini-mart shortly thereafter, but POS must not have had much to drink that day because she had to wait over an hour for him to make an appearance. Finally, at 10:15, Fat Eddie exited the SUV again and headed around to his boss's side. Gwen got into firing position. Fat Eddie opened the passenger door. POS stepped out and walked around Fat Eddie toward the front of the car. As Eddie closed the door, Gwen had a clear shot.

Trash, she thought.

Boom. POS went down. She hit him square on the left knee.

Boom. Her second shot was a bit off, missing his knee but shattering his right femur. The shots were so fast that the second shot hit before Fat Eddie could respond. He dropped to the ground, gun pulled, searching wildly for a target.

Gwen threw the rifle and empty iced tea bottle into the duffel, threw the duffel over her shoulder, pulled up her hood, and left the apartment as quickly and quietly as she could. The old lady was opening her door as Gwen hit the bottom level. "Damn."

"What the fuck is going on out here?"

"I think it's the hooker," Gwen replied. "I need to get in there and make sure she's okay."

The old lady watched as Gwen used her card to get into the apartment. "I knew she'd get herself killed someday," muttered the woman as she went back into her unit, shutting the door behind her.

Gwen ran to the window, not bothering to lock the door, pulled it up, and was out in a matter of seconds. She could hear yelling coming from the front of the building but didn't stop to listen. She made her way down the alley and out onto the side street. Once on the street, she turned right and headed toward the bar she spotted earlier in the day on her walk here. She would have the bartender call her a cab. It was a bit farther than she wanted to be on the streets at night but thought this was her best option. She had walked about two blocks when she heard the sirens.

She was almost to the bar when two young men approached her, one with a knife. "Gimme that bag, bitch."

Gwen pulled out her pistol and pointed it at the head of the knife-wielding thug, "I would like nothing better than to shoot you both in the face, so drop that knife, turn, and run. Now."

"You ain't gonna sh—" *Boom.* Gwen shot the knife holder in the upper arm. He went down; the friend turned and ran.

Gwen stood over the injured thief. "Get up. You're okay," she ordered. "*Get up and run now!*" She loomed over him, gun pointed at his face. This was all the encouragement he needed. He scrambled to his feet and took off just as people were running over to see what was happening.

"Thief!" she yelled, pointing at the running men, distracting attention to that direction as she ran for the bar. Inside, patrons were trying to look out the windows to see where the shot had come from.

"What's happening?" one asked her.

"Somebody tried to rob me! I ran, but he shot at me."

This elicited concern from all those within hearing. Once it was determined that Gwen was okay, someone bought her a drink, and the bartender offered to call the police.

"Don't bother. They're gone by now, but if you could call me a cab, I'd be grateful."

The bartender called the cab. "What are you doing around here this time of night, if you don't mind my asking?"

"My car broke down, my cell phone is dead, and I was trying to find a phone."

"You're having a rough night," commented the man beside her, perhaps the person who bought her a drink.

"You're tellin' me."

"You're lucky to be alive, lady."

"That I am." Gwen downed her drink.

Apparently, the sound of gunfire was not uncommon because things went back to normal in the bar. Everyone was back at the bar, and conversations resumed. No one asked her any more questions, and there was no more talk about the police. Gwen ordered another drink as she waited for the cab. Her hands were shaking, but that was understandable considering she had just been shot at. Gwen smiled to herself.

She had the cab drop her at the upscale housing development down the street from her apartment in Timonium, and she walked the few blocks home. As she sat on the bed, she thought, *This was just too easy*. She laid back and slept for the next twelve hours.

Chapter 26

I Am Happy to Help

This time, Gwen didn't even wait for the police to show up at her door. She didn't give it much of a thought. She just didn't care. She hoped POS was in pain; actually, she was sure he was. She hoped he would never walk again. She would wait a month or two and drive by that corner to see if POS and Fat Eddie were back. If so, next time, she might shoot for the elbow. That thought made her smile.

In the meantime, she had another project, and all the supplies she needed were still in the corner of her living room. She had a half dozen sleeping bags, a few new men's coats, a few new women's coats, hats, gloves, socks, toothbrushes and toothpaste, soap, men's underwear, women's underwear, sweat suits, T-shirts, cargo pants, and tennis shoes of various sizes. She also had a few lawn chairs, identical to the one she used in her downtown apartment.

She waited for a full week and then summoned an Uber, hoping and praying she would get the same West African driver. She smiled when she saw him and waved as he pulled up in front of her building.

The driver hopped out. "Nice to see you again! And where are we headed today, miss?"

"No place, I have a favor to ask of you."

The driver looked unsure and waited for an explanation.

"There is a small group of homeless people that hang out every evening on Fayette near Shipley. Do you know where that is?"

"Yes, I do. I am familiar with the area, ma'am. I don't like to go there though. They had a shooting just last week."

"Did they? Hmmmmm. Well, if you get there before the sun goes down, you can be out of town before its dark. I'll make it worth your while."

"What is it exactly that you need from me?"

"I have supplies that I would like delivered. I will pay for the trip there as though I were in the car, and then I will give you two hundred dollars extra."

"Why will you not come and deliver these items in person?"

"I don't want them to know who it's from. I know that sounds silly, but it means more if you do good deeds in secret. I don't want thanks, and I don't want them to feel awkward." He still didn't look convinced. "You are welcome to look through the items so that you can see there is nothing illegal." She smiled.

"Okay, I will help you. You don't have to give me extra though. I am happy to help."

"Great! Can you help me bring everything down, please?"

The driver followed Gwen up the stairs to her apartment where he saw a large box and several trash bags full of items.

"There are sleeping bags in the box. Feel free to look through them. In the bags, you'll find clothing and hygiene items. In this one bag, the one with the yellow Twistee on it, on the very top there is a red coat. There is a woman in the group named Meg. Can you make sure she gets this coat? If she is not there, please bring the coat back, and I'll try again another time. I want her to have that one. I'll pay you for the return trip if that happens."

"Okay, I will ask for Meg."

They carried the box and bags down and loaded up the car.

"Thank you very much," said Gwen as she reached out her hand with a substantial tip.

"No, no, no, this is not necessary, miss."

"Please take it. I'll feel better if you allow me to pay you extra. I know this is not an ordinary request."

The driver shrugged and took the money, then shook Gwen's hand.

"You are a nice lady. I am happy to help. Thank you." He got in the car and drove off. Gwen trusted that he would make sure the delivery reached its destination and intended recipients.

Gwen slowly took the stairs back up to her apartment. That was done. What now?

It had been nine months since the death of her daughter.

Chapter 27

Why Was He on the Street?

Detective Mandato had already spoken with Gwen's landlord. It didn't take long to determine that the shots came from his building. Mr. Keene had led the detective to the third floor apartment and was surprised to find it unlocked. The detective looked around the apartment, noting the folding chair in front of the open window, trash in the kitchen, and towels in the bedroom closet. "Tell me about the tenant."

"Old woman by the name of Madeline Kahn. Short, maybe five feet two inches. Two hundred pounds easy. Paid her deposit and first month's rent with a money order."

"Do you have a copy of her ID?" He knew the answer before he asked. First of all, Madeline Kahn was a famous comedienne from the '70s and '80s. No doubt this landlord had been given a fake name, and in this area, ID was seldom supplied.

"No."

Mandato shook his head. "You'll need to stay out of this unit for a while." He then called in the CSI unit to bag and test all items in the apartment. His next task was to interview any locals he could find.

The only tenant home today was the old lady on the first floor. "What do you want?" she greeted as she opened the door.

"I want to talk to you about a shooting last night. Did you hear anything?"

"Of course I heard it. I'm not deaf, for Christ's sake." The old lady took a long drag off her cigarette and blew the smoke into the detective's face.

"Did you see anyone or anything unusual?"

"Yeah, I saw Fatty from upstairs break into the hooker's apartment," she answered, pointing to her neighbor's unit. "Said she needed to make sure she was okay. I knew that was bullshit, but what was I gonna do?"

Detective Mandato asked the lady to describe "Fatty" and was not surprised to hear a similar description to that of the landlord's description of Madeline Kahn.

"Did you notice anything else?"

"No, but if you find fatty, tell her I can buy my own damned fruit!"

"She bought you fruit?"

"Yeah, a few days ago, left it at the door."

"How do you know it was her?"

"I've lived here for thirty years, no fruit. She moves in and that very day, fruit. I'm not an idiot."

"Thank you for your help." And with that, Detective Mandato had the door slammed in his face. He smiled as he walked away from the door. "Sweet old lady."

He had to hit a few local marts before he found one who recognized his description of "Ms. Kahn." The lady bought a few things, items that Detective Mandato recognized from the apartment trash, paid in cash, then bought some fruit, paying in cash again. Not much help but made it likely that the sweet old lady was right—"Fatty" had bought her fruit.

Mandato had more work to do, cameras to review, cab companies to contact, and Uber records to subpoena. He felt like he knew who the shooter was but was far from proving it.

In the meantime, Gwen carried on with her life as though nothing had happened. She worked, emailed Claire a few times a week, and researched local addiction-counseling centers. Now that Leah was gone, she had no heirs, no one to pass on her small fortune to. She wanted that money to be used for good, and this was her new cause. Every few weeks, she would summon her Uber driver, whose name she learned was Julius Akwashiki, for a trip downtown. She always had bags of clothing and hygiene supplies, and they would find homeless people to whom they would deliver their packages. Gwen always made it a point to talk to the people she helped. She would not just drop a dollar in a hat or hand someone a bag and walk on. She wanted to talk to them, ask their names, and see if she could find out how they got to this point. She found that most were open to chatting. The most engaging, she would take to lunch. She enjoyed her time with Julius and her new friends. And Julius didn't seem to mind. Gwen didn't know if that was because she tipped him more for these trips than he probably made in a day or if she truly enjoyed the time. She suspected it was a little of both. Either way, he was a nice man, and she appreciated the company.

Nearly six weeks had passed since the shooting before Gwen received the anticipated contact from the police. This time, however, it was not a knock on the door. This time, it was a phone call inviting her to come in for a visit. Gwen agreed to come in that very afternoon and added that she hoped they were calling her in to tell her that Leah's pusher had been arrested.

Gwen arrived at the police department on Edison Highway at the scheduled time. She was escorted to an interview room where she had to wait for about ten minutes for Detectives Mandato and Davis.

"Detectives," greeted Gwen, nodding, "I assume you kept me waiting because you were busy booking my daughter's drug dealer?"

"No, ma'am, attending to other matters. Sorry to keep you waiting," answered Mandato. Detective Davis just nodded a greeting to Gwen as they both took a seat on the other side of the table.

Gwen waited patiently.

Detective Mandato laid a portfolio on the table. He opened it and pulled out a few pictures, one by one, and laid them on the table facing Gwen. Gwen looked at pictures of herself in the gray wig, looking quite fat. The photos were a bit blurred, obviously pulled from street cameras downtown.

"Another short fat woman, detectives?"

"We think this is you," commented Detective Davis.

Gwen chuckled. "No, doesn't even look like me."

Detective Mandato pulled out a few more photos. This time, they were pictures of the SUV that Gwen had watched for weeks, a picture of the building where Gwen had rented an apartment, and finally a picture of a short woman in a hoodie carrying a tray of coffee across Shipley Street. She looked at the pictures and then back up at the detectives.

"Does this SUV look familiar to you?"

"Yeah, I see dozens like it every time I'm on the road."

"What about this apartment building?"

Gwen shrugged. "No, not specifically."

"Have you ever been in the area of Fayette and Shipley?" Detective Mandato already knew the answer to this question. He had seen pictures of Gwen's car driving near the corner of the shooting.

"Yes."

"What was your business there?"

"I had no business there. I've taken quite a few drives around Baltimore since my daughter's death. I spot drug dealers on pretty much every block. I then would drive the same route a few days later, only to see the same drug dealers in the same places."

"How do you know these individuals are dealing drugs?"

"Common sense. You only need to watch them for a minute to realize what they're up to."

Detective Davis pointed to the picture of Gwen carrying the tray of coffee, "Is this you?"

"No." She looked Detective Davis in the eye. "Can I expect to get called in here every time you have a picture of a short fat woman? Is there a point to all this?"

"The point is, there was a shooting in this area about a month ago," answered Mandato, pointing to the pictures of the SUV and apartment building. "The victim was a local drug dealer. The description of the shooter closely matches the person in this picture. We think this picture closely resembles you." The detective paused for a second, gauging Gwen's reaction but seeing nothing. "Do you own a rifle, Miss Marsh?"

"Yes, I do."

"What type of rifle?"

"308."

"Why would someone living in Towson need a rifle?"

"I enjoy target practice. I find it to be a great stress reliever."

"Would you be willing to let us examine that weapon?"

"Sure, stop by anytime."

Detective Davis chimed in, "Ever take a cab downtown?"

"A few times over the years."

"How about an Uber?"

"Yes, frequently."

"Can I ask the reason for these trips downtown?"

"Which ones particularly?"

"Start with the cab rides."

"It's been a while, but I have taken a cab downtown for shopping, to visit potential clients, and to visit the aquarium. But again, that's been quite a while ago."

"How about Uber?" The detectives had already spoken to Mr. Akwashiki. He told them how caring Miss Marsh was. He knew exactly where she lived as he had picked her up a few times. This fact made Mandato wonder if Gwen was really the perp. Miss Marsh obviously wasn't stupid. Would she really make it so easy for an Uber driver to identify her? Or was this planned to make him ask himself that very question?

"In my drives through the streets of Baltimore, I also noticed a lot of homeless people. I've used Uber to deliver packages to those people."

"Why use Uber? Why not drive your car?"

"I felt safer. I don't like to park in Baltimore or walk the streets alone."

"That must get expensive for you."

"Yes, it does."

"So you've never delivered your packages on your own?"

"I did once, the very first time. I had the Uber drop me off and then walked until I found the homeless ladies I had seen a few days earlier."

"What did you deliver that time?"

"I had warm clothing, antibacterial wipes, some cash, and a lawn chair as I recall."

"Why a lawn chair?" asked Davis.

"I always see them standing or sitting on the ground. I thought a chair would be nice to have."

"How about the next trip?"

"I felt uncomfortable walking around those streets, so the next time, I asked the Uber driver, Julius, to deliver the packages for me." Anticipating the next question, Gwen continued, "This time, I sent more lawn chairs, sleeping bags, clothing again, more of the same. I suspected that this particular group slept in the abandoned buildings nearby and thought the sleeping bags would come in handy."

"That group was near where the shooting took place?" Mandato was trying to get Gwen to acknowledge that she knew about the shooting.

"That group was on Shipley Street as I recall."

"And how did you come to know this group."

"I didn't. I saw them on my drives down that street." Mandato had spoken to this little group of people and shown them pictures of Gwen. None acknowledged having ever seen her.

"And after that?"

"After that I went with Julius and hand-delivered my packages."

"Why?"

"Why what? Why do I give to those in need? Because I can. Why did I decide to do it myself? I thought it was more meaningful. I wanted to treat the people I was helping like human beings. Face-to-face."

The three sat silent for a moment.

"If there is nothing else, I have a few questions for you," said Gwen.

"We have no other questions at this time but will stop by for that rifle."

"Good. If I can drive down the streets of Baltimore a few times and spot drug dealers, why can't the Baltimore City PD? If you knew this guy who got shot was a drug dealer, why was he on the street and not in jail?"

"Fair questions," answered Detective Mandato. "Arresting these dealers is not as easy as it would seem. We need more than common sense. We need probable cause to make an arrest. This means we need evidence. We have to catch the dealer in the act. We need to have someone report the dealer by name. Drug users are seldom willing to do that. Locals are afraid to do that. Our leaders are more interested in getting the main suppliers and are hesitant to arrest low-level dealers, thinking they might lead us to the suppliers. And we are grossly understaffed. There are over 620,000 people in Baltimore and 2,500 officers. Recent riots have made our jobs even more difficult."

"Was the dealer who got shot killed?" asked Gwen

"No, but he won't walk again."

"Well, hopefully that keeps him off the streets at least. When you catch the shooter, you should thank them." Gwen paused for a minute. "Allow me one more comment. I am not nearly as fat as that woman in the pictures." Gwen stood to leave.

"Thank you for coming in, Miss Marsh." Detective Mandato stood and opened the door for Gwen.

Gwen looked up at him. "Please don't take me wrong. I appreciate the work you do. I know your job isn't easy. I just want the son of a bitch responsible for my daughter's death, and it bothers me to think that you are spending more time on the shooting of this drug dealer than you are finding the one who killed my baby."

"It may look that way, but that's not the case, ma'am."

Gwen nodded and walked away.

Detective Mandato sat back down. "Thoughts?"

"Well, she cared this time."

"What do you mean?"

"Last time, she said she didn't care enough to ask about Donna's assault. This time, she asked if the victim was killed."

"True." Mandato thought for a moment. "I don't know what to think. Part of me is convinced she's guilty, and the other part of me believes her completely." He looked at Detective Davis. "She's either innocent or a really good liar."

"There are a lot of really good liars out there," responded Davis.

"And a lot of short fat women," replied Mandato, chuckling. "That woman is a piece of work. I'll give her that."

Chapter 28

I Think We've Made a Decision

The Baltimore PD did indeed stop by and pick up Gwen's rifle. She made a show of pulling out a locker from under her bed, unlocking it with her thumbprint, and removing the rifle. The officers gave her a receipt and took the rifle for examination. The actual weapon they were looking for was in an unlocked plastic container under the same bed, other side. *They'll need a search warrant if they want that one*, she thought.

Gwen then waited a few days before hopping in her car and driving back down to Southwest Baltimore. She didn't expect to see the SUV. It was too early in the day for that, but she was hoping to spot Meg. It was a bit warm for Meg to be wearing the red coat, but Gwen kept an eye out for red anyway. It took a few trips around the area, but she finally saw a glimpse of red a few blocks ahead on the right. She pulled over into the right-hand lane and, as she got closer, slowed down. She could see a woman ahead carrying a red coat over her shoulder. She was pretty sure it was Meg.

Pulling up alongside the woman, she rolled down the passenger window. "Meg!" she called out.

Meg turned to look, surprised to hear someone calling her name. Recognizing the woman she knew as Madeline, she approached the window. "You need to get out of here. They lookin' for you."

Gwen knew immediately who "they" were. "I know. I've already talked to them. Hop in. I'll buy you lunch."

Meg looked uncertain.

"I promise I won't bite." Gwen smiled.

"Yeah, I heard that one before." Meg laughed as she opened the door and got in.

Once in the car, Meg didn't waste any time. "Did you shoot that drug dealer?"

"Yes."

"Nicely done." Meg held up her hand for a high five. Gwen slapped it, smiling.

"Did you send me this coat?"

"Yes."

"Thought so. Thank you, and thank you for the cash in the lining. I knew you'd be back."

"I'm sorry I lied to you. I think you understand now why I did."

"I do. I wasn't bothered by it."

"My name is Gwen."

"Nice to meet you, Gwen." Meg smiled. "Where we gonna eat?"

"You pick."

"There's a deli down in the main part of town, lots of businesspeople around lunch. I used to hang there, hoping one of them would give me money or bring me a sandwich. They didn't. Do you think their sensibilities would be offended by an old dirty, smelly homeless woman sitting at the table next to them for lunch?"

"I do." Gwen smiled.

"I think we've made a decision then. There's a parking lot a block from there."

Fifteen minutes later, the two women walked into the deli and took a table in the middle of the room. As Meg had predicted, the other patrons were all local businesspeople, dressed accordingly. Gwen could have passed for one of them, though a bit more casually dressed. Meg, however, stood out. Her clothing was dirty and torn. It was apparent by sight and by smell that she hadn't seen a shower in quite a while.

They perused their menus and were ready to order by the time a waitress came to the table.

"Can I help you, ladies?" The waitress was a young girl, probably in her twenties, and Gwen decided right then and there to tip her well. There were plenty of waiters and waitresses in this town who would have been very snooty in this situation.

The ladies placed their orders.

"If you'll excuse me, I'm going to use the restroom." Meg stood up and headed toward the back. Gwen watched as those around them followed Meg with their eyes. She saw some whisper to their colleagues or make a show of holding their noses. A few made the mistake of meeting Gwen's look and quickly looked away.

The food came before Meg returned to the table. Gwen was just about to go check on her when she finally returned, looking refreshed. "Sorry to keep you waiting. I don't get access to running water very often and wanted to take advantage of it."

"No problem." Gwen noticed that her new friend's hands and face were now clean. "Bon appétit," she said, smiling.

Meg didn't waste any time; she dug right in. Between bites though, she said, "I lied to you too, Gwen. My name is Margaret. I hate the name Meg."

"Then why do you use it."

"Because I hate this life." She shrugged. "It seemed to fit."

Gwen nodded her understanding. "Do you mind if I ask how you came to this point?"

"Not at all, but not here. Too many ears," Meg replied, glaring at those seated around them.

"We'll eat now and talk later then," agreed Gwen. So they ate with very little chitchat. Gwen noticed that Margaret—she refused now to think of her as Meg—had impeccable table manners.

Finished lunch, they both ordered coffee, mostly because they enjoyed sitting here together. As they sipped their coffee, Gwen noticed that it had started to rain outside. "Margaret, would you like to come back and stay at my condo tonight?"

Margaret looked taken aback for a second. "Look, Gwen, I like you, but I don't go that way."

"Neither do I. I'm not interested in your black ass. I'm offering you a night's sleep in a real bed." Gwen was a bit annoyed at her new friend's assumption.

Margaret threw back her head and laughed. "Calm down there, girl. I'm sorry. If you knew the propositions I get, you would understand my reaction. Yes, I would love to accept your invitation. And for your information, my black ass is mighty fine."

Gwen laughed. "I'm sure it is, Margaret, but it's safe from me." They both laughed. "Good, we'll go to my place, and you can sleep in my daughter's room."

"Where's your daughter going to sleep then?"

"She passed away about a year ago."

"Oh, Gwen, I am so sorry." Margaret reached across the table and grabbed Gwen's hand. They held on tightly to each other for a moment. Letting go, Margaret continued, "Girl, we have a lot to talk about."

Chapter 29

That Would Have to Wait

They got back to Gwen's place midafternoon. The first thing Margaret wanted was a hot shower, so Gwen set her up with everything she needed in the full bath off the hallway. As her friend showered, Gwen made sure that Leah's room had clean linens. She also looked through her clothing to find some things that might fit Margaret. She pulled out a few shirts that she thought would work, but her pants would all be way too short for the much taller Margaret. She then went through Leah's things and found a few pairs of casual pants and some undergarments that she thought would fit. Maybe tomorrow they could go shopping so Margaret could get some clothes of her own.

Margaret stayed in the shower until the hot water ran out. As she was drying off, she heard Gwen yell to her, "There are some clothes on your bed that should fit. Hair dryer is under the sink if you need it. Take your time."

Margaret joined her friend in the living room about fifteen minutes later, dressed in ill-fitting clothes but otherwise looking refreshed and relaxed. "I can't thank you enough for that. If you made me leave right now, I would still be forever grateful for that shower!"

"Glad you enjoyed it. Can I get you anything?"

"A nice tall glass of ice water would be great."

"C'mon then, let me show you where everything is. I'm not waitin' on your ass while you're here." She smiled at Margaret to show she was kidding. "Feel free to help yourself when you want something, okay?"

Eyes welling over with tears, Margaret asked, "Why are you being so kind to me, Gwen?"

Gwen stopped and turned toward her new friend. "A short time ago, you saw a woman standing alone, and you didn't just walk by." Margaret understood. Sometimes, it's the simple acts that make the biggest difference.

Gwen gave her a short tour of the kitchen, prepared a nice tall glass of ice water for each of them, and led her guest back into the living room.

After taking a long drink of her water, Margaret said, "I was looking at the pictures of your daughter in the bedroom. She was very beautiful."

"Yes, she was."

"Tell me about her."

Gwen took a deep breath. "She was my life. Everything I did from the day I knew I was pregnant was for her." Gwen told her about T&H, talked about how she came to start her own business, and talked about her hopes and dreams for Leah. She held nothing back. She told about her fears of losing her daughter when Leah started school, Leah's growing popularity, and her diminishing importance in Leah's life. She cried as she told Margaret about Leah's drug use and how she always thought it was just a phase, that Leah would turn things around.

As she prepared dinner, she talked about the day Leah died. "Identifying my child's body was the hardest thing I have ever done. I wanted to scream. I wanted to beat on something. But all I could do was shake my head that, yes, this was my daughter. And then the officers led me upstairs to tell me how Leah died and to ask me some questions, and Leah's friend Donna was sitting in the lobby there, crying, and I knew, I just knew, that she was to blame. I didn't know how. I just knew it was *her* fault. She ran over to me, yelling, 'I'm sorry. I'm sorry,' and I wanted to kill her. I wanted to grab her by her skinny throat and squeeze until nothing was left of her. But the officer blocked Donna from getting close to me, so that would have to wait.

"They told me that Leah had passed out as the result of a combination of heroin and alcohol. She was on her back on Donna's couch. At some point during the night, she had vomited and choked on her own vomit. She didn't overdose. She didn't suffer a heart attack or a stroke from the drugs. She choked to death. She could have been saved."

"And you blame this friend, Donna?"

"You're damned right I do. She was there. She could have called for help. She could have rolled Leah over. She didn't."

Margaret thought it likely that Donna had also been passed out, that she didn't know her friend was dying, but she didn't speak those words. She knew Gwen didn't want to hear them.

"Donna waited until morning to check on my girl and found her *unresponsive*." This last word was accompanied with air quotes. "Finally, she called for help, but it was too late. Leah was long gone."

"I am so sorry."

Gwen just nodded as she placed food on the table.

"Gwen, when you said you wanted to kill Donna, you also said, 'That would have to wait.' What did you mean?"

"I didn't kill her. I thought about it, but I wanted her to suffer. I wanted her to feel the pain that I was feeling." She prepared Margaret's plate for her. "Eat up."

Gwen sat down, prepared her plate, and continued. "I blame myself mostly for what happened. I should have insisted that Leah get help. I should have stopped it right at the very beginning. I should have been stricter with her as a teenager. I should have stopped bailing her out of trouble. I should have stopped giving her money. There's a lot I should have done and a lot I shouldn't have done."

"You can't blame yourself, Gwen."

"I do blame myself, but I blame others as well. By the time Leah was buried, I had made the decision to get retribution. For me and for Leah. I bought a gun, I bought a rifle, and I learned to shoot."

"Damn, girl! Remind me never to piss you off."

Gwen smiled. "You don't seem to have it in you to do something bad enough that would make me want to hurt you." She continued, "Donna was first because I knew where to find her. I watched her for a bit to find a good time to make my move. I wanted her unconscious like my Leah was. I went into her apartment with the intention of shooting her in the knees, but once I was in there, I changed my mind. I figured that losing her beauty would be the most painful thing to her, so I cut up her face."

Margaret stared openmouthed at her new friend.

"I know that sounds crazy, like something a crazy person would do, but I'm not crazy. At least I don't think I am." Gwen shrugged. "Maybe I am, but I look at it as payback, not just for what she let happen to my daughter but for her life, her useless life and the damage that has caused to those around her."

"Do you know how she's handling it?"

"I haven't seen her or heard about her, but I know in my heart she is not handling it well."

"Weren't you worried about getting caught?"

"No. I was very careful. The police did come to see me the next day, I think because they knew how I felt about her. But nothing ever came of it. So I moved onto my next project—her drug dealer."

"Which brought you to my neighborhood."

"Right. It took me a while to figure out who the dealer was and where to find him, but I found it finally in a text message on Leah's phone. So when we met, I was stalking him." Gwen smiled, as though reminiscing about meeting her friend at a party.

"So you bought those coffees so you could follow him into the store?"

"Yes," Gwen admitted. "I wanted a look at that piece of shit, and that's how I thought of him—POS. I had to wait until I could rent an apartment across the street from his hangout, but it was worth the wait. I had the perfect vantage point."

"Wow. I didn't know it was you until a few cops came around with a picture of a woman with blond hair, heavier than you, and then a picture of you, asking if we had seen either person. We all said no, of course, but that night we talked about it, wondering if that was you or not." Margaret shook her head in amazement. "He was alive when they took him away, but I hope he's dead now."

"Nah, killing is too easy. I want him to suffer. I want him to suffer like he makes his customers suffer, like he makes their families suffer. If I see him back at it again, I'll shoot his elbows out." Gwen stopped for a minute and looked at her friend. "I'm not a violent person…normally. I just couldn't let him continue to destroy lives with immunity. I couldn't let Donna get away with the death of my daughter."

"So you shoot to maim, not to kill."

"Yup." Gwen nodded.

Margaret didn't know whether to be impressed or frightened. "Wow. Does anyone else know about this?"

"No. My friend Claire was here when the police came about Donna, so I think she suspects I had a hand in that, but otherwise no."

"Why are you telling me? Aren't you afraid I'll go to the police?"

"I don't know why, to be honest. I think I just needed to talk, to tell someone. And no. I don't think you will, but if you do, I'm okay with that. I have nothing left in this life, and I just don't care what happens to me. If I end up in jail, it will be worth it."

Margaret reached across the table and gently grabbed Gwen under the chin, lifting her head up just a bit higher. "You *always* have something left in this life, my friend. Always. God has plans for you, and maybe that plan was just to help this old homeless woman get a shower and a good meal, but there is *always* something."

Nodding, Gwen replied, "I do have a few projects in mind. Actually, you might be able to help me with those, but we can talk about that later." Gwen got up to start clearing the table.

"No way!" Margaret stopped her. "You sit. I'll clean up." As Gwen sat back down, Margaret started to clear the table.

"So…were you there that night? The night I shot the POS?"

"Yes, I was. I was sleeping. We were all inside by that time. We slept in that abandoned building."

"I figured that."

"Shots woke us all up. We hear shots a lot, but this time, they were close. Elijah, the big one, went to look, and when he came back to tell us who had been shot, we all went out. The fat driver was keeping everyone back, threatening us all with his gun. Police got there pretty quick, cuffed the driver, and threw him into the back of the police car. More cops showed up. A few tended to the dealer until the ambulance got there. He was screaming and writhing around on the pavement. Almost felt sorry for the guy." Margaret chuckled. "Not really. The rest of the cops blocked off the area and stood around talking. I could see them looking up at the apartment building across from QuikMart and figured that was where the shots come from. Didn't take long for one of those cops to approach us to ask if we seen anything. Of course, we hadn't. They went in the apartment building, then behind it. I went back to bed. Show was over.

"Was the next day or maybe two days later when we were shown your picture. Like I said, we lied, but I was worried that maybe a camera in the mart got you when you were buying coffee."

"I was pretty careful. I was always careful. And it helps to be invisible."

"Invisible? I see you just fine." Margaret smiled.

"Most people don't see me. If they do, they look away. I guess there are some advantages to being ugly."

Margaret swung around from the sink. "You are not ugly! Don't ever say that. God don't make ugly."

"God sees things differently. He looks at the soul. People look at the face. *This...*," Gwen pointed to her face, "tends to repulse people."

"Bullshit, you just need to smile more. You have RBF, girl. That's cured by smiling."

"RBF?"

"Resting bitch face. You always look mad."

Gwen roared with laughter. "I've never heard that before, but I guess I do have RBF."

The new friends talked well into the night.

Chapter 30

How Did I End up on the Streets?

"Can I ask you a question?"

"How did I end up on the streets?"

Gwen nodded. "If you don't want to answer, that's okay. You just don't seem like someone—"

"Who would be homeless?" Gwen nodded again. "Girl, I can tell you from firsthand experience that homeless people come from all walks of life. Many are drug addicts, and many are mentally ill, sure, but not all. I am neither, but yet—"

"What happened?"

"No one thing, Gwen. It was a series of events. I grew up in a nice middle-class family in a nice middle-class neighborhood in Woodlawn. I did well in high school and went to work at social security right after I graduated. I had a good job. After a few years there, I met a man, Tyrell, at a party. We got married. We had two boys, Terrence and Theodore. They were good boys. Beautiful boys. Life was good. We bought a house in the same area where I had grown up. When the boys were in elementary school, Tyrell started staying out late, and then eventually, he started staying out all night. I would ask him where he had been, and of course, the son of a bitch lied. I knew he had a whore. We fought about it. Every time he came home, we fought, till eventually I was just glad when he didn't come home. Finally, one day, I came home from work to find he had packed up this stuff and was gone. Never saw the bastard again, which was fine with me. But the worst part was that my boys never saw their dad again. That was not fine.

"I couldn't manage the mortgage by myself, so I sold the house, and we moved into an apartment that I could afford, and life was okay for a while. I was able to make ends meet. I could take care of my boys." Margaret stopped talking for a bit and sipped her tea. Gwen waited.

"Then one day, the bottom fell out. My boys were in high school by this time, and I thought they were both in school that day. I was at work, and I looked up to see two police officers walking toward me. I knew in that split second that one of my beautiful boys was gone. They asked if there was some place private where we could talk, and I took them into a conference room. They told me that Terrence had been cutting school with friends, and the kids had gone to the state park. A fight broke out over a girl, shots were fired, and my son was hit in the head. He wasn't involved in the fight, but he was dead. Wrong place, wrong time, and my beautiful son was dead." Gwen reached out and grabbed Margaret's hand.

"I'm so sorry."

"Thank you." Margaret gave Gwen's hand a squeeze and then let go. She wiped the tears from her face and continued. "Somehow, I kept going. We buried Terrence. I went to the trial of the kid who shot him and kept my cool when the little shit was only sentenced to juvenile detention for a few years. I prayed for solace and for peace and for strength, and God was good. He fortified me, and I kept going. I sent Theodore to counseling too. I wanted to make sure he was okay, and I thought he was.

"Two years later, there was a knock on the door in the middle of the night. Again, I knew. As soon as I heard that knock, I knew." Tears were streaming down Margaret's face. "My boy was dead. I knew he had been hanging with the wrong crowd. I knew it, and I should have put a stop to it. He died of an overdose. He still had the needle in his arm."

Gwen had her hand over her mouth, tears streaming down her face as well.

"I'm so sorry, Margaret. I don't know what to say."

"There's nothing to say, sweetie. Words don't mean anything anyway. You helped me feel like a human being again. Thank you for that, and thank you for listening. I've never told anyone all that before."

Gwen wiped her eyes. "You will never be out there again, Margaret. You have a home now."

"That's very kind, but I can't take advantage of you like that."

"It's not taking advantage. You're doing me a favor too. I'll enjoy the company. And we'll get you back on your feet. I'll help you find a job. We'll get you clothes. I know a lot of business owners. Surely one of them could use help."

Margaret chuckled. "Ain't nobody going to want an old lady like me, plus I haven't worked in years. What experience can I say I have?"

"You worked before, and then you took time off. Tomorrow, we'll start some lessons on the computer. I'll teach you the basics. You can type?"

"It's been a while, but yes, I can type. I'm sure it will come back."

The next day, the ladies went shopping and bought Margaret a small wardrobe, and then they started with Margaret's computer training. She learned quickly. Meanwhile, Gwen called each of her customers to see if any of them were hiring. After speaking to about a dozen of them, Gwen finally found one who was hiring. It was a small electrical service company. The receptionist had just turned in her resignation. Gwen told them she had the perfect person to replace her, and sight unseen, Margaret was hired simply based on the trust this client had for Gwen.

Chapter 31

You're a Pain in the Ass, You Know That?

The satisfaction that Gwen felt after shooting her daughter's drug dealer lasted only a few weeks. Chances that he was the dealer who killed Margaret's son were slim, so there was another dealer out there who needed to be dealt with. But Gwen had to accept the fact that she would never know who that was. She brooded on this for a while. Margaret noticed and would ask if she was okay, if she wanted to talk about anything, but Gwen would always respond, "Nope, I'm fine."

The new roommates had settled into a routine. Margaret started her job and would use Gwen's car to go to and from work each day. Gwen would work during the day as well. They made dinner together in the evening and then would talk or watch TV. Gwen, though she enjoyed the company and her time with Margaret, was getting antsy. It weighed on her that she hadn't actually killed Leah's dealer, that there were many more dealers out there, killing the children of other women. Gwen thought of little else. Finally, one evening, as they watched a movie, Gwen made a decision.

The next morning, as soon as Margaret left for work, Gwen called her Uber driver, Julius.

"Miss Gwen! So good to hear from you. It's been a long time."

"I know. I've been busy. Can you pick me up this morning? I just need a short ride today, but I do want to start going back downtown soon. There are many more people who need help."

"You are a wonderful person, Miss Gwen. I'm happy to pick you up. Give me an hour, and I'll be there."

"Thank you, Julius."

Gwen used the next hour to move money from her savings account into checking. She then called her attorney and made an appointment to see him that afternoon. Now that Leah was gone, Gwen needed to revise her will. A lot of the money Gwen had saved during her life had been spent on failed attempts to deal with Leah's addiction, and a lot had been spent digging Leah out of one situation after another, but there was still over five hundred thousand that Gwen had put away, with the intention of taking care of her daughter after Gwen was gone.

Gwen was ready and waiting when Julius arrived. She hopped into the front passenger seat. After the usual pleasantries, Gwen said, "I need to go to the Ford dealership on Joppa Road, please."

"Sure thing, Miss Gwen. Are you buying a new car?"

"Yes, I am. My first car was a Mustang. That was a long time ago." She chuckled. "I want to drive a Mustang again. Do you think that's crazy for someone my age?" She looked at Julius, wondering if she should have blurted that out.

"Miss Gwen, I think that if you want a Mustang, then you should have a Mustang!" He turned and flashed his beautiful smile her way. "Those are beautiful cars. I would like to have one myself someday!"

"I think so too, Julius. When I have it, I'll give *you* a ride."

"I would like that very much."

"I won't want to take my new car downtown though, so I'll still need you for trips into the city."

"You call me, and I will be there. No problem."

"I know I can count on you, Julius, and I hope you know I appreciate it."

"I do, Miss Gwen."

They were silent for the rest of the short trip. As they pulled into the parking lot, Julius offered to wait.

"No need," answered Gwen. "I intend to drive away in my new Mustang this morning."

Julius laughed. "Then I believe you will. But please call me if you need me to come back for you."

"Will do," said Gwen as she paid for her ride on her phone. She tipped Julius in cash though, wanting to make sure he got the full tip.

"You know you can tip me on the app too, Miss Gwen."

"I do know, but I want you to get it now, and if it goes through Uber, you'll have to pay taxes on it."

Julius smiled and shook his head. "Thank you. I hope to see you soon."

"You will, Julius. Thanks." And with that, she closed the door and headed into the dealership.

Three hours later, Gwen drove out of the dealership in her new, fully loaded, black Mustang GT fastback. She left behind her one very happy car salesman. Gwen knew she probably overpaid. She could have bargained more, but she was in a hurry, and she wanted the car. What was another few thousand anyway?

She drove straight from the dealership to her attorney's office, where she spent the next hour revising her will. She also wrote three letters while she was there and asked her attorney to deliver them upon her death. The lawyer at first resisted taking the letters from Gwen, but she manipulated his emotions by reminding him that she had no one else in her life that she could ask this of.

Done with the attorney, Gwen still had a few hours before Margaret would be home. She decided to take a drive into the city. This would allow her to enjoy her new car and scope out a few targets at the same time. And so the next hour was spent getting to know her Mustang and taking note of where she saw the most homeless people and where she saw suspected dealers.

As she turned a corner onto Paca Street, she was shocked to see an SUV that she immediately recognized. It was parked on the other side of the street. Gwen passed by without looking too closely but then went around the block, coming back down Paca on the same side of the street. Though she didn't slow down as she went by, she did take a good look, and sure enough, Fat Eddie was sitting behind the wheel. Gwen was furious. That piece of shit was back at it. He changed locations, but he was back at it.

"Nope. No way," said Gwen out loud. "That son of a bitch!" Gwen briefly considered just going home, grabbing her gun, and coming back and blowing this asshole away. But as she drove out of the city, she realized that she needed to plan this out. She couldn't just kill this piece of shit in broad daylight and expect to get away with it. She needed to think. She would come back this evening and see if the car was there. Better if she could plan her attack at night, just after dark. Gwen drove home, deep in thought.

Knowing she was too pissed off and too preoccupied to make dinner that night, Gwen stopped and picked up pizza on her way home. By the time Margaret walked in the door, the table was set and waiting.

"Girl, did you see that new Mustang outside?" Margaret asked as she blew into the kitchen.

"It's mine."

"Whaddya mean, 'It's mine'?"

"Whaddya mean 'Whaddya mean'? The car is mine." Gwen smiled.

"Hot damn, girl! Let's go for a ride!"

"We will." Gwen laughed. "Let's eat first, and then we'll take a ride."

As they ate, Margaret got quiet for a moment. Then she said, "Please tell me you didn't buy a new car just because of me...just so I could use the other car."

"Nope. My very first car was a Mustang, and I loved driving that car. It wasn't really suitable though once I had Leah, so I traded it in then for a more *family*-type car. I decided it was time to drive what I want again."

"I agree, Gwen. You deserve the car you want! Are you going to sell the Toyota?"

"Nope. On Saturday, we're going to head down to the DMV and change the title over to you. We'll get you a legal driver's license too." She ignored the look of disbelief on Margaret's face and continued. "The DMV is going to expect you to pay tax on the value of the car. I'll cover that for you."

"Gwen. You don't have to do this. I'm working now. It may take me a little bit, but I'll be able to buy my own car."

"I know. It doesn't make sense for me to sell that car. First, selling a car is a pain in the ass. Second, I want you to have it. You need a car to get back and forth to work. And I like that car. I have a lot of memories of Leah tied to that car, so I don't want to get rid of it."

"I think you're full of shit, Gwen. Don't you try to play on my emotions." Gwen started to object, but Margaret held up her hand to stop her. "I appreciate you helping me, but I insist on paying you for the car. I'm already living in your home for free."

Gwen thought for a moment. "Okay, let's handle it this way. We'll look up the Blue Book value of the car. Whatever it is, that's how much you pay for it, okay? And you pay what you can, when you can. No set payment schedule. Okay?"

"Okay. I need to start paying you rent too."

"We'll talk about that later," answered Gwen, having no intention of bringing the topic up again. Changing the subject, Gwen said, "You're going to have to get car insurance. I'll call my agent tomorrow. I need to let him know I have a new car anyway. I'll see if he can come out tomorrow evening and get you set up too."

"Thank you, Gwen. I don't know how I can ever repay you for all you're doing for me."

"You can hurry up and eat so we can take a ride!" Gwen smiled at her friend.

"That I can do!"

After dinner, the ladies took a drive. Gwen took some back roads to Hunt Valley, then hopped on 83, and drove south into the city. She drove past Paca Street and looked down to see if she saw the SUV. Sure enough, it was there. The sun was just beginning to set. Gwen was ready to head home. "Wanna drive home?" she asked Margaret.

"Hell no. I'd be a nervous wreck. You just keep driving, and I'll enjoy the ride."

The next day, Gwen prepared dinner and ate early. She left Margaret's dinner in the oven to stay warm and left a note: "Sorry, had to run out for a bit, shouldn't be late. Dinner is in the oven."

Gwen then, carrying a brown bag full of trash, waited out front for Julius. He pulled up shortly, flashing his usual beautiful smile as Gwen hopped into the front passenger seat. "Hello, Miss Gwen, where are we going today?"

Nodding toward the bag on her lap, she said, "I have a delivery to make. If you can drop me at Baltimore and Light, I should be able to find my new friend."

They chitchatted as Julius drove. He always had stories from home that he loved to share, and he could usually make her laugh. In a way, he reminded her of David. Until now, only David had been able to make her laugh like that.

When they pulled up to the corner at Baltimore and Light, Gwen pointed down the road a bit and lied, "I think I see her just ahead."

"Would you like to drive around the block and then pick you right back up?"

"No, but thanks, Julius. I'll probably take her out to dinner and spend some time. I'll text you when I'm ready, okay?"

"Okay, but please be safe, Miss Gwen. You should text me before it gets dark, please."

Gwen smiled at him. "I will, Julius. And I promise to stay safe." Yes, he did remind her of David.

As Julius drove away, Gwen walked in the direction in which she had pointed. She had a bit of a hike to get to Paca, and she was a bit out of shape. It had been a while since she had done any serious stalking. After a block or two, Gwen dropped her bag into a trash can. She then put her hands in her jacket pockets. In her left pocket, she had cash in case she ran into any homeless on her walk, and in her right, she had her pistol.

As she approached Paca Street, she pulled her hood up over her head. She didn't have a way to change, and honestly, she was past caring. If she got caught, she got caught. She was doing the city of Baltimore a favor, and certainly, a jury of her peers would agree.

Standing at the corner, she could see the SUV sitting a block or so down the street. There was very little foot traffic. No one was standing near the car. She walked toward the car but on the other side of the street, never taking her eyes off Fat Eddie sitting in the driver's seat. When she was directly across from Fat Eddie's door, she crossed the street and knocked on the window.

It took a second or two, but Fat Eddie lowered his window. "Da fuck do you want, pugface?"

"I hear you can hook me up."

"With what, dog food?" Fat Eddie and POS laughed.

Gwen gripped her pistol and had a quick flashback to the two assholes in colleges referring to her as a dog. "Oxy."

"How much cash you got?"

"How much do I need for five?"

"One grand."

As Gwen nodded, Fat Eddie smiled and looked toward POS. When he looked back, Gwen had pulled her pistol and, pointing directly at his face, fired once, hitting him directly in the forehead. As he fell back toward the passenger seat, POS leaned forward to grab the door handle, just enough to give Gwen a clear shot. She fired three more times, hitting him twice in the side and once in the head. POS fell forward against the dashboard. She knew they were both dead. She put her pistol back in her pocket, turned, and headed back down Paca Street. She took her time and didn't look back. She could hear a lot of activity behind her and even thought she heard someone yell, "Stop that guy!" but she kept going. After a few blocks, she took her coat off, keeping her pistol pocket easily accessible. As she neared Baltimore Street, she summoned Julius and, within thirty minutes, was safely in his car and on her way home.

Margaret was reading the newspaper when Gwen got home.

"You don't have to make my dinner if you're going out, Gwen," she scolded.

Gwen chuckled. "Settle down. I made myself dinner too and ate before I left."

Margaret wanted to ask where her friend had gone and why she hadn't taken her car but didn't want to overstep any boundaries, so she just said, "Well, thank you. I just don't want you to think I'm helpless."

"Didn't think that for a minute."

The next morning, the expected knock came. Gwen had been waiting. She opened the door. "Good morning, detectives."

"Good morning, Miss Marsh. Can we come in?"

Gwen stood aside and waved them in. She was in a good mood that morning. "Can I get either of you a cup of coffee?"

Detective Mandato answered for both of them, "No, thank you. We'd like to ask where you were last night."

"What time?"

"Around eight."

"I was either downtown, in the area of Baltimore and Light, or on my way home by that time. Not exactly sure of the timing."

"And why were you downtown?"

"I was delivering a package to a homeless woman. I did that and spent some time with her."

"How did you get there?"

"Uber."

"Do you have the contact information of the driver?"

"Sure do. I use him all the time." She pulled out her phone, pulled up Julius's contact info, and passed the phone to the detective.

As Detective Davis jotted down Julius's name and number, Gwen asked, "Is that it?"

"Were you near Paca Street last night?"

"No."

"I think you were."

Gwen shrugged. "You're wrong. Let me guess. There was another fat lady in the area?"

"Do you own a .45 pistol?"

"Yes, I do."

"May I see it?"

"No, you may not. I've been very patient with this nonsense, but that's about to run out. Instead of coming here to tell me you found my daughter's drug dealer, you harass me every few weeks about some random event. You want my pistol, get a warrant."

"We'll do that." The detectives stood. "Oh, when we do get that warrant and we're close, we'll also be getting a sample of your DNA."

"That's fine. Do what you have to do." Gwen paused. "Can I ask what happened near Paca Street?"

"Double murder."

Gwen's eyebrows went up. "And you think I did that? Why?"

"One of the victims was the same victim from last month's shooting on North Avenue."

That day after dinner, Margaret was reading the newspaper. Gwen knew exactly what was in the paper as she had read it earlier. As she read a book, she could feel Margaret's eyes on her occasionally. Finally, Margaret spoke. "This is interesting. That dealer you shot a while back. Well, apparently, he was back on the streets and got himself shot again last night. This time, he's dead."

Gwen looked up. "Yeah, I read that. Good."

"Where did you go last night, Gwen?"

"I don't want to talk about it, Margaret."

Margaret nodded and went back to reading, or at least pretending to. She knew in her heart that Gwen did this, and she also now knew that the ride downtown in Gwen's new Mustang was more of a reconnaissance mission than a joyride. Gwen was going to end up in jail. This shooting happened way too fast. No way Gwen took the same precautions she did the first time. And now she killed two people. Margaret wondered who the second person was.

"Someone else was killed with the dealer, Gwen. Who was it?"

"I said I didn't want to talk about it." Gwen glared at her friend.

"I know you been good to me, Gwen, but don't think for one minute that you can intimidate me. Answer the question."

Gwen stood and looked down at Margaret. "I don't know."

Margaret stood as well, face-to-face with her friend. "Bullshit. Now sit your ass down and tell me what happened." The two ladies stood staring at each other for a moment, neither wanting to be the first to look away. Finally, Gwen took a deep breath and sat down.

"It was his driver. Same driver as last time."

Margaret nodded, glad it wasn't an innocent bystander. "Listen, I don't give a rat's ass about those two, but I care about you. You have to stop this. You're gonna end up in jail, and I don't want to have to visit your ass in jail."

"I'm not done, Margaret. I want to kill every drug dealer I can."

"I know you do. So do I. But we can't do that."

"Why? Why can't we do that?"

"Because there is always someone else to take their place, Gwen. As long as there are addicts, there will be drug dealers." Gwen didn't respond. "Don't you think I would love to kill whoever gave my baby heroin? I would like to kill that son of a bitch with my bare hands. But what good would it do? Will it bring my baby back? No. Will it save someone else's baby? Probably not. Don't get me wrong. I'm glad you killed that piece of shit, but I also know that someone else will take his place, make that money, and kill those addicts. So you're gonna end up in jail or get killed yourself, and for what, Gwen? For revenge? Is it worth it?"

Gwen stood up, shaking. "You're goddamned right it's worth it! It's definitely worth it. They prey on the weak, and nobody gives a damn!"

"You think you're the only one who cares? Bullshit, Gwen! I care! Lots of people care! They just handle it in a different way." Margaret realized she was yelling and took a deep breath. "Look, Gwen, I know your heart is in the right place, but I worry about you. I don't want to have to see you in jail, and I surely don't want to have to bury you. You are one of the best people I have ever met in my life. I mean that. And as long as there are addicts, you will have dealers to kill."

"And as long as there are dealers, there will be addicts."

Margaret thought for a second. "Maybe if you focus on healing the addicts, the dealers will go out of business. You reached out and helped this homeless woman." Margaret pointed to herself. "I bet you could help a lot of people if you put your mind to it. Use your time to do that, Gwen."

Gwen sat back down.

"Promise me, Gwen, that you're done, that you won't go lookin' for other dealers. You've got Leah's dealer. Be done with it."

"I can't promise that, Margaret. I sit here, and I think about those pieces of shit out there, and I get so angry."

"You keep at it, you're gonna get caught."

"I know."

Margaret thought for a minute. "Part of the problem is that you sit here in this apartment all day, day after day, and you brood. You need to get out. You need to keep your mind occupied."

"I work," Gwen defended herself.

"Yeah, you work a few hours a day. I've seen you. That leaves a lot of time on your hands."

"Where do you want me to go?"

"I want you to get a job outside of this house."

"I don't need another job."

"I disagree. You need to do something. I happen to know that the bank we use is looking for another teller."

"How would you know that?"

"Because when I go in there, I actually talk to the people there. I converse. I ask questions. I get to know them."

"I don't want to know them. That's why I use the ATM or drive-through."

Margaret shook her head. "Gwen, there are good people out there. Nice people. You just have to take the time to get to know them. Let them get to know you."

"That's never really worked out well for me, Meg."

Margaret knew she was getting to her friend when she called her Meg. She ignored it and continued on, "So it must be everybody else in the world then, right? Couldn't possibly be you?"

"Fuck you."

"Have you ever thought that *you* could be the problem? I know you, and I know you are a wonderful person. You saved my life! Why don't you show that side of yourself to anyone else?"

"It's never really worked out well for me," Gwen repeated.

"Well, here's what you're going to do. Right now, you're going to update your résumé. Tomorrow morning, you're going to haul your ass down to that bank and apply for the teller job. Whether or not you make friends is up to you, but you're going to apply for that job."

"And why would I do that?"

"You'll do that for me, Gwen. Because I love you, and I need my friend. Please do this for me."

Gwen sighed and put her head in her hands for a moment. Margaret moved over and sat next to Gwen and put her arm around her. She gave Gwen a gentle squeeze and said, "Please."

With her head still in her hands, Gwen responded, "You're a pain in the ass, you know that?"

"Yes I do."

They both chuckled. "Okay, you win. I'll do it. They probably won't hire me anyway. I've never worked in a bank."

"If that happens, we'll find another job opening for you."

"Great," replied Gwen less than enthusiastically.

Within an hour, Gwen had updated and printed her résumé. The next morning, a few minutes after 9:00 a.m., Gwen knocked on the bank manager's door, résumé in hand. She talked to the manager for a bit; took a math test, which she aced; and gave the manager a list of references. That afternoon, the manager called Gwen and offered her the job. She was to start training the next week. Training went well and fast, though Gwen didn't exactly make any friends along the way. She learned fast though and was quickly on her own, at her own station.

Chapter 32

Gwen Slept Soundly That Night

Two weeks into her new job, Gwen was getting antsy. The job was boring, and she didn't like the people she worked with. She knew that Margaret was right and that she needed to keep busy, but she really wanted to find something else. So that Saturday, she spent the afternoon looking online for open jobs. While she was looking, she came across one job for an office manager, and that contact's last name was Goldfeder. Goldfeder. David. Thoughts of David would pop up briefly in her thoughts often, but she would always suppress those. She wouldn't allow herself to think about him, but seeing that name brought back that ache in her heart. She had a wonderful man, someone who loved her, and she threw that away. Just threw it away. Margaret was right; it was *her* fault. Her pride cost her the only man who ever loved her.

Gwen opened Facebook. Leah had set up an account for her about five years ago, but Gwen never used it. She logged in and went right to the search box and typed in "David Goldfeder." Surprisingly, there were quite a few David Goldfeders out there, and her David was among them. She recognized his picture immediately—older, of course, even less hair, larger jowls, thicker glasses, but it was her David.

She clicked on his account. Apparently, he wasn't really an active Facebook user either, but he was certainly tagged in a lot of pictures. Gwen began to go through them. David's wife was a short, fat, unattractive woman named Raquel, and they looked incredibly happy. In every picture, they were holding hands, or David had his arm around Raquel. From what Gwen could see, they had three teenage sons. There were family pictures taken around the table, on vacations, and in what was probably their backyard. They had a beautiful home. She even found some pictures of David's parents and brother, the people she was supposed to meet the week or so after she walked away from this man who loved her. They looked like happy people. Gwen's heart hurt. That should have been *her* life.

Gwen slammed down the top of her laptop, laid her head down on her desk, and cried. She cried for a long time, only pulling herself together when she heard Margaret return home from running errands. Gwen pulled herself together, washed her face, and went into the kitchen where Margaret was putting away groceries.

"Any more bags in the car?"

"No, but there are some just outside the door, if you don't mind getting those."

Gwen went and brought in the rest of the groceries and helped put things away. "I've decided to look for a different job. Being a teller is just boring."

"Okay, but please don't quit until you are ready to start another job." She looked at Gwen. "Please."

Gwen nodded. "I saw a few things today on Monster. I'll email my résumés and see what happens."

Margaret smiled at Gwen. "Well, I know one thing—any company would be lucky to have you."

Gwen fought back tears. "Thank you, Margaret."

"For what? That's the truth."

"For making me get a job and get out of the house. For having faith in me. For caring about me."

Margaret threw her arms around this woman who pulled her off the streets, "Of course I care about you!" She could feel Gwen shaking and pulled back to see Gwen crying. "Are you okay? What happened?"

"I'm just having a bad day. I'm just feeling emotional." Gwen smiled, "Don't worry. This too shall pass." Margaret didn't look convinced, so Gwen continued, "I promise, I'm okay."

"Okay then. If you want to talk, I'm here. You know that, right?"

"I do. Thank you." And to change the subject, she asked, "So what's for dinner tonight?"

"Shrimp creole! I've been craving that for weeks. I hope you like spicy!"

"You know I do." Gwen smiled.

The rest of the afternoon was uneventful. Gwen pretended to read while Margaret made dinner, but she was deep in thought. She was angry. Her life had been wasted. The only good thing she had done, Leah, was gone. Out of seven billion people in the world, she had two friends. Two. And one of those she hardly ever saw. Was that her fault? She had to admit to herself that it was probably was.

Her thoughts turned toward Leah, her daughter. How she missed her. What could she have done differently? She should have been a better mother. She recalled one of her last conversations with Leah. She had woken Leah up that day. It was well past noon, and her daughter was still sleeping. Gwen was concerned. She knew that Leah was drinking way too much and that her drug use had increased. She was concerned because Leah should have been at work that morning and was probably going to lose her job. She was concerned about the people whom Leah was hanging out with. So Gwen had gone in to wake her daughter and talk some sense into her. That conversation hadn't gone as expected.

She had opened the blinds to let light into her daughter's room. That didn't work, so she shook Leah until she woke.

"What the fuck, Mom?"

"Aren't you supposed to be at work?"

"I'm sick, okay? Call them and tell them I can't work today."

"No, I'm not covering for you this time. You're not sick. You're hungover. Get up and get yourself together. I'll make you some coffee."

"I'm not getting up. Now get the fuck out of my room."

"Your room?" yelled Gwen, turning on her daughter. "This is *my* house, and everything in it is *mine*."

"Fine, then I'll move out of *your* house!" Leah threw back the covers and jumped up.

Gwen sighed. This was not going well. "I don't want you to move, Leah. I want you to get your life together. I want you to take your job seriously. I want you to find good friends, friends who don't spend their nights in bars, who don't use drugs. I want to help you, Leah."

"Help me? That's a laugh. You have lied to me my whole life!"

Gwen looked at her daughter. "When have I ever lied to you, Leah?"

"Every day. My entire life, you told me 'You're beautiful, Leah,' 'You're so smart, Leah,' 'You can do whatever you want, Leah,' 'The world is at your feet, Leah,' 'The world loves beautiful people, Leah.' Well, guess what, Mom? The world doesn't give a shit whether I'm beautiful or not. You know what it's gotten me? Nothing. Not a damned thing." By this point, Leah was screaming with tears running down her face. Now she just wanted to hurt her mother. She needed to turn the conversation away from her failures. "And who's my father? Huh? Have you ever told me the truth about that? Just some guy you had a one-night stand with? Seriously, Mom? Who would want a one-night stand with you?"

Gwen stood frozen in her daughter's room. She was accustomed to Leah being disrespectful and hateful, but never like this. She didn't know how to respond.

"I'm this way because of you, Mom. Now get out of my room and let me go back to sleep." Leah plopped back down in her bed, confident that she had won that battle, that her mother was emotionally defeated and wouldn't bother her again today. She could apologize later.

Gwen remembered that she had just turned and left the room. She knew at that very moment that she had lost her daughter. It wasn't long after that that Leah died. In the time between, they had never spoken about that fight. Maybe if Leah had had more time, they would have talked about it. Maybe with more time, she would have been able to get through to her daughter and get her help. But there wasn't more time.

And this was where Gwen's mind turned back to the dealer. He was dead now, and Gwen was glad. But did she know for sure that POS was the guy? Did she know for sure that the dealer who really killed her daughter wasn't still out there? She wondered if the dealer who killed her daughter also killed Margaret's son.

By the time dinner was on the table, Gwen had worked herself up into a fury. She was very quiet during dinner, but Margaret didn't pry. She knew her friend was having a bad day, so she just tried to keep the conversation light. After dinner, they cleaned up together and then assumed their usual positions in the living room, in front of the TV. They watched the news for a bit and then switched to ID. Shortly after 10:00 p.m., Margaret announced that she was done for the day and headed to bed. "Yeah, me too," said Gwen and headed to her room as well. But once there, she dug into her closet and pulled out the small safe with her handgun, then sat on her bed and waited until she heard Margaret finish in the bathroom and climb into bed. Gwen grabbed her keys and left the house. She took some mud and used it to cover her license plate, then got in her car and drove away.

She drove straight downtown and to the areas where she had seen drug dealers in the past. As she was sitting at a light on North Avenue, she saw a clean-cut young man walking down the street. He looked out of place, and she wondered why he was there. She saw him approach one group of what appeared to be homeless people, but at this point, the light changed, and she needed to drive away. She went around the block and found this same young man talking to just one person, and she thought she saw them discreetly exchange something, and then the young man walked on. *Definitely a dealer*, she thought.

She continued to drive around the block as she followed this young man on his walk. He would approach nearly everyone he saw, and sometimes, she would catch him handing something to the other person. Gwen's anger rose. The final straw was when she saw him approach a young woman. When Gwen came around the block again, she saw him leaning into the woman and handing her something. Gwen pulled out her handgun and made one more trip around the block. This son of bitch was preying on the young and the homeless. No way he could walk down this street dressed like this and not get robbed if these people didn't know and fear him. As she came up the block, she could see her target now walking alone. She hit the button to roll down the car window. As she reached her target, she took aim and fired one shot at the young man. He immediately went down, and she sped off.

Gwen slept soundly that night.

There was nothing in the morning paper about the shooting, but in the afternoon, Gwen did find an article online. Her heart stopped when she read the headline, "Local homeless advocate shot down on North Avenue. A young homeless advocate was killed in a drive-by shooting last night. At around 11:00 p.m., twenty-four-year-old Matthew Streilein was shot and killed as he walked down North Avenue. Locals interviewed said that he was a frequent visitor to that area. One homeless man who declined to give his name said, 'Matt was good people. He ministered to us. Never saw him pass by a homeless person without giving them money or food. He would recommend shelters. Whatever he could do to help.' Tea Smith, was also interviewed: 'Matt prayed with me just minutes before he was shot.'"

Gwen stopped reading. She could barely breathe. "What did I do? Oh my God, what did I do?" She closed her computer and laid down on her bed. For the first time in years, she prayed. She begged for forgiveness. She cried. "What do I do now? God help me."

Margaret knocked on Gwen's bedroom door. "Are you okay in there?"

"I'm fine. I'm sick. Don't come in here. I don't want you to get it." Gwen covered her face with her pillow and cried. She stayed in her room the rest of the day.

She was sure there would be a knock at the door, but it never came. The next day, she went in to work, and that was when she met Larry.

Chapter 33

"They Had Me, and I Was Failing Them"

Gwen and Larry were sitting on the floor behind the counter. They could see the lights from the police cars hitting the back wall of the bank.

"I hope you're thinking because we're about out of time. I should have never listened to you. I should have turned and walked right out of this damned bank."

Gwen snorted. "Well, you didn't, and here we are, so shut up and let me think."

The phone rang. Larry and Gwen looked at each other. Gwen silently pointed to herself and then crawled down to where she could reach up and grab the phone on the counter. "Yeah."

There was a split second of silence on the other end. She knew the "negotiator" was surprised to hear her voice and not Larry's. "We just want to make sure everyone is okay in there."

"Everyone is fine, okay?"

"What can we do to end this so no one gets hurt?"

"You can leave me alone for ten fucking minutes so I can think."

"Okay, we can do that." replied the negotiator. His job was to stay calm and to keep the suspect calm.

"Then do it," she yelled. "And if you call before the ten minutes is up, I start firing." With that, she hung up.

Larry was looking at her in disbelief. "What the hell are you doing?"

"I have no idea," she replied calmly. She looked at Larry. He put his head in his hands and cried without making a sound. "What were you thinking today? Look at you. You're not a thug. This is *clearly* the first time you've robbed a bank. You looked terrified when you walked in here. I knew immediately what you were up to. You seem intelligent, but this…this is just stupid." She shook her head. "Talk to me while I think. I think better with background noise."

Looking up and shaking his head, Larry said, "I don't know what to make of you. I'm trusting you with my life right now, and I have no idea why."

"Because you don't have a choice." Gwen looked at him and, for the first time today, smiled. Nudging him in the side, she said, "How the hell did an all-American guy like yourself end up trying to rob a bank?"

And so Larry told his story.

"Three years ago, I had a wife, lived in a nice place in Lutherville, had my kids in Catholic school, and had a great job as a controller for an HVAC company. Things were good. We weren't rich, but we were comfortable. My wife, Anna, and I were happy. The kids were happy and getting a good education. They were involved in rec sports—soccer and baseball mostly. My older son, Dylan, also took karate, and the little one, Danny, took art lessons. Danny is an amazing artist for a nine-year-old. He really is. We had a busy life, but we loved it.

"Then Anna was diagnosed with pancreatic cancer. I was missing a lot of time at work taking Anna from one doctor's appointment to another, from one test to another. It took a few weeks to determine that the cancer had progressed past the point where they could help her. It was in her liver. She went downhill fast." Larry wiped his face with his hands and took a deep breath. Gwen remained silent.

"At first I had home care come in during the day to take care of her while I was at work, but I wasn't happy with the level of care she was getting. I could tell they hadn't bathed her. I didn't know how much attention they paid to her, but I was sure it wasn't enough. I refused to put Anna in hospice. I wanted her home. She wanted to be home. So I started going into work a bit later each day and leaving earlier. I would take care of Anna, take the boys to school, pick them up, drive them to where they needed to be, or arrange carpooling with other parents.

"As Anna required more and more care, it was hard to keep up, so I asked for a leave of absence. Instead of granting that leave, they fired me."

"They *fired* you? Can they do that? You need to sue somebody!" Gwen couldn't believe that a company could do that.

"Well, they did, and I can't afford a lawyer. They said that I was missing too much time, and they weren't firing me because I had asked for leave. They were going to do it anyway. They needed a full-time controller, not a temp and not someone who could only give them four or five hours a day. They did give me a small severance package, but between Anna's medical bills and basic living expenses, we went through that in no time. I couldn't worry about that though, for the next month or so, my focus was completely on my wife. It was only a little over six months from the day she first went to the doctor until the day she died.

"After the funeral, I pulled myself together and started looking for work. Problem was, I was overqualified for pretty much everything. Nobody wants to hire a middle-aged man. Why pay someone with twenty years of experience what they're worth when you can hire a kid out of college for half the price, right? Early on, one small family-owned company offered me about half of my previous salary to come work there. I turned it down, sure that I could find something better. I should have taken that damned job. It would have been better than nothing." Larry sighed and shook his head.

"I had to pull Danny out of art lessons and Dylan out of karate. I just couldn't afford it. I went through my severance and my savings within that first year. I had to sell the house because I couldn't afford that either. We had very little equity in that house, so I walked away with only a few grand. I was living off unemployment, and the only apartment we could afford was in Brooklyn. I don't know if you're familiar with Brooklyn, Maryland, but it's no Lutherville, I can assure you.

"When we moved, I naturally also had to pull the boys out of private school and enroll them in public schools. This time was difficult for me, but it was really hard on the boys. They went from a nice house in Towson where they each had their own room and a nice yard to play in to an apartment in a bad part of town where they shared a bedroom and had no yard whatsoever. They went from a nice Catholic school to run-down, overcrowded public schools. They had to leave all their friends behind. Everything they loved was gone—their mother, their house, their friends, their school."

"They had you," Gwen pointed out.

Larry snorted derisively, "Yeah, they had me, and I was failing them. Danny tried to make the best of things. He went to school, came home, did his homework, and then drew. He made a few friends, but I also think he's getting bullied at school. He's a nice boy, not a fighter, and the area we live in is tough on nice boys.

"Dylan is in middle school, and it's a tough school. He started getting in fights almost immediately. Thank God he knows karate. He could handle himself well, and it didn't take long for kids to steer clear of him and pick on somebody else. Problem was, Dylan started hanging out with those bad kids. He started getting in trouble at school. I swear, last year, I spent as much time in that school as he did. Seems I got called down there nearly once a week for an audience with the principal." Larry shook his head and thought for a moment. Gwen waited, wanting to hear the rest.

"At the end of that first school year in Brooklyn, I found weed in Dylan's pocket. I confronted him, punished him, and threatened him. I thought that was it. Then about six months ago, I found pills. I confronted him again, but he gave me the usual bullshit answers that kids come up with."

Yeah, Gwen knew those all too well. "It's not mine." "I'm only holding them for a friend." "It's the first time I ever tried it, and I won't ever do it again." "I'm not high. I'm just tired." She knew those lies.

Larry continued, "That was when I knew that I had to do something. I had to get my kids out of that area. I still couldn't find a job. Well, I could find a job, but the ones I found were less than the unemployment I was getting. My brother-in-law lives in North Dakota. He's in construction and said that if I could get out there, he could get me a job. A good-paying job. Not my field but I'm handy, and at this point, a job in construction sounded great. I figured I needed about five thousand dollars to get out there and put down a deposit on an apartment. That's why I'm here."

He looked at Gwen for the first time since he'd started speaking. She was just watching him. They both sat silently for a minute. She grabbed the bag of phones and started going through them.

"What are you doing?" he asked.

"They're going to call back in about one minute. When they do, you pick up. Tell them I said I'm diabetic and need food. Tell them I want two pizzas and two two-liter Cokes. *No* diet, I want the real thing. Tell them, everyone is fine, and I'm going to let you all go."

"*You're* going to let us go?"

"Yes, they need to think I'm the one orchestrating this. You're an innocent party."

"How the hell are you going to pull that off? And why?"

"It's going to be okay. Trust me." She looked him in the eye. "Please. You don't have a choice. But more importantly, I can do this. I promise you that you will get home to your boys."

The phone rang.

"Pick it up," she said. And while Larry gave the negotiator instructions, Gwen tried each phone. She was able to unlock the third one she tried. *What idiot uses 1234 as their password*, she thought. She then typed out a text to Margaret. "M, it's Gwen. I'm using a coworker's phone. Please go into my desk and get out my address book. Mail it to—"

When Larry hung up the phone, he said, "They promised pizza in $1/2$ hour."

"Good, what's your address and last name?"

"Why?"

"Just tell me, please." Larry gave her the information she requested, trusting her but not understanding why. Gwen continued her text. "Larry Gorman, 8623 Eighth Avenue, Brooklyn, Maryland.

Please do that ASAP. Let me know you got this and then delete this text."

Larry sat there, wondering what Gwen was doing and not knowing what he should do. He looked around, and that was when he finally thought about the cameras. "*Shit!*"

"What?" Gwen looked up.

"Cameras. Never thought about the fucking cameras!"

Gwen thought for a second. She had a new plan, and the cameras would help. "Don't worry about those."

Larry looked at her, incredulous. "Don't worry about them? You *are* out of your mind, aren't you?"

"It's too late to worry about them, right? So why bother at this point?" She softened her tone. "Please trust me on this." Again, what choice did he have?

They planned out how to handle the pizza delivery and were ready when the police called back to announce that lunch was ready.

Chapter 34

That Woman Is Evil

The hostages in the closet could hear Gwen yell from time to time but couldn't always make out the words. They had debated among themselves whether or not they should try to get out but decided against it. They had heard the phone ring a few times and had guessed correctly that it was the police.

The guard, feeling bad for letting down his employer, tried to make up for it by keeping everyone calm. "We're going to be okay. It may take some time, but the police are pros. They'll get us out of here in one piece."

"I think she's in on it. Gwen," said Karen, looking at the group around her. "I was watching her with this guy. They were talking for quite a bit before he pulled that gun."

"I never did like her," answered Lindsay. The other two tellers nodded in agreement. "And when she was taking our phones, she looked at me with pure hatred. It wasn't fear I saw in her eyes. It was hatred."

Sue, the other teller, agreed, "Lindsay is right. Gwen hates us. I see it every time I look at her. I feel the hate coming off her. Other than when she first started here, she has not said one nice word to me. Not one."

"Okay, let's not jump to conclusions," said the guard. "We don't know that she's involved. He did have a gun to her head. Don't forget that." He didn't have a problem with Gwen; he didn't even know her.

They had never spoken, but he was as much to blame as she was. He never paid attention to what he thought of as homely tellers. He always spoke to Lindsay. Every chance he got. The others, he would respond if spoken to. And of course, he was always nice to Karen. She had the power to ask that he be replaced, and he always kept that in mind.

"Defend her if you want," shot back Lindsay, "but I know what I saw. That woman is evil, and mark my words, she is *in* on this."

When no one disagreed, Lindsay felt emboldened. "Think about it. She just started here. She said she had never been a teller before, but when I trained her, she seemed to already know what she was doing. *Nobody* picks the job up that quickly. And she's not young. Who starts a new career at her age?" Lindsay looked to Karen. "What did she do before coming here?"

"She has her own bookkeeping business. She said she needed the extra income. I did call her clients that she listed as references. They all liked her." Karen sounded a bit defensive.

"Yeah," countered Lindsay, "and do you know for sure that these people really were her clients? I bet they weren't."

"No, I guess I don't," answered Karen, wondering if she had made a terrible mistake.

"I need to sit." This came from the elderly lady whom Gwen had been helping when this whole situation started. "I'm not feeling well."

Everyone quickly made room for her to sit, and the guard piled up boxes of forms that could be used as a seat. Sue grabbed a brochure from the shelf. "Here, Mrs. Kelso, let me fan you. There's not much air in here. We shouldn't be stuck in here much longer." Sue began to fan the older lady and tried to soothe her, continuing to speak quietly to her, assuring her that everything would be okay.

Lindsay continued, "So she connives her way into a job and then makes no effort at all to fit in. She had no intentions of staying here for long. You can all see that, right?" Lindsay looked right at Karen.

"You might be right. I don't know," said Karen, looking down. "I just don't know. I just thought she was odd. Other than her abrupt personality, she's a good teller."

"Of course she is!" snapped Lindsay. "She knows exactly what she's doing." She said this firmly, as though this proved her point.

Suddenly, they heard movement at the door, and a second later, the door opened. There stood Gwen, pointing the gun into the storage room.

"It's lunchtime," said Gwen. Pointing the gun directly at Lindsay, she said, "Come with me, blondie."

Lindsay froze, and the guard spoke up, "No, take me instead."

"Settle down there, Kojak. I'm not going to hurt her." Turning to Lindsay again, she said, "Come with me now." As she waited for Lindsay to make her way forward, she noticed Sue fanning Mrs. Kelso. Mrs. Kelso was not looking well. "Bring Mrs. Kelso with you and get a move on."

Lindsay helped Mrs. Kelso to her feet. Both women were shaking. As soon as they were out of the storage room, Lindsay noticed Larry standing there, waiting. Gwen nodded to him, and he shut the door, then pushed the copier back in front of it. Gwen nudged Lindsay toward the front of the bank.

"Lunch is here. You're going to unlock the front door. Larry will hold it open for you, and you will stand right at the opening. Someone will hand you pizza and sodas. I will be right behind you and would have no problem shooting you in that empty head of yours. Understand?"

Lindsay nodded. She was terrified. The cockiness she had felt just a few minutes earlier was completely gone.

Gwen spoke softly to Mrs. Kelso. "You are free to leave, ma'am. When the door is opened, just walk out. Put your hands up so there is no mistake." Mrs. Kelso nodded her understanding. "Ask them to have a doctor look you over, okay? You don't look well." Mrs. Kelso nodded again. Gwen looked her in the eye and whispered, "I'm sorry you had to go through this."

Gwen turned away before Mrs. Kelso could respond and looked at Larry. "It's showtime."

Larry handed Lindsay the keys. "Unlock the door now and don't move past the doorframe. She's crazy, and she *will* shoot you." He looked Lindsay in the eye to make sure she understood. She did.

Lindsay unlocked the door and handed the keys back to Larry. Larry pulled the door open and stood there, keeping it open. Gwen stood a few feet behind Lindsay, using her as a shield from any sharpshooters outside and keeping Larry's gun aimed at Lindsay.

Larry motioned for Mrs. Kelso to walk through the door. "Put your hands up, ma'am."

As Mrs. Kelso began to move, Larry yelled out, "Gwen's letting this lady come out. She needs medical help." He admired the old woman as she walked past him. She was scared, you could see that, and she was weak, but she walked out on her own accord, back straight, arms up, eyes ahead. *One tough old lady*, he thought. He looked at Gwen, but her eyes remained on Lindsay.

Mrs. Kelso walked right to the first police car where she was immediately, and a bit roughly, pulled to safety. Larry hoped she was okay. Once Mrs. Kelso was safe, a plain-clothed officer approached the door carrying two pizza boxes and two sodas. Gwen yelled out, "Hand the boxes to Blondie first." The officer followed instructions, and Lindsay turned and put the pizza down on the ground behind the front wall. "Now give her the soda and then move away quickly. Any wrong moves, I shoot." Again, her instructions were followed.

Larry quickly shut and locked the door. He and Lindsay picked up the pizzas and sodas and carried them behind the counter. Gwen made sure to keep them both between her and the police out front.

She held the gun on Lindsay and instructed Larry to get cups from the break room.

Lindsay started to speak. "Listen, Gw—"

Gwen cut her right off. "No. Don't say a word." Gwen's mind was racing, and she didn't want to have to listen to this woman's squeaky voice.

Lindsay nodded silently and then looked around, everywhere but straight back at Gwen.

When Larry returned, Gwen said, "Take a slice for yourself. We'll send the rest back with Blondie here." Larry grabbed a slice and poured himself a drink. Gwen took nothing.

The trio then walked back to the storage closet. "Lunch is served," sang Gwen as they opened the door. Lindsay walked in with the pizzas, and Larry placed the sodas and cups on the floor. The door was then closed, and the hostages stood silently as they listened to the copier being pushed back in front of the door.

As Larry ate, Gwen checked the phone, waiting for Margaret to respond. Larry shook his head. "You are one strange woman. I cannot figure you out. I come in here to rob the place, one look at you, and I'm scared shitless. Then somehow, you take over the entire operation, and I'm sittin' here, still scared shitless, while you sit there calmly checking for text messages. I don't know if you're helping me or trying to get us both killed."

Gwen smiled. "Looking at me made you scared?"

Larry shook his head. "Don't misunderstand me. It was the *way* you looked at me. That scared me."

She chuckled at that. "Good, I knew I was ugly but didn't think my face was scary. The look, however, that's a learned response."

"You're not ugly. You should never say that, Gwen."

She finally looked up at him, just lifting her eyes but keeping her head down. "I have a mirror, Larry. I know what I look like, and it's okay. I have adapted, but let's not lie about it."

Larry shook his head a bit. "You're wrong. You just need to smile a bit. That's all."

Gwen looked up, and though she didn't want to, she smiled. "I know. I have RBF, right?"

Larry laughed out loud. "Ha! Yes, you do!"

They smiled at each other for a second, and then Gwen continued. "We need to be honest about our situation right now, okay?" Larry nodded. "Chances are, you're not getting out of here with any cash. Even if they think you're an innocent party here, you're gonna get searched. I thought about moving some funds into your account, but I don't think I can do that without them being able to trace it.

I don't want to leave them any reason to believe you had a hand in this."

"But I did *have a hand in this*. I started this whole fiasco."

Gwen waved her hand at him. "Yeah, yeah, yeah, but no one has to know that."

"How are they *not* going to know that?"

"Listen to me. When you came in, you hesitated a bit. You're going to be asked about that. You tell them the truth. Something about me scared you. You wanted to wait for another teller but decided you didn't want to be rude. Right?"

"Okay," Larry answered doubtfully.

"So you approached my station and said you wanted to make a withdrawal." Gwen stopped and thought for a second. "Do you have an account with this bank?"

"Yes, but I never come into this branch."

Gwen sighed. "You tried to rob your own bank, Larry?" She shook her head and bit her tongue. The words *shit for brains* were sitting right there, begging to be let loose, but she held them in.

She didn't give Larry a chance to respond. She continued, "Okay, do you have any money in your account?"

"A little, yes."

"Okay, so you were coming in to make a withdrawal. They are going to ask you why you didn't fill out a withdrawal form at the front of the bank, and your answer is…"

"Uhhhhhhhhh, I normally go to the ATM, so I didn't know I needed one?"

"Good! Okay, so you come up and ask to withdraw funds. Now here is where the cameras come into play. Ever notice how at each teller station the wall between the lobby and the tellers gets higher so that you can't see what is going on at the next station?"

Larry nodded.

"Well, that wall also keeps the cameras from seeing exactly what's happening on that counter in front of the teller, for obvious reasons. No one wants their bank transactions on camera. So that's in your favor. When you reached the counter, you gave me your account number and said you wanted to make a withdrawal. You then made the mistake of putting your arms on the counter. I grabbed your hands and told you that you were going to rob the bank, and now that I knew your account, if you didn't, I was going to shoot you here and then go to your house and kill your family."

Larry looked at her in disbelief. "What the fuck are you talking about? Nobody is going to believe that."

"Trust me, they will. Those people we have locked up in the storage closet will back you up. They hate me, and before you ask, they hate me because I hate them. It's irrelevant. Just know they will be more than willing to believe the worst of me." Gwen took a breath. "So I threatened you and then put a gun in your hand. You don't know where it came from, but you think I had it under the counter."

"Why would you have a gun?"

Gwen raised her voice a bit. "Shut up and let me finish! I'll explain all that." She thought for a minute. "Is this gun registered?"

"No, bought it on the street."

Gwen breathed a sigh of relief. That would have been a problem. She continued, "Okay, so I told you to round up the people in here and put them in the closet. The camera will back you up on that because I did tell you to do that. Everything that happened after that point will show me as being involved and, no offense, being in charge."

Larry sat silent, shaking his head. "Why would you do this?"

"You have children to go home to, that need you. I have nothing."

"I can't let you do this for me. You have a life. You have family."

"I have nothing, Larry. Trust me on this. I'll explain, but you have to promise me not to react. No pity. No tears. No judgment. No drama."

Larry nodded. "I promise."

"I have one person in my life. A friend. No family. I had a daughter, but she died two years ago." Larry took a breath, and Gwen shot him a look, warning him to stay silent. "My parents died nearly twenty years ago, no siblings, no cousins, no nuthin'. Never married. I've had only two friends in my entire life. I'm almost forty-five years old, and I have had only two friends. Three if you count a teacher I had in high school. I just could never trust anyone. I learned early in life that people hurt you, that people hated me because I look like I do. So I stayed away from them for the most part. The two friends I have are people that I helped. We became friends because I could help them, and I could see they were truly good people. My first friend moved away in middle school. We keep in touch, but she has her own life and family. So no, I have no one, really."

"Look," Larry spoke up and ignored Gwen's glare. "I'm gonna say something here whether you like it or not. There is nothing wrong with the way you look! People back off because you scare the shit out of them! You glare at people. Smile and lighten up."

Gwen sighed. "You're the second person to tell me that, but it's too late."

"It's never too late, Gwen."

"It is. Listen, chances are pretty good I'm going to end up in jail in the near future anyway. Do you follow the news?"

"Yeah."

"Then you've heard about the drug dealers who have been shot in the street?"

Larry looked at Gwen in disbelief. "Yeah."

"Well, I'm the prime suspect."

"Bullshit." Larry shook his head. "No way."

"It's true. My daughter died of a drug overdose. That was my response."

"Shooting people was your response?"

"Yes." Gwen sighed. "Let's get back to business. In addition to this job, which my friend suggested I get to keep busy, I also have a bookkeeping business. I asked my friend to mail you my address book. All my clients and contact information are in there."

"I don't understand."

Gwen rolled her eyes. "You're an accountant. You are out of work. I'm not going to be able to run my business anymore. You should start one. That address book is a list of leads you can start with. Every one of them is going to be left high and dry without a bookkeeper or accountant. You won't be able to get my computer, but that's okay. Each client gets a thumb drive with everything on it. You can start with that."

"I don't know how to respond to this, Gwen. You're sacrificing too much for me."

"Just say thank you and don't get all emotional on me. I'm doing this more for me than for you."

The two were still sitting on the floor behind the counter. Gwen reached over, opened a file drawer under her teller station, and pulled out her purse. Reaching into a side pocket, she pulled out her keys and removed a small key from the ring. "I have a storage unit at Stack and Store on Joppa Road, unit 326B. Can you remember that?"

"Yeah."

"This is the key. As soon as you can, go there. There is some old furniture in there. There is a trunk where I store my weapons and ammo. Leave that alone. You'll see a desk, and if you open the top right drawer, you'll see some folders. One of those folders has about 10,000 in cash. It was money I hid from my daughter. Take it. Buy yourself a nice computer. You're going to need it. Use the rest to take care of your kids. When you go to the storage unit, wear a hoodie and hide your face as much as possible. Wear gloves. Once they find the unit, the police may look over the security videos. You don't want them to see you there."

Larry reached out to touch Gwen, but she backed away. "I don't need your sympathy or appreciation. Just tell me that you understand and can remember what I told you."

Larry pulled his hand back and said, "I understand, and I'll remember."

"Good, thank you."

They both sat there for a moment, silent, and were startled when the phone rang. Gwen reached up and grabbed the phone. "Yeah."

"Everything okay in there? Everyone fed?"

"Yeah, we're all good."

"Good. Now what can we do to end this?"

"Give me fifteen more minutes, and we'll all be out."

"Why not come out now? Let your hostages go. I'm sure they are scared and—"

Gwen shouted into the phone, "Because I said fifteen minutes, that's why. Now does that work for you, or do I need to make myself more clear?" She literally growled out that last phrase.

"Okay, fifteen minutes. But then what?"

"Call me back in fifteen, and I'll tell you 'then what.'" Gwen slammed down the phone.

Gwen turned to Larry. "So you're clear on what to say and do, right?"

"No, I'm not clear on why you are doing this, but yes, I know what to say and do."

"Good. I explained why. I don't know what else to tell you."

Larry took a breath and decided to let that go. "Okay, so how do we end this now?"

"When they call back in fifteen minutes, we say we're coming out. We let everyone out of the closet and walk them to the front door. We can have Blondie unlock the door again, and they all walk out. Once they're all out and past the line of police, then you and I walk out. They will probably arrest us both, but you'll be home by tomorrow morning. They will have nothing to hold you on."

"And what about you?"

"I told you, I'm headed for jail anyway." She looked at Larry and grabbed his hand. "You should call your kids. Let them know you are here and will probably not get home until late. Tell them not to worry. You will be okay."

Larry nodded, grabbed the phone, and dialed. "Dylan, it's Daddy...yes, I'm in that bank...no, don't believe what you are seeing on the news. It's going to be okay...yes, I'm a hostage but we'll be getting out soon. I may not be home until late though, so you take care of your brother, okay? Stay home, you make dinner, get to bed on time...it's going to be okay, I promise you. I love you both. I'll try to call again as soon as I get out of here...Bye, I love you." Larry slowly hung up the phone.

Gwen sat beside him, thinking. "I think we've thought of everything." Larry sat still and thought about his boys and wondered if he would really get home. Would he lose his sons? He put his head in his hands and cried. Gwen laid a hand on his back.

"It's going to be okay, I promise you."

Larry wiped his face and rose to his knees. "I hope you're right, Gwen. I really do." He slowly worked his way toward the men's room.

Gwen sat motionless on the floor. This would have been so much easier if this idiot had just shot her. Just her luck that a bank robber would turn out to be a nice guy. Damn it! She hoped she was right, and he could go home before the end of the day. She didn't give a thought to the people in the closet. She knew they were fine. They'd be fine, and they would go on with their useless lives, counting other people's money and gossiping about one another every chance they got. Claire was fine. She didn't need anything from Gwen, and Gwen explained her state of mind in the letter she left with the lawyer. Margaret would be taken care of. In about fifteen minutes, Gwen would have nothing to worry about; things would be taken care of for her. She wouldn't come into this piss-pot bank anymore. She wouldn't have to go home to memories of Leah. She wouldn't have to hunt anymore, though admittedly she would miss that. Her pain had been her constant companion. She nurtured it and fed it. It was a part of her.

She sighed. Life could have been different, but it wasn't. She could have smiled more and been more open with people. Maybe she could have been happy. "Oh, stop it, you old lunatic!" she yelled at herself. "Life was what it was. You were dealt a bad hand, and you dealt with it." Gwen sat up straight, wiped her hands over her face, and stretched. When Larry returned, she said, "I have one more thing I want to do."

She crawled down to Lindsay's teller station, opened the file drawer, and pulled out Lindsay's purse. She rifled through it until she found what she wanted and then stood. "I'll be right back." She saw the look in Larry's eyes, but she didn't care if they shot her through the window now. It was okay. She turned and walked back to the ladies' room.

Gwen looked at herself in the mirror. She smiled. Yes, that did improve her face. She chuckled a little. "RBF. Who knew?"

Gwen put the cosmetics that she took out of Lindsay's purse on the sink. The colors were not ones that she would have chosen, but they would work. Gwen slowly applied the blush and then put on some lipstick. She admired the results in the mirror. "Not half-bad, Gwen, not half-bad." Gwen used her hands to brush out her hair and frame it around her face as best she could.

She took one last look at herself in the mirror. "This is it, Gwen." She had a flashback to a summer when her parents, "against their better judgment," allowed Gwen to go to vacation Bible school with Claire. She remembered what she learned about God that week and heaven and hell and sin. Gwen got down on her knees. "Dear God, I'm sorry. I'm sorry that I killed that innocent man, and I'm sorry that I'm not sorry about the others I killed. I know I'm a terrible person, but please forgive me. I wish I had known you better. Forgive me for what I'm about to do, Lord."

Gwen got up and, leaving the cosmetics on the counter, walked out of the ladies' room.

Larry looked up as she approached. Gwen said, "Okay, let's get this over with,"

Larry smiled. "Well, look at you! You got a boyfriend on the police force?"

"Nah, just anticipating a photo shoot." Gwen smiled.

"Well, you look lovely," Larry told her sincerely.

"Thank you." She looked at Larry. "Are you ready?"

Larry nodded. "I guess so. I know what to do. I know what to say. I have your key. I just want to go home."

"And you will," Gwen said reassuringly. Still standing, Gwen waved her arm to the police out front. Within fifteen seconds, the phone rang. "We're ready," answered Gwen. "I'll send out four hostages first."

"Which four?" replied the officer.

"The guard, Karen the manager, and the tellers, Lindsay and Sue. Once they are out, I'll walk out with the last hostage to make sure you don't shoot."

"We're not going to shoot. Who is the last hostage?"

"A customer."

"What about your accomplice?"

"I don't have an accomplice, just someone who ended up in the wrong place at the wrong time. I'll explain later." Gwen hung up the phone.

"Okay, Larry, let's open up that closet. I'll hold the gun on you. You guide them all to the door. Have Blondie open the door. Let them all out, then close the door. Okay?"

"Got it." Larry grabbed the keys to the front door, and he and Gwen walked to the closet, pushed away the copier, and opened the door. Everyone inside was sitting on the floor.

"Get up!" shouted Gwen. "Does anyone need to use the bathroom?" They all nodded. "Okay, one at a time. If you're not back in two minutes, I start shooting, got it?" They all nodded. Gwen let Karen go first, then each teller individually, and finally the guard. No one was gone for more than a minute or so.

Once that was done, Larry herded the group toward the front door. He handed the key to Lindsay. "You unlock the door and leave the key in the lock." Larry was shaking as he handed over the key. He looked back at Gwen and continued, "Then you all leave, one by one. Walk to the police with your hands up. They'll take care of you from there." As he spoke, Gwen held the gun pointed at the group. She wanted there to be no mistake in their minds as to who was in charge.

Lindsay gave Gwen one last look, not of hatred or contempt, but really of confusion, then she unlocked the door, pulled it open, and walked through. The remaining bank employees followed her, and then Larry shut the door.

"I'm going to go get a picture of my daughter out of my purse. I want her with me," Gwen said. Larry nodded.

Gwen went behind the counter and knelt down. She put the gun in the back waistband of her pants. She then pulled her wallet out of her purse and took Leah's picture out of the wallet. She kissed the picture and looked into her daughter's eyes. "See you soon," she whispered.

As she came back around the counter, Larry said, "Where's the gun?"

"I left it back there," answered Gwen, nodding her head toward the counter. "I don't want it on me when we leave here." Larry looked suspicious, but she didn't give him time for more questions. "You ready?"

He nodded.

"Let's go then."

"Wait. Before we go out there, thank you. You could have left me on my own, but you didn't."

"Don't get all mushy, Larry." Gwen smiled. "It's going to be okay. Like I said, I'm doing this as much for me as for you. You just take care of those boys, okay?"

"Okay."

Gwen grabbed Larry by the arm and guided him to the door. As he opened the door, she slowly reached back to get the gun. Larry pulled open the door and walked through. Gwen, still holding his arm but slightly behind him, followed along. She heard the door close behind them. She let go of Larry's arm and, as hard as she could, pushed him aside. He lost his footing and fell sideways. As he fell, as if in slow motion, he could see Gwen pull out the gun from behind her and point toward the police officers in front of them.

Larry screamed, "No!" but his voice was drowned out by gunfire. He watched helpless as Gwen was hit repeatedly, bullet after bullet slamming her body back up against the bank door. His own gun, never fired, flew from her hands. In seconds, she was on the ground, motionless.

Larry heard himself screaming "No, no!" over and over again. He felt himself being grabbed roughly under the arms and dragged to the line of police cars. He could hear a woman screaming in the background, "He's a victim. He's a victim!"

Chapter 35

Twenty Years Later

Larry

Larry sat in his study with his sons. His daughters-in-law and grand-kids were outside, but Larry had pulled his sons away because he wanted to talk to them. He was dying. He'd been fighting cancer for a few years. He had turned over the business to his son Dylan who had been working with his father now for quite a few years. Dan was settled as an art teacher and a writer. His sons were happy and successful, with good families of their own. His work was done. He was tired of fighting and ready to see his beloved Anna again. They argued with him and tried to encourage him to keep fighting, but he refused. It was time, and he hoped they would accept his decision.

And he also wanted his sons to know exactly what happened that day at the bank. The guilt of letting Gwen take the blame for what he started ate at him always. He wanted those he loved to know the truth. So today, after he let them know of his decision to stop chemo, he told them exactly what Gwen had done for them. He explained why he had felt that robbing a bank, though it sounded crazy now, at the time seemed to be his only option. Then he told them everything that happened from the minute he walked into that bank.

"So not only did that woman keep me out of jail, but she also gave me what I needed to start my business and get back on my feet. She saved my life, and she saved yours. I should have told you this years ago, and I'm sorry I didn't."

Larry's sons never said a word as he spoke and sat in silent disbelief for a few seconds when he finished. Dylan kept his eyes on his father, his heart breaking for this man who loved him so much. Dan was looking at the ground.

"And the police never had any idea that you were involved?" asked Dan, looking up, trying to process what he had just heard.

"I think they did, but they couldn't prove it. Gwen was right. The cameras actually worked in my favor. I told them that she handed me the gun and then forced me to participate under threat of pinning the act on me. She was already under suspicion for much worse crimes, so they believed her capable of that. I felt awful letting them believe that about her. *She had saved my life*, but I just couldn't risk being taken away from you." He looked as his boys. Men now. Good men. "I thank her every day. I thanked her after I signed on about half of her customers. I thanked her when I used *her* money to set up an office and put a deposit down on our apartment in Lutherville. I thanked her when I could move you out of Brooklyn. I thanked her when I could enroll you in good schools again. I thanked her on the days you graduated from high school and then from college. I thank her every time I look at you and every time I look at your beautiful children." Larry sighed deeply. "I knew she was going to take the blame and try to protect me, but I didn't know...I didn't think for second that she going to get herself killed. I wouldn't have let her do that."

"Wow. I just don't know what to say, Dad," said Dylan, shaking his head.

"You don't have to say anything. It was just important to me that you know what this woman whom you never met did for you, did for us. I know what's been written about her, but she was a good person, and she saved us. Every bad word that I read about her in the weeks following that day tore at my heart. She didn't wake up that morning planning to rob a bank. I did. She didn't walk into that bank that day with a gun. I did. It was me." Larry began to cry. His sons came and knelt beside him and wrapped their arms around him, trying to comfort him. "And I know she did some bad things before that day. I know she did, but I also understand. If anyone had hurt either of you, I may have done the same." Larry shrugged and shook his head. "I don't know. We never know what we're capable of until we feel that our backs are against the wall. It's easy to say, 'I would never...' but I would have said that I would never buy a gun. That I would never rob a bank. And yet I did both...or tried to." Larry sat up straight and looked at his sons. "So now you know the truth, I hope you don't hate me, but I also hope you remember Gwen and what she did to save us."

"We don't hate you, Dad," both men replied at once.

"Thanks for telling us, Dad," said Dylan. "Thank you for what you did for us, and I promise we'll never forget Gwen either."

The young men helped their father to his feet, and he hugged each in turn.

"Dad, I'd like to write a book about this someday? Would that be okay with you?" asked Dan.

"As long as you make Gwen the hero," Larry answered.

*****

Julius

Julius took the cover off his prized possession—his Mustang. He kept it covered all the time, unless of course he was driving it, even though it was also parked in his garage. His wife and kids teased him about it, but he didn't care. This car meant a lot to him, and he wasn't going to let anything happen to it.

He opened the passenger-side door and slipped into the front passenger seat. Opening the glove box, he pulled out a worn envelope. He slowly pulled out the contents and read them for the hundredth time.

Dear Julius,

As you know by now, I left you my Mustang. Probably not a good car for Uber driving, but I'm sure you can use a second car just for fun. I want you to know how much I appreciated your help but, more importantly, how much I enjoyed our time together. Spending time with you was one of the few joys of my life.

Depending on the circumstances of my death, you may read some bad things about me. Some will be true, but believe me when I tell you that I never put you in a position where you could be abetting my crimes. Never. You helped me to help others. That's what we did, and I hope you remember that each time you get into the Mustang,

Enjoy it, my friend, and thank you for everything.

Gwen

As always, Julius shook his head. This was an expensive car, and she left it to *him*. Why? Yes, he drove her around and helped her when he could, but she paid him. When they were together, he didn't realize how much that meant to her, and he certainly didn't know what she was up to. Not until he read about it in the newspaper. He probably wouldn't have even read the article because the headline referred to a "Gueneviere Marsh." But he did recognize the last name and wondered if it could be his good client. If the article hadn't included her address, he never would have believed it was about the kind woman he knew. That woman was generous, kind, and thoughtful. She went out of her way to help people she didn't know, to make them feel loved. He could never reconcile this with what he read about Gwen in the paper.

Julius felt someone standing next to him. It was his daughter Abbie. "Why are you sitting here, Daddy?"

"Just thinking, sweetheart. Did I ever tell you about my friend, Gwen?"

Abbie rolled her eyes. "Only about a thousand times, Dad."

Julius laughed. "You exaggerate, but I tell you a lot because I want you to remember. There is good and evil in each of us, and we have to nourish the good and stomp out the evil."

"I know, Daddy." Abbie smiled at her dad.

"Good, never forget it." Julius looked at his daughter. "Want to go for a ride? I have a delivery to make."

"In the Mustang?"

Julius nodded, smiling.

"Yes! I'll go tell Mom, and I'll be right back." Julius smiled as his daughter excitedly ran into the house.

He got out of the car, opened the trunk, and began to load boxes.

Julius met Margaret in the weeks following Gwen's death. They began meeting for coffee often and became very close. Margaret had even introduced Julius to his now wife, and she had become an important member of their family, a surrogate grandmother to his children. He loved her dearly, so when Margaret decided to open a homeless shelter and drug treatment center, he gladly assisted in any way he could. He started a ministry at his church to raise money and collect supplies for the shelter, and each week, he delivered the collections. And every trip, he thought of Gwen.

That was what he would do on this trip, and yes, he would tell his daughter about Gwen, again.

*****

Claire

Claire sat in her dining room with her teenage granddaughter. Gueneviere looked just like her grandmother, petite and blond, and was every bit as sweet. She loved to visit with her grandmother whenever she could. Today, Claire, or Nana as Gueneviere called her, had pulled out some old photo albums for them to go through.

They came to a picture of Claire at the age of ten or eleven standing with a chubby young friend. "Who's that, Nana?"

"That's my friend, Gwen. She was my dear, dear friend."

"Gwen?"

"Yup. Her real name was Gueneviere."

"Is that why you chose that name as Mom's middle name?"

"Yes, it was." Claire sat back in her chair. "I met Gwen in the fourth grade. I was bullied a lot back then. I was small and limped and was just a perfect target. But that all stopped when Gwen stepped in to protect me. One bully had my books and was holding them up over his head, so I couldn't reach. I was embarrassed and angry and close to tears when Gwen walked by, punched the boy in his stomach so hard that he dropped the books and fell to the floor." Claire chuckled at the memory. "I picked up the books and walked away. I suspect there were others she punched, but I never saw it." Claire shook her head. "Anyway, a short time later, I invited her over after school, and from that day for the next two years, we were together daily."

"What happened after two years?"

"My mother and I had to move here to Ohio to take care of my Nana. We only saw each other a few times after that, but we kept in touch."

"Do you still keep in touch?"

"No, Gwen died before you were born." Claire's eyes filled with tears. "Life had been hard on Gwen. She didn't let people see the same side of her that I did. I think things would have been different for her if she had."

They both remained quiet for a moment. Claire wiped her eyes. "But I'll tell you this, if it wasn't for Gwen, I wouldn't be the person I am today. She taught me to have confidence in myself. She pointed out to me that I was stronger than I thought I was. She taught me that it was okay to be different. I miss her."

"I'm sorry, Nana."

"The last time I heard from her was by letter. She had left it with her attorney to send me upon her death. Life had beaten her down, and she was suicidal. She asked me to forgive her. Me forgive her!" Claire shook her head. "I didn't know what for. She had never been anything but good to me."

"Do you still have the letter?"

Claire nodded.

"Can I read it?" Claire thought for a second, then got up and went into her bedroom. She returned a minute later with a worn envelope, which she handed to her granddaughter.

Gueneviere slid the pages out of the envelope and began to read aloud: "Dearest Claire…"

Claire held up her hand to stop her granddaughter. "You don't have to read it out loud, sweetie. I know it by heart."

Gueneviere nodded and continued to read silently.

Dearest Claire,

If you have this letter, that means I'm dead. Chances are I did it myself. I think about it every single day. And if that's the case, just know that I died happy to do so. Once Leah was gone, life lost all meaning. I'm sorry.

There are a few things I want you know though.

I love you with all my heart. Every good memory I have from childhood involves you. The best two years of my childhood were the two years that we were together. Thank you for that. Even though I wasn't great at keeping in touch, I never stopped thinking of you as my best friend. If I didn't come visit when I should have, that was never because of you. It was me. I was a mess, and I never wanted you to see me like that. I was ashamed of who I had become. I'm sorry. Maybe I would have been a better person if

I had spent more time with you. You always came for the important events in my life—when Leah was born, when my parents died, and when Leah died. Thank you. I'm sorry I didn't do the same for you. It was selfish and probably stupid of me to worry about what you would think of me.

After Leah died, my intention was to leave everything to you, hoping it would help send your kids to college or keep you comfortable later in life. A lot happened after Leah died, and I did some terrible things (I hope you never find out, but if you do, please don't hate me) and decided it would be better if the money I had left was used to help lots of people. I hope you meet my new friend, Margaret. She can explain.

I do want you to have the few pieces of jewelry that I have, especially my high school ring…

Gueneviere stopped reading and looked at her grandmother's right hand. She had a gold ring that she always wore on her middle finger. The ring had a black stone, and "OLS" was written diagonally across the stone in gold. She looked at the ring and then at Claire, who simply nodded.

…especially my high school ring. I also want you to have my mah-jongg set. I haven't played since "the ladies," but I could never part with it. I hope that you can use it and that you'll think about me, the me you knew back then, when you play. Lastly, I want you to have my book collection. I thought about you every time I started a new book and wondered if you would like it.

Not a day went by, Claire, that I didn't miss you and your mom. Thank you for being my friend. Thank you for loving me. I know I could be terribly unlovable.

Forgive me, please.

Love,

Gwen

"Wow." Gueneviere looked up from the pages to see her Nana quietly crying. "I'm sorry, Nana. I shouldn't have asked to read that. I didn't mean to bring up sad memories for you."

Claire reached out and took her granddaughter's hand. "It's okay, sweetie. I know I'm crying, but I do love to talk about her, so thank you. She was a good friend when I was in desperate need of one."

"Do you mind if I ask how she died?"

"Honestly, I'm not sure. The newspapers said she was robbing a bank and got shot. I never believed that. Gwen wouldn't have robbed anything. I don't know how it happened, but I know that she allowed herself to be killed. Her friend, Margaret, told me a few things about Gwen's last days, and I'm sure of it."

"I'm sorry, Nana."

Claire wiped the tears from her eyes and sat up straight. "Thank you, sweetie. I prefer to remember Gwen the way I knew her." She smiled at her granddaughter, "How about a game of mah-jongg?"

*****

Margaret

"And now I would like to introduce our guest of honor, without whom Gwen's Place would not exist. This place that we all know and love, that has fed and housed thousands over the past two decades. This place that has given addicts a safe place to go for help. This addict right here…," continued the speaker as he pointed to himself and took a breath to control his emotions, "this addict right here was saved because of this place and because of this woman. Ladies and gentlemen, let's hear it for Margaret Gray!"

As Margaret was helped up the steps to the stage, every person in the room stood and clapped. As she slowly walked across the stage to the podium, she looked out over the crowd. Many, many faces whom she knew and loved. Many faces who came through the doors of Gwen's place looking lost and hopeless, now happy and full of life. "Thank you, Jesus," she whispered as she took her place at the podium. The crowd stayed on their feet, clapping.

Margaret enjoyed the joy for a moment and then held up her hands, asking everyone to quiet down. "Please sit. Thank you so much. I can't tell you how much that welcome means to me. But y'all are gonna wanna sit because I have a lot to say!"

The crowd laughed as they all took their seats, and one young lady in back called out, "You can keep us here all night, Miss Margaret!"

"I promise I won't do that," Margaret chuckled, "but I do have a lot that I want to tell you. There is so much that you don't know about how this place got started. Over the years, a lot of you have asked me, 'Who's Gwen?' and I always say..." And as she finished her sentence, quite a few members of the audience quoted with her. "'Gwen was a dear friend of mine.'

"Well, tonight, I'm going to tell you just who Gwen is. And truth be told, Gwen should be standing here instead of me tonight. This place was her idea, her creation. She gave birth to it. She funded it. Gwen gave me the confidence to build it. Without her, we wouldn't be in this room tonight. Without her, I just don't know what would have happened to a lot of you here tonight." Margaret took a moment to pull a handkerchief out of her pocket and wipe tears from her eyes.

"Yes, Gwen Marsh was a dear friend of mine. And if you research her name, you'll read a lot of bad things about her. Some true. The main accusation false. You'll read that she robbed a bank. She did not. She was helping a desperate father who came into that bank that day to rob it. She was helping him to find another way, to get home to his family, to survive. Gwen died that day. She died helping someone she had just met. Someone who, I found out later, had threatened her with a gun. She helped him. She saved him. And you know what? She saved me too.

"When I met Gwen, I was living on the streets. Some of you know that. I had been in the streets for a number of years. I honestly don't remember how long. One evening, I saw a woman standing by herself, and she looked so lonely and sad. I spoke to her. I didn't know who she was. I assumed she was homeless as well. I just knew she looked sad.

"Well, she wasn't homeless. And from that night on, the group I hung with in Baltimore started receiving gifts—sleeping bags, sweaters, hats, gloves, tissues, wipes, you name it. I knew it was her. She sent the supplies with a young man, Julius, who most of you know." And with that, the crowd was on their feet again. They all knew Julius. He spent a lot of time at Gwen's place and got to know all the residents. He would do whatever he could for any one of them. Margaret held up her hands again and waited for them to quiet down. "Yes, that Julius." She smiled.

"Julius would deliver the supplies, and he had a red coat that he said was specifically for me. For me." Margaret shook her head at the memory. "Someone gave me a coat. And I knew in my heart who it was. And later that night, when I covered myself with that coat, I felt a lump in the lining. I ripped the seam to find a few hundred dollars there. A few hundred dollars! I hadn't seen more than a few dollars at one time in years, and here I had a fortune." She chuckled again. "I didn't know what to do with it, so I kept it there, and little by little, I would pull some out and get food and drinks for our little group. And then one day, Gwen came back. She found me walking down the street carrying that red coat, took me to lunch, and brought me back to her place. She gave me a place to stay and helped me find a job. She gave me my life back, and when I asked her why, she said, 'Because you didn't just walk past me.' People had just walked past Gwen her entire life. Remember that. Never just walk past someone. We *need* each other." Margaret looked around the room. "*We need each other.*

"As we got to know each other, I found out that Gwen had lost her only child to drugs. Her daughter. And the night I met Gwen, she wasn't just hanging around looking for people to help. She was looking for her daughter's drug dealer. She wanted to kill him, and she eventually did." Many in the crowd started to clap, happy to hear that a drug dealer had been killed, but Margaret held up her hands and admonished them. "No, that's nothing to cheer. I know I was happy when I found out, but now that I look back on that time with clear eyes, violence is nothing to cheer. Yes, I'm glad that man was taken off the streets, but as we all know, there were plenty to take his place. And in killing that man, as satisfying as the vengeance may have been to Gwen, she also killed a piece of herself. See, goodness and evil don't go together. Goodness and evil shouldn't live in the same house. Goodness and evil shouldn't occupy the same soul." Margaret stopped for a moment and thought about her friend. "I think in the end, goodness won out in Gwen. She's remembered by most for the evil, but those of us who knew her know that the goodness won out.

"But killing that man took its toll on Gwen's soul, and she wanted to die. She knew her time was short. She left me a note. I won't read the entire letter to you, but I do want to read the part that is the foundation to Gwen's place.

"'I left some money to the Sisters of Notre Dame to use to care for retired nuns. I left my car to Julius because I think he'll love driving it, and he was good to me. And I left some jewelry to my friend Claire, but the rest I leave to you. The condo and everything in it is yours, and everything in my bank and investment accounts is yours. The lawyer will give you the exact amount, but it should be about half a million.'" Margaret stopped reading and looked up. "My first thought was, 'What am I going to do with a half million dollars!'" She chuckled. "But in typical Gwen fashion, she told me exactly what I was going to do with that money." Margaret continued reading. "'Don't squander that money like I squandered my life. I was so blinded by rage and hatred, I felt that I had been so wronged by the world that rather than use that money for good, I hid it. And by the time I realized that most of the bad in my life was my own fault and not everybody else's, it was too late. Don't wait, Margaret. Use that money for good. Open a homeless shelter or a rehab facility. Use it for good. I know you will, Margaret.'"

Margaret folded the letter and looked up again. "And do you know this woman went on to thank *me*? She thanked me for being her friend. All that she did for me, and she thanked *me*." By this time, tears were streaming down Margaret's face, but she didn't care. "Well, I took my friend's words to heart, and I started with the homeless shelter and a few years later added on the rehab facility. And in the beginning, I couldn't tell anyone just why I named it Gwen's Place. If I had, this place would have been tied to the bad things Gwen had done. I knew that, so I kept it to myself. But today I can tell you because today you know that Gwen was good, that the good in her won out. And I thank God for that each and every day. Thank you."

*****

Sister Mary Francis

The retirement of Margaret Gray was a big deal in Baltimore, and her speech made the local news. Sister Mary Francis, long retired, read the speech in its entirety.

When she finished, she put down the paper and smiled. "I knew you would do good things, Gwen."

About the Author

Maryland native E. D. Lippert is the first-time author behind *Gwen*. She's married to an amazing man and has four wonderful adult children and twelve beautiful grandchildren. In addition to raising a family, Ms. Lippert has spent her adult life working in accounting and then technology while always wanting to write. That desire to create meaningful stories and characters has been bubbling just below the surface for decades.

She and her husband are dedicated to addiction recovery, and both sit on the board of a local halfway house for recovering addicts and alcoholics.

When not fixing technical issues or writing, E. D. loves to read, crochet, and above all, spend time with family. Her big bucket list item (in addition to writing a best seller, of course) is to spend an extended vacation in Italy with her family.